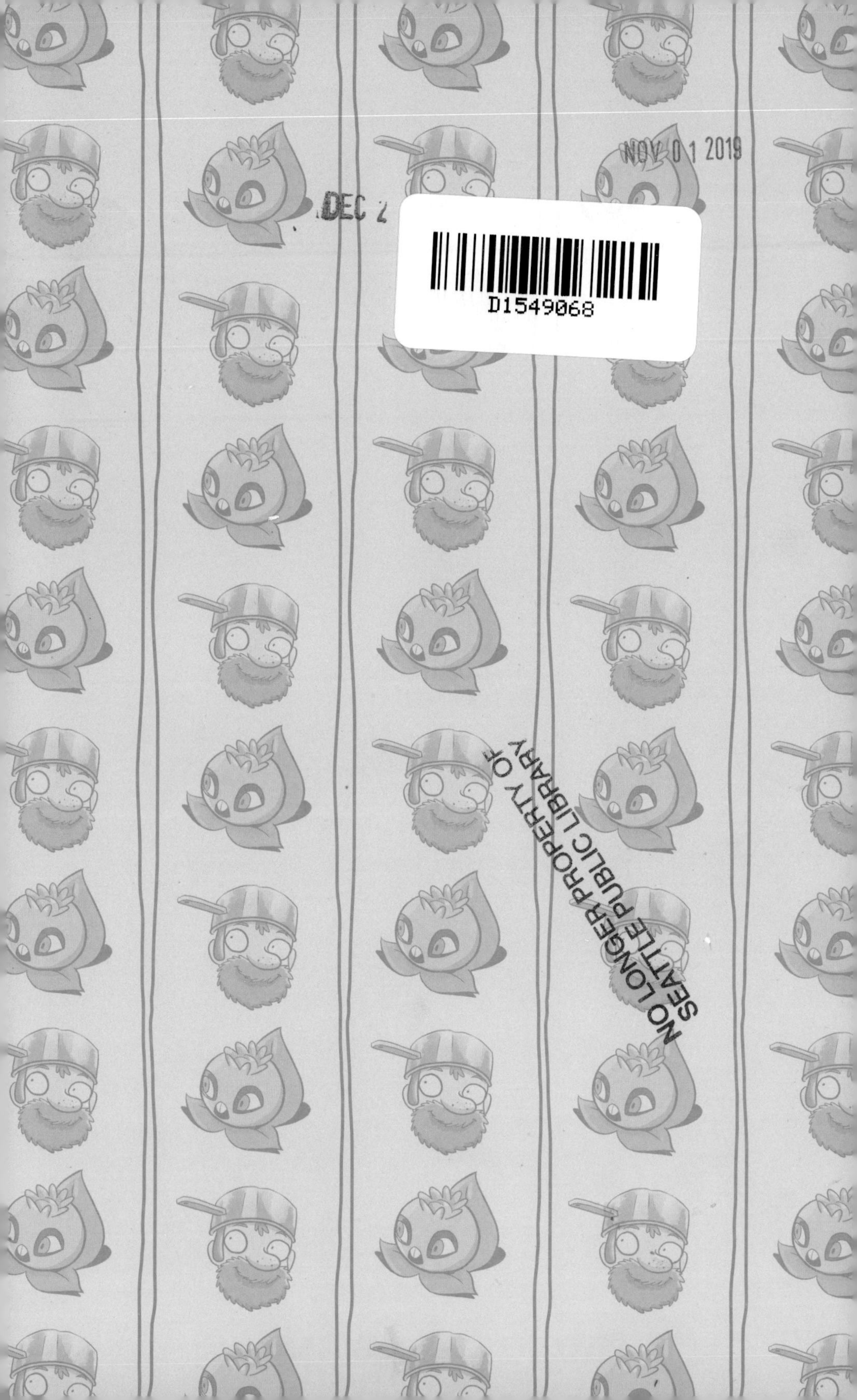

PLANTS VS. ZOMBIES

A LITTLE PROBLEM

Written by PAUL TOBIN
Art by SARA SOLER
Colors by ADI CROSSA
Letters by STEVE DUTRO
Cover by SARA SOLER
Bonus Story Art and Colors by RON CHAN

DARK HORSE BOOKS

PLANTS VS. ZOMBIES™

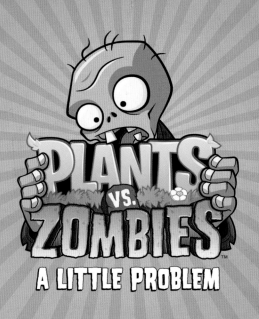

A LITTLE PROBLEM

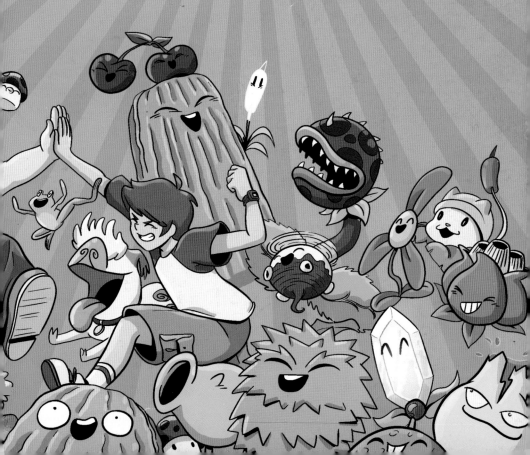

Publisher **MIKE RICHARDSON**
Senior Editor **PHILIP R. SIMON**
Associate Editor **MEGAN WALKER**
Assistant Editor **JOSHUA ENGLEDOW**
Designer **BRENNAN THOME**
Digital Art Technician **CHRISTIANNE GILLENARDO-GOUDREAU**

Special thanks to A.J. Rathbun, Kristen Star,
and everyone at PopCap Games and EA Games.

First Edition: October 2019
ISBN 978-1-50670-840-9

10 9 8 7 6 5 4 3 2 1
Printed in China

DarkHorse.com
PopCap.com

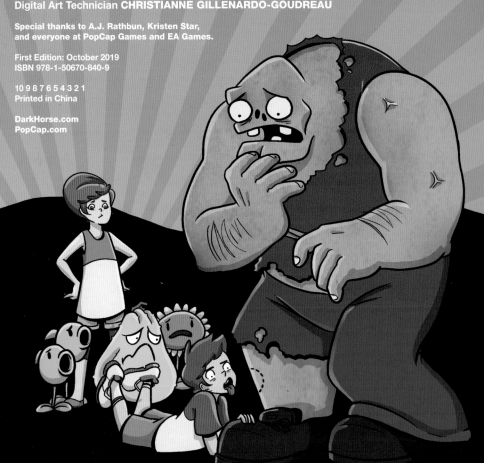

No plants were harmed in the making of this graphic novel. Several zombies, though, attempted to make themselves very small in order to break into the Dark Horse Comics candy and soda machines in the lunch room. Now those vending machines are broken. Great. Thanks, zombies.

Library of Congress Control Number: 2019941874

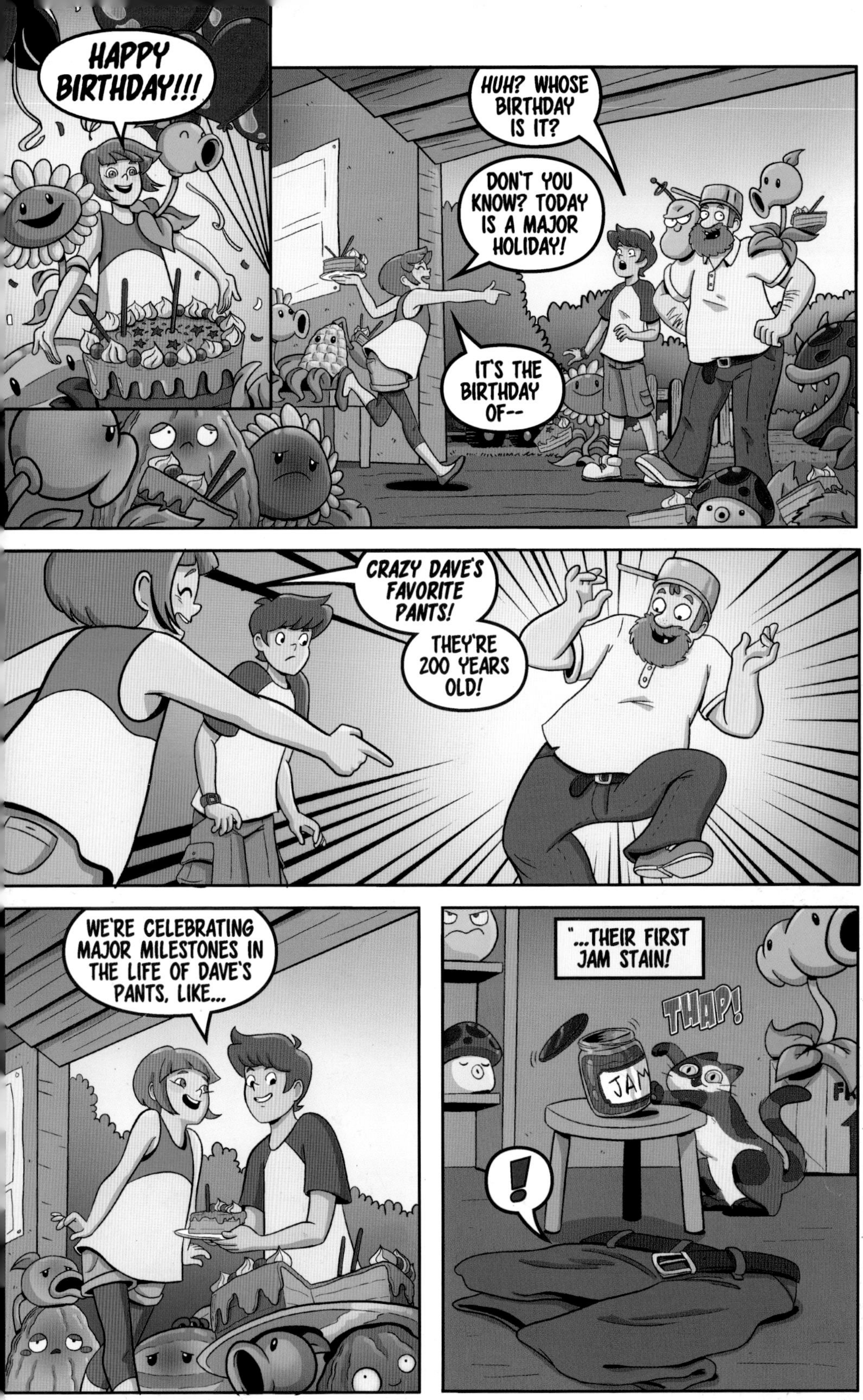
HAPPY BIRTHDAY!!!
HUH? WHOSE BIRTHDAY IS IT?
DON'T YOU KNOW? TODAY IS A MAJOR HOLIDAY!
IT'S THE BIRTHDAY OF--
CRAZY DAVE'S FAVORITE PANTS!
THEY'RE 200 YEARS OLD!
WE'RE CELEBRATING MAJOR MILESTONES IN THE LIFE OF DAVE'S PANTS, LIKE...
"...THEIR FIRST JAM STAIN!
THAP!
JAM
!

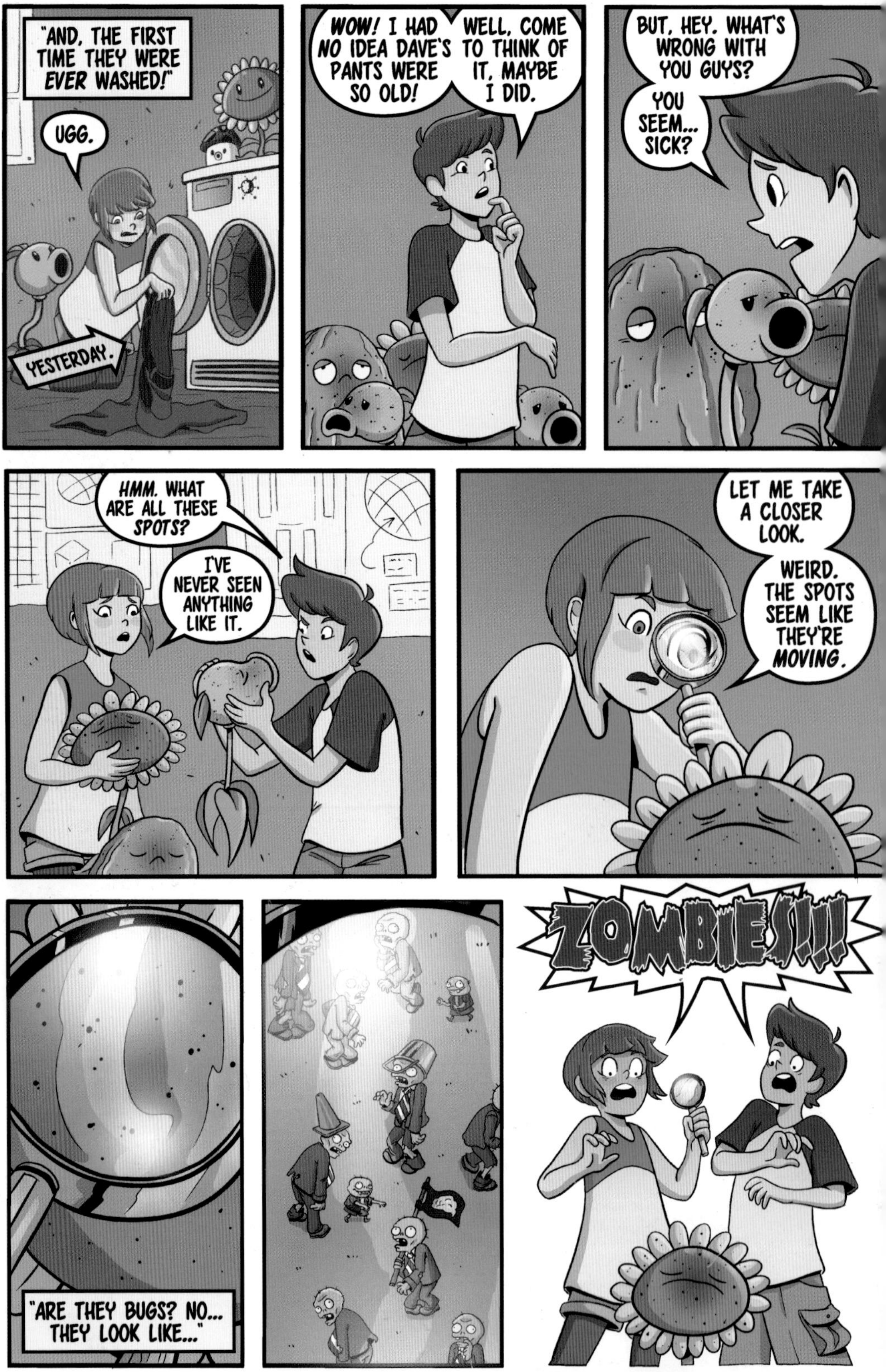
"AND, THE FIRST TIME THEY WERE *EVER* WASHED!"
UGG.
YESTERDAY.
WOW! I HAD *NO* IDEA DAVE'S PANTS WERE SO OLD!
WELL, COME TO THINK OF IT, MAYBE I DID.
BUT, HEY. WHAT'S WRONG WITH YOU GUYS?
YOU SEEM... SICK?
HMM. WHAT ARE ALL THESE *SPOTS?*
I'VE NEVER SEEN ANYTHING LIKE IT.
LET ME TAKE A CLOSER LOOK.
WEIRD. THE SPOTS SEEM LIKE THEY'RE *MOVING*.
"ARE THEY BUGS? NO... THEY LOOK LIKE..."
ZOMBIES!!!!

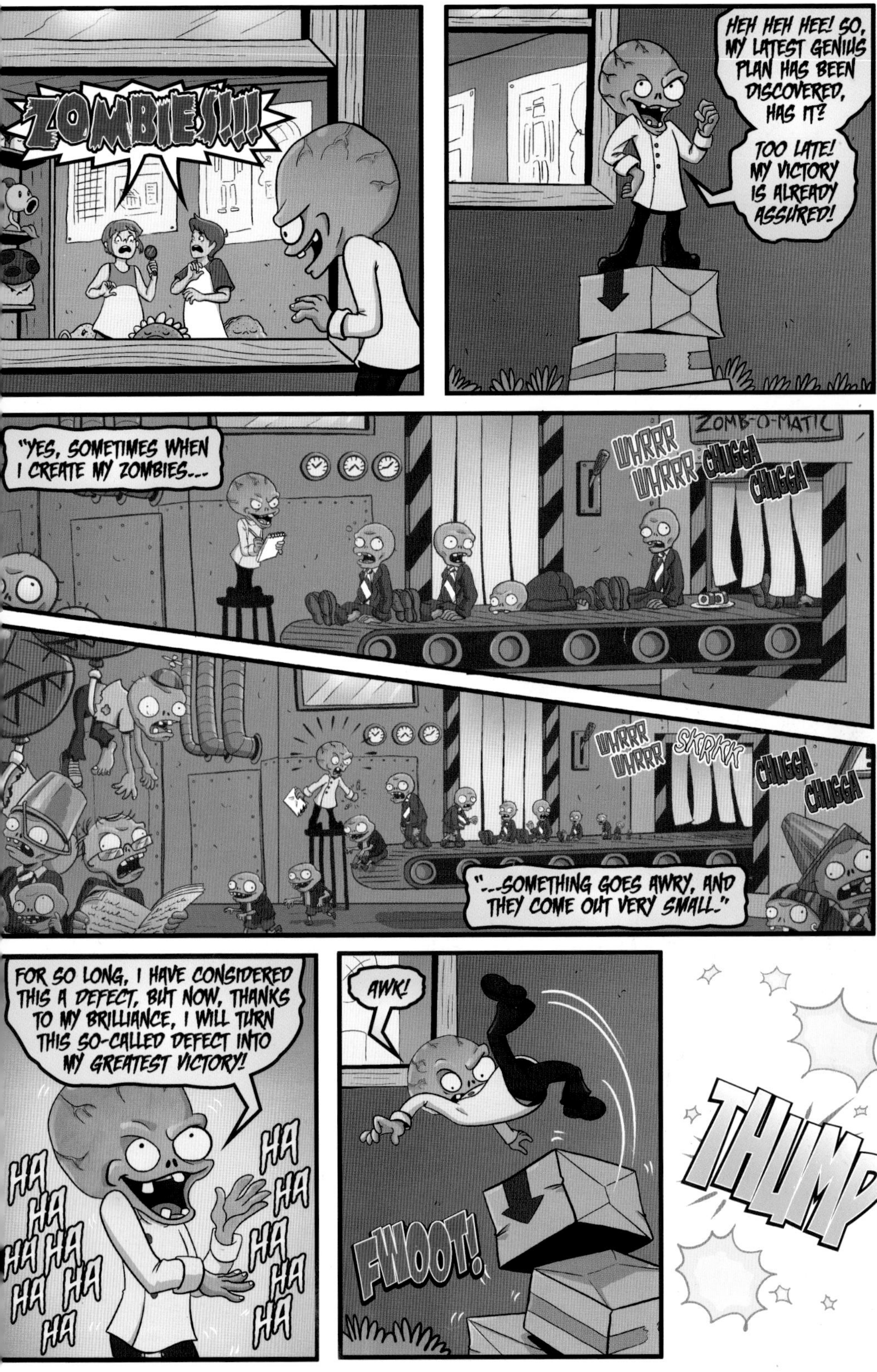
ZOMBIES!!!
HEH HEH HEE! SO, MY LATEST GENIUS PLAN HAS BEEN DISCOVERED, HAS IT?
TOO LATE! MY VICTORY IS ALREADY ASSURED!
"YES, SOMETIMES WHEN I CREATE MY ZOMBIES...
ZOMB-O-MATIC
WHRRR WHRRR CHUGGA CHUGGA
WHRRR WHRRR SKRKK CHUGGA CHUGGA
"...SOMETHING GOES AWRY, AND THEY COME OUT VERY SMALL."
FOR SO LONG, I HAVE CONSIDERED THIS A DEFECT, BUT NOW, THANKS TO MY BRILLIANCE, I WILL TURN THIS SO-CALLED DEFECT INTO MY GREATEST VICTORY!
HA HA HA HA HA HA HA HA HA HA HA HA HA HA HA
AWK!
FWOOT!
THUMP

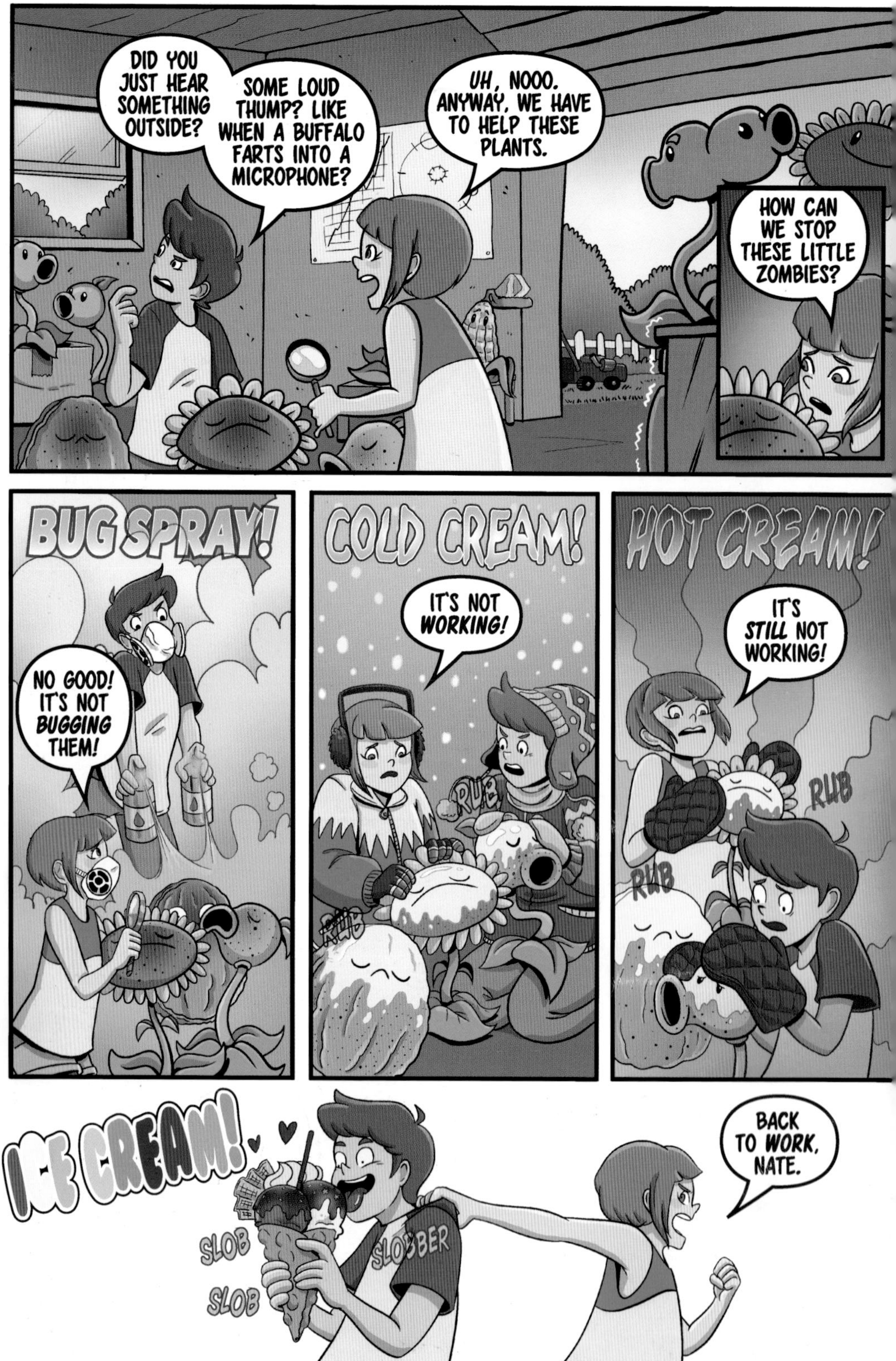
DID YOU JUST HEAR SOMETHING OUTSIDE?
SOME LOUD THUMP? LIKE WHEN A BUFFALO FARTS INTO A MICROPHONE?
UH, NOOO. ANYWAY, WE HAVE TO HELP THESE PLANTS.
HOW CAN WE STOP THESE LITTLE ZOMBIES?
BUG SPRAY!
NO GOOD! IT'S NOT BUGGING THEM!
COLD CREAM!
IT'S NOT WORKING!
RUB
RUB
HOT CREAM!
IT'S STILL NOT WORKING!
RUB
RUB
ICE CREAM!
SLOB
SLOB
SLOBBER
BACK TO WORK, NATE.

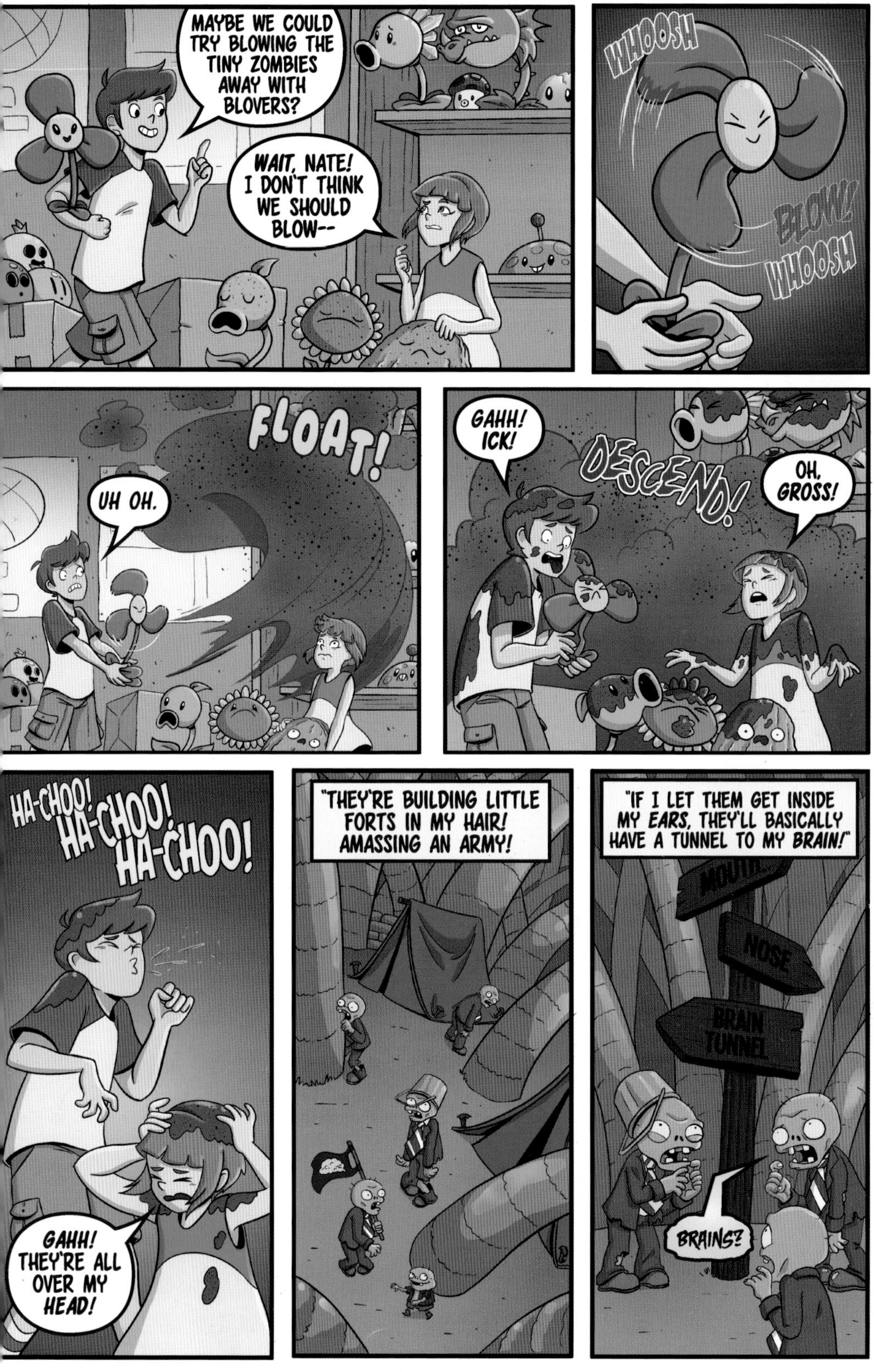
MAYBE WE COULD TRY BLOWING THE TINY ZOMBIES AWAY WITH BLOVERS?
WAIT, NATE! I DON'T THINK WE SHOULD BLOW--
WHOOSH
BLOW!
WHOOSH
FLOAT!
UH OH.
GAHH! ICK!
DESCEND!
OH, GROSS!
HA-CHOO! HA-CHOO! HA-CHOO!
GAHH! THEY'RE ALL OVER MY HEAD!
"THEY'RE BUILDING LITTLE FORTS IN MY HAIR! AMASSING AN ARMY!
"IF I LET THEM GET INSIDE MY EARS, THEY'LL BASICALLY HAVE A TUNNEL TO MY BRAIN!"
NOSE
BRAIN TUNNEL
BRAINS?

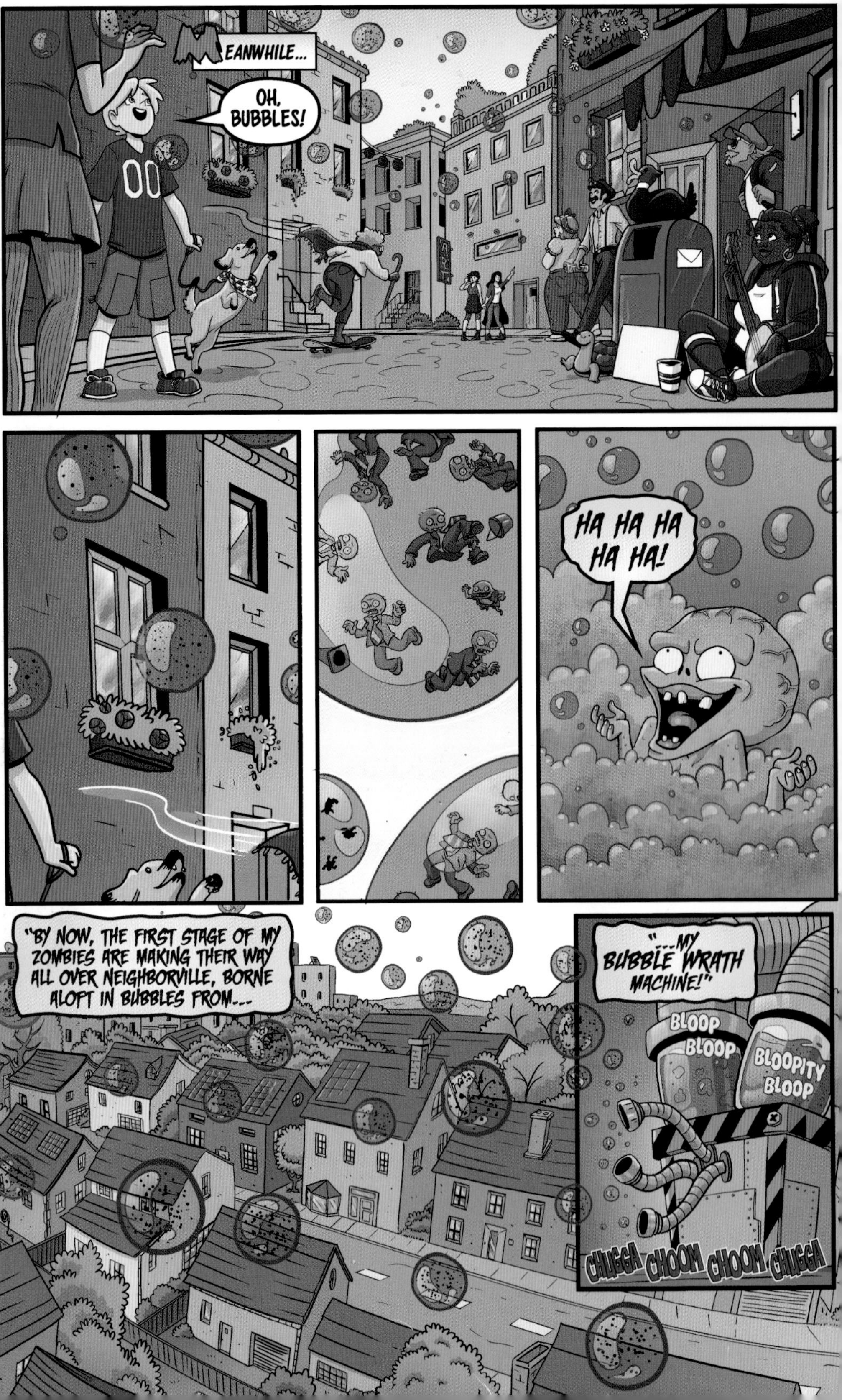
MEANWHILE...
OH, BUBBLES!
ART
HA HA HA HA HA!
"BY NOW, THE FIRST STAGE OF MY ZOMBIES ARE MAKING THEIR WAY ALL OVER NEIGHBORVILLE, BORNE ALOFT IN BUBBLES FROM...
"...MY BUBBLE WRATH MACHINE!"
BLOOP BLOOP
BLOOPITY BLOOP
CHUGGA CHOOM CHOOM CHUGGA

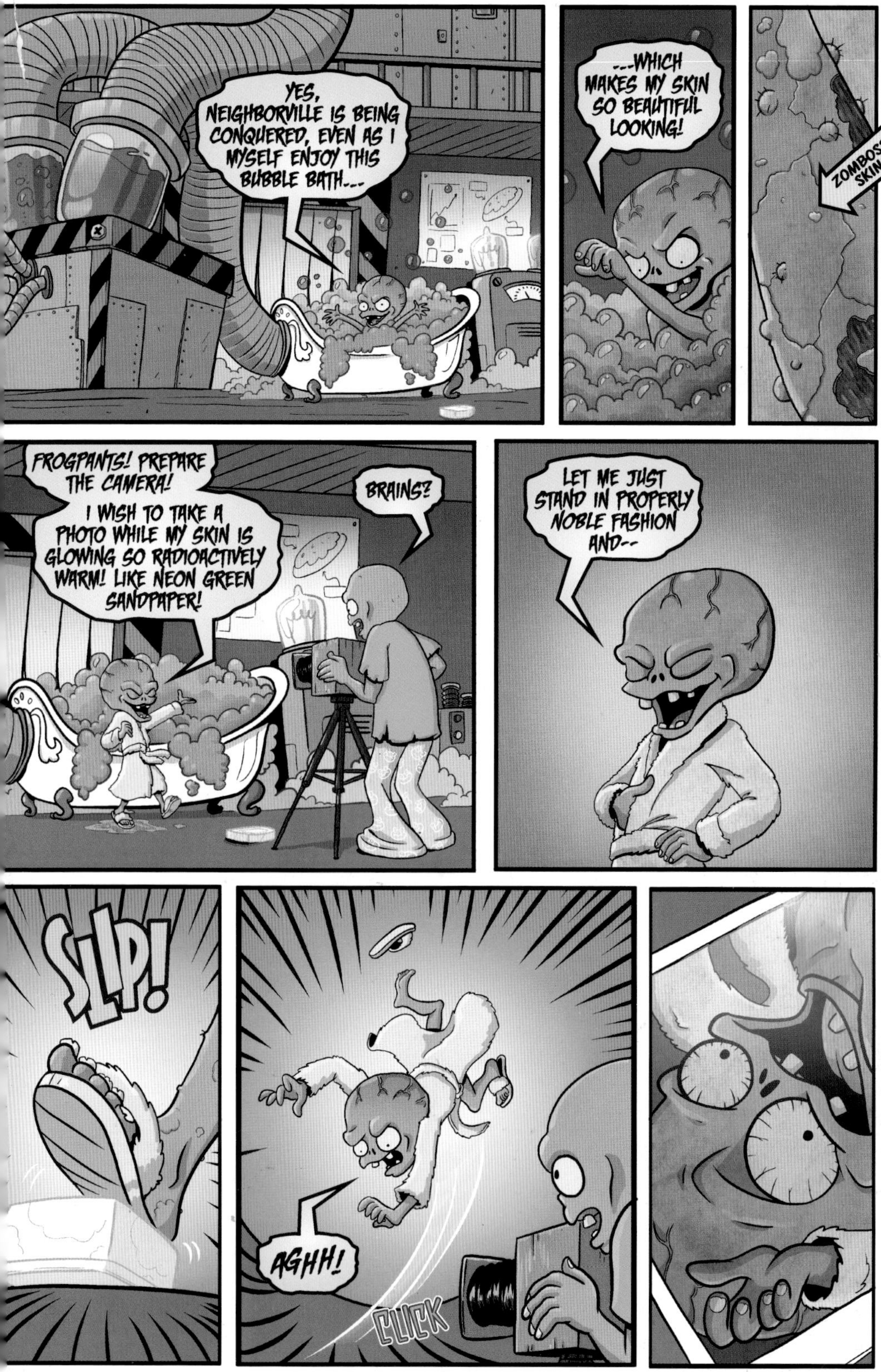
YES, NEIGHBORVILLE IS BEING CONQUERED, EVEN AS I MYSELF ENJOY THIS BUBBLE BATH...
...WHICH MAKES MY SKIN SO BEAUTIFUL LOOKING!
ZOMBOSS SKIN
FROGPANTS! PREPARE THE CAMERA!
I WISH TO TAKE A PHOTO WHILE MY SKIN IS GLOWING SO RADIOACTIVELY WARM! LIKE NEON GREEN SANDPAPER!
BRAINS?
LET ME JUST STAND IN PROPERLY NOBLE FASHION AND--
SLIP!
AGHH!
CLICK

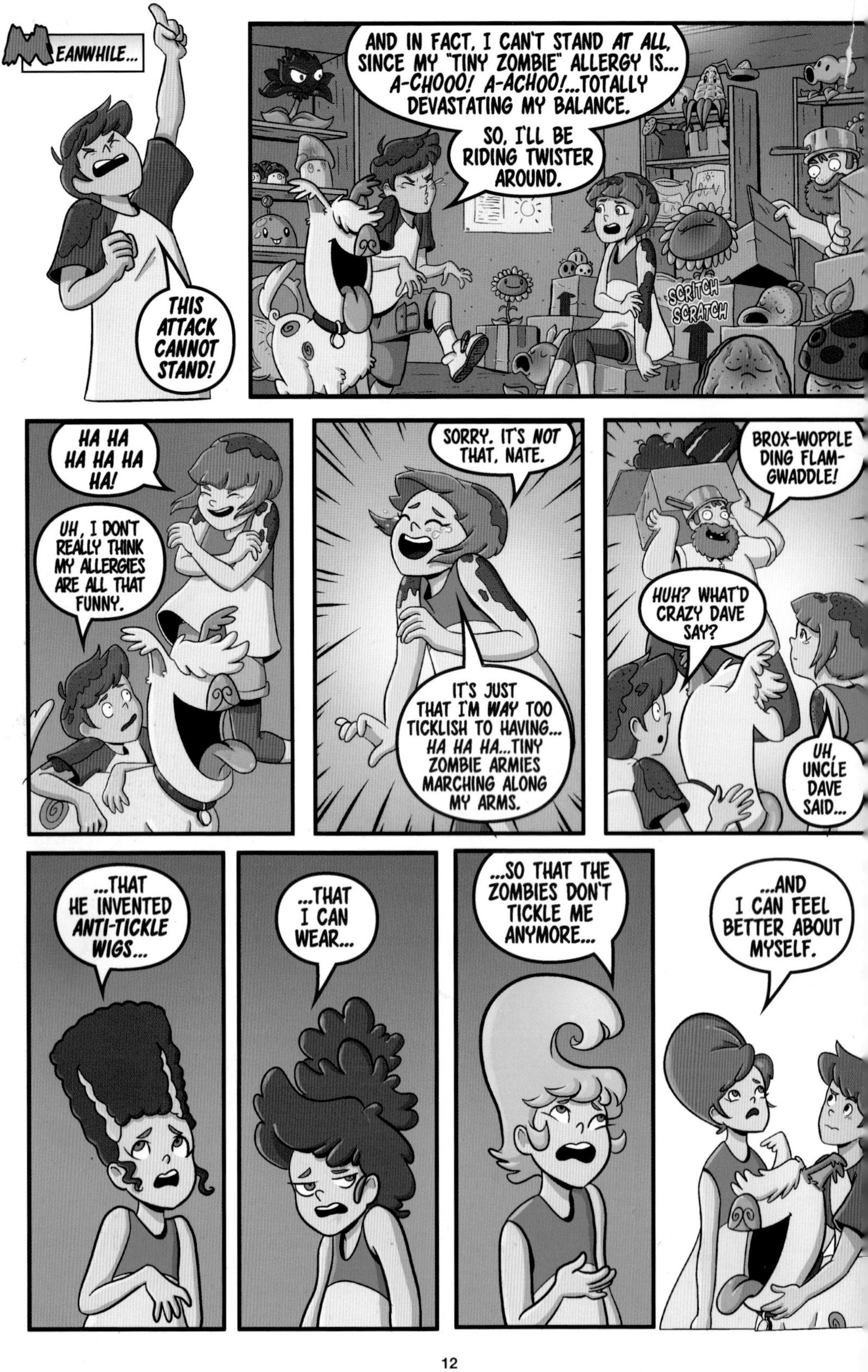
MEANWHILE...
THIS ATTACK CANNOT STAND!
AND IN FACT, I CAN'T STAND AT ALL, SINCE MY "TINY ZOMBIE" ALLERGY IS... A-CHOOO! A-ACHOO!...TOTALLY DEVASTATING MY BALANCE.
SO, I'LL BE RIDING TWISTER AROUND.
SCRITCH SCRATCH
HA HA HA HA HA HA!
UH, I DON'T REALLY THINK MY ALLERGIES ARE ALL THAT FUNNY.
SORRY. IT'S NOT THAT, NATE.
IT'S JUST THAT I'M WAY TOO TICKLISH TO HAVING... HA HA HA...TINY ZOMBIE ARMIES MARCHING ALONG MY ARMS.
BROX-WOPPLE DING FLAM-GWADDLE!
HUH? WHAT'D CRAZY DAVE SAY?
UH, UNCLE DAVE SAID...
...THAT HE INVENTED ANTI-TICKLE WIGS...
...THAT I CAN WEAR...
...SO THAT THE ZOMBIES DON'T TICKLE ME ANYMORE...
...AND I CAN FEEL BETTER ABOUT MYSELF.

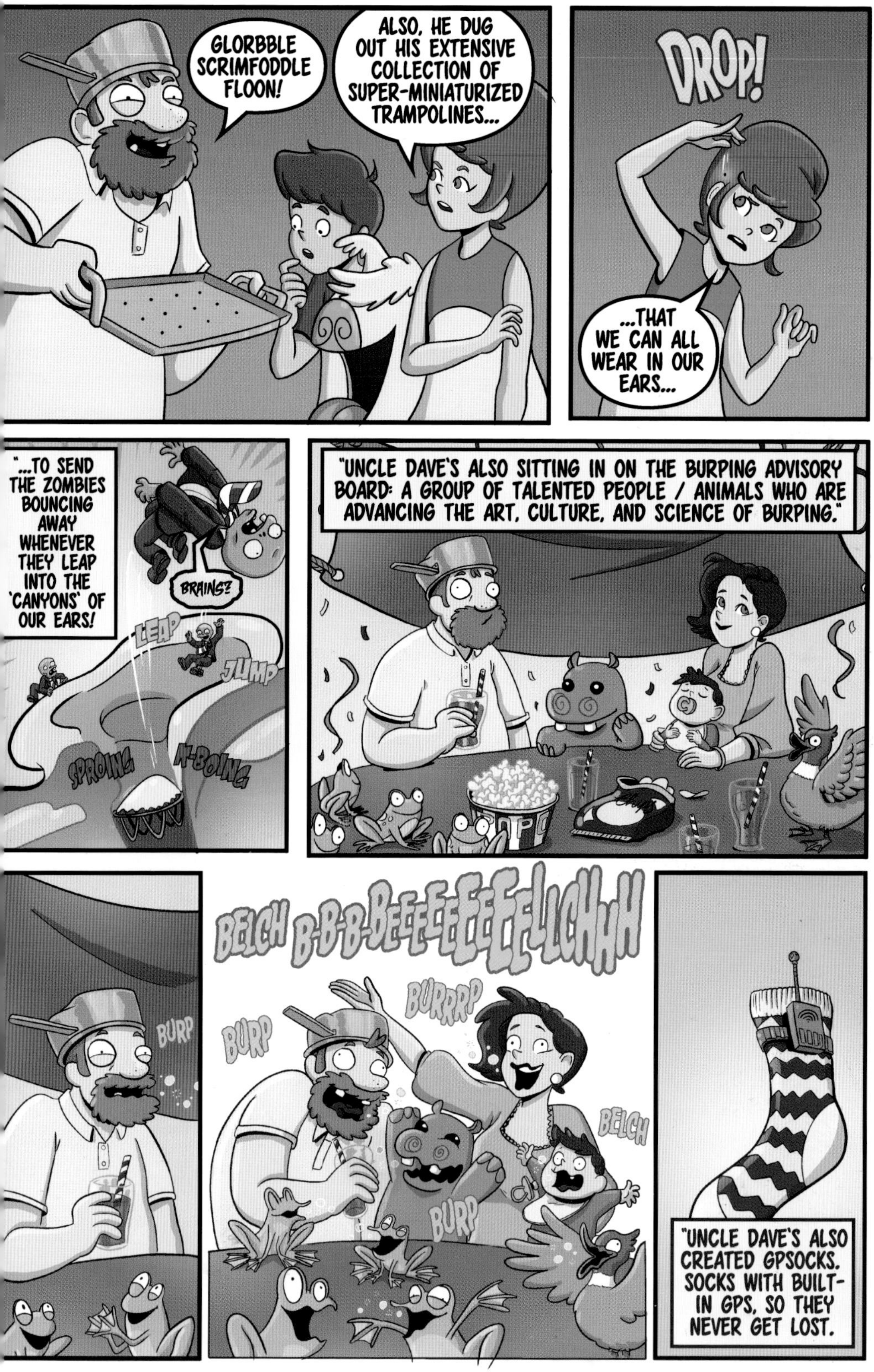
GLORBBLE SCRIMFODDLE FLOON!
ALSO, HE DUG OUT HIS EXTENSIVE COLLECTION OF SUPER-MINIATURIZED TRAMPOLINES...
DROP!
...THAT WE CAN ALL WEAR IN OUR EARS...
"...TO SEND THE ZOMBIES BOUNCING AWAY WHENEVER THEY LEAP INTO THE 'CANYONS' OF OUR EARS!
BRAINS?
LEAP
JUMP
SPROING
N-BOING
"UNCLE DAVE'S ALSO SITTING IN ON THE BURPING ADVISORY BOARD: A GROUP OF TALENTED PEOPLE / ANIMALS WHO ARE ADVANCING THE ART, CULTURE, AND SCIENCE OF BURPING."
BURP
BELCH B-B-B-BEEEEEEEELLCHHH
BURRRP
BURP
BELCH
BURP
"UNCLE DAVE'S ALSO CREATED GPSOCKS. SOCKS WITH BUILT-IN GPS, SO THEY NEVER GET LOST.

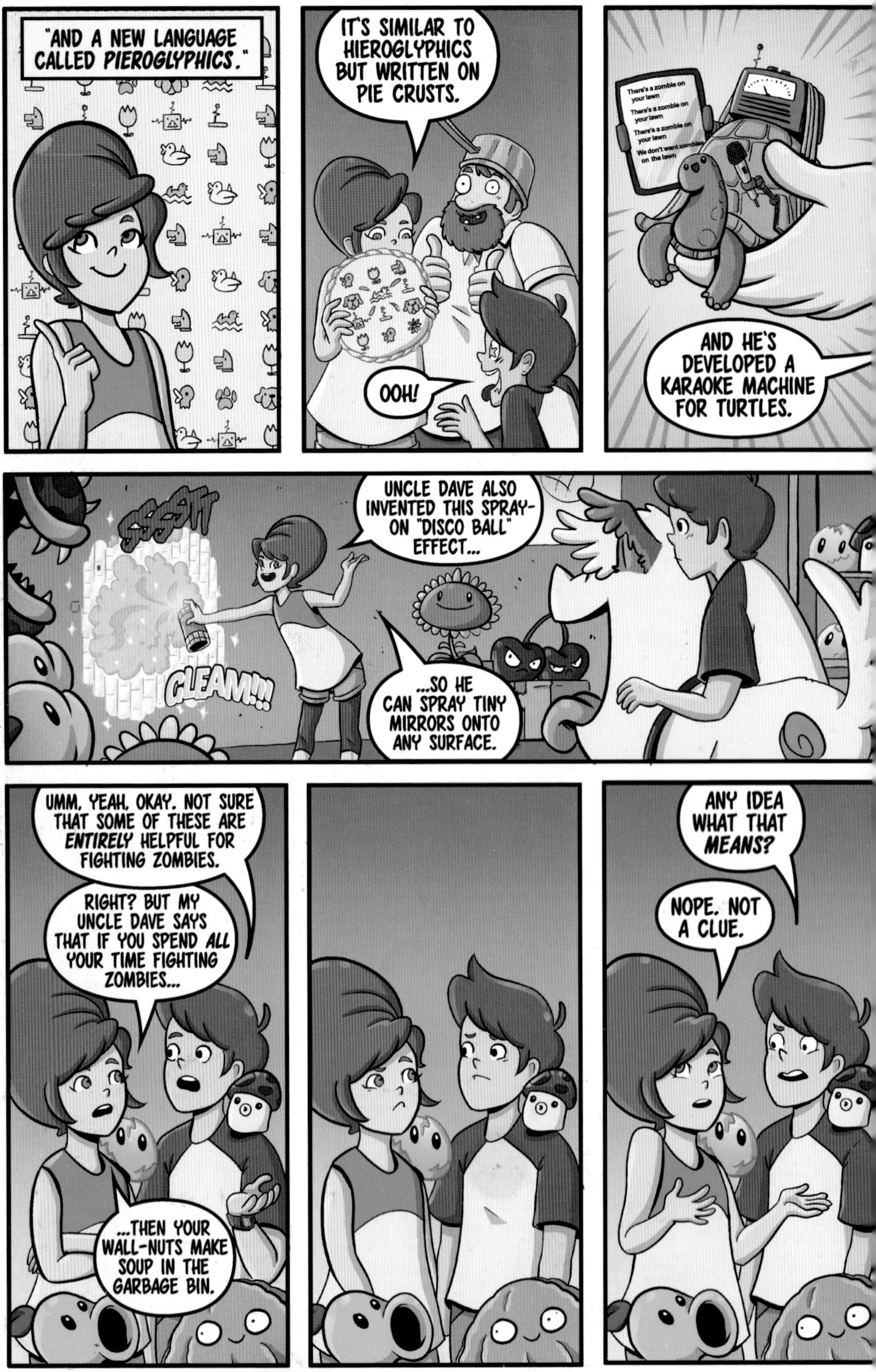
"AND A NEW LANGUAGE CALLED PIEROGLYPHICS."
IT'S SIMILAR TO HIEROGLYPHICS BUT WRITTEN ON PIE CRUSTS.
OOH!
There's a zombie on your lawn
There's a zombie on your lawn
There's a zombie on your lawn
We don't want zombies on the lawn
AND HE'S DEVELOPED A KARAOKE MACHINE FOR TURTLES.
SSSSTTT
GLEAM!!!
UNCLE DAVE ALSO INVENTED THIS SPRAY-ON "DISCO BALL" EFFECT...
...SO HE CAN SPRAY TINY MIRRORS ONTO ANY SURFACE.
UMM, YEAH, OKAY. NOT SURE THAT SOME OF THESE ARE *ENTIRELY* HELPFUL FOR FIGHTING ZOMBIES.
RIGHT? BUT MY UNCLE DAVE SAYS THAT IF YOU SPEND *ALL* YOUR TIME FIGHTING ZOMBIES...
...THEN YOUR WALL-NUTS MAKE SOUP IN THE GARBAGE BIN.
ANY IDEA WHAT THAT *MEANS?*
NOPE. NOT A CLUE.

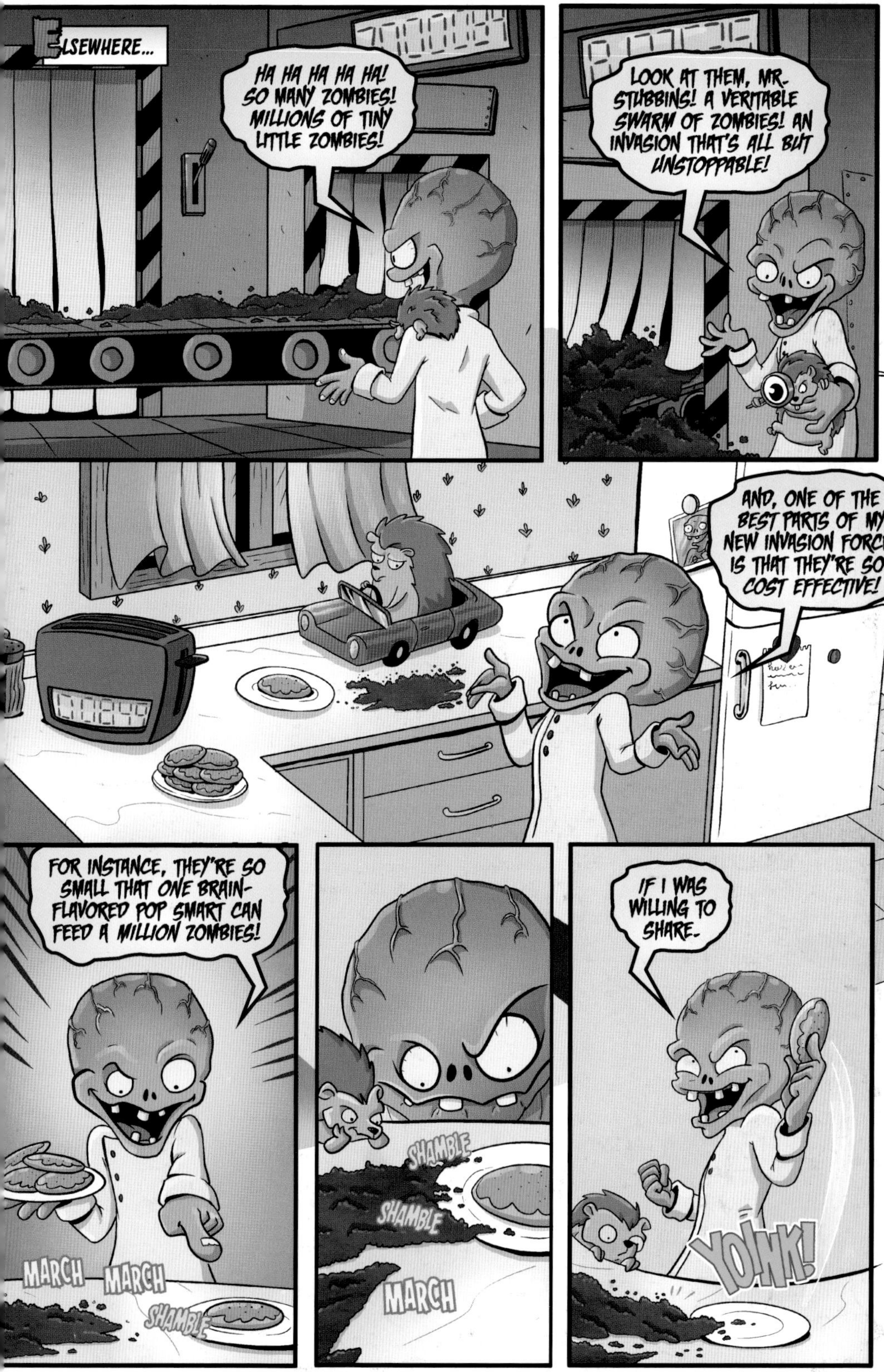
ELSEWHERE...
HA HA HA HA HA! SO MANY ZOMBIES! MILLIONS OF TINY LITTLE ZOMBIES!
LOOK AT THEM, MR. STUBBINS! A VERITABLE SWARM OF ZOMBIES! AN INVASION THAT'S ALL BUT UNSTOPPABLE!
AND, ONE OF THE BEST PARTS OF MY NEW INVASION FORCE, IS THAT THEY'RE SO COST EFFECTIVE!
FOR INSTANCE, THEY'RE SO SMALL THAT ONE BRAIN-FLAVORED POP SMART CAN FEED A MILLION ZOMBIES!
MARCH
MARCH
SHAMBLE
SHAMBLE
SHAMBLE
MARCH
IF I WAS WILLING TO SHARE.
YOINK!

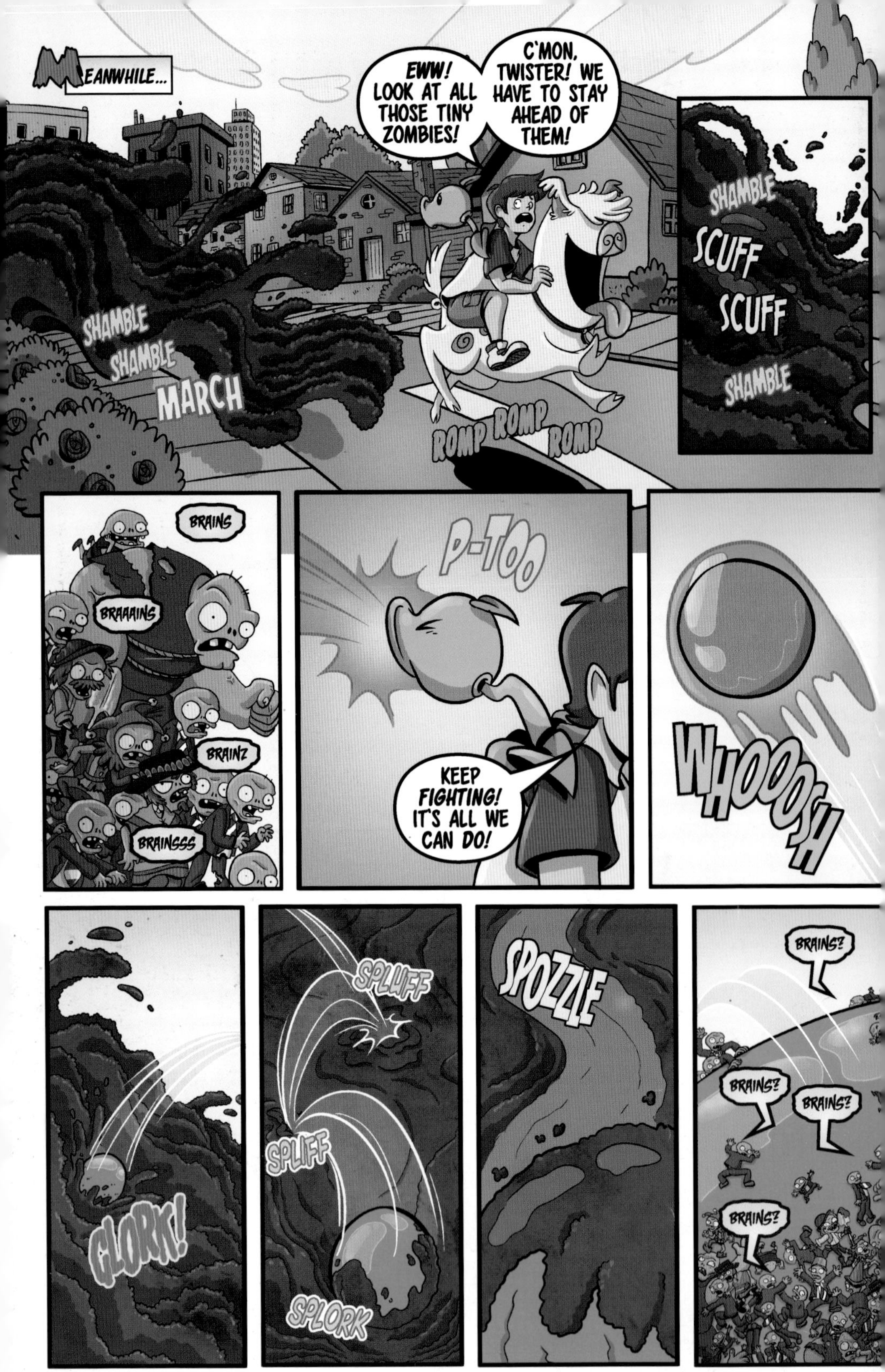
MEANWHILE...
EWW! LOOK AT ALL THOSE TINY ZOMBIES!
C'MON, TWISTER! WE HAVE TO STAY AHEAD OF THEM!
SHAMBLE
SHAMBLE
MARCH
ROMP ROMP ROMP
SHAMBLE
SCUFF
SCUFF
SHAMBLE
BRAINS
BRAAAINS
BRAINZ
BRAINSSS
P-TOO
KEEP FIGHTING! IT'S ALL WE CAN DO!
WHOOOOSH
CLORK!
SPLUFF
SPLIFF
SPLORK
SPOZZLE
BRAINS?
BRAINS?
BRAINS?
BRAINS?

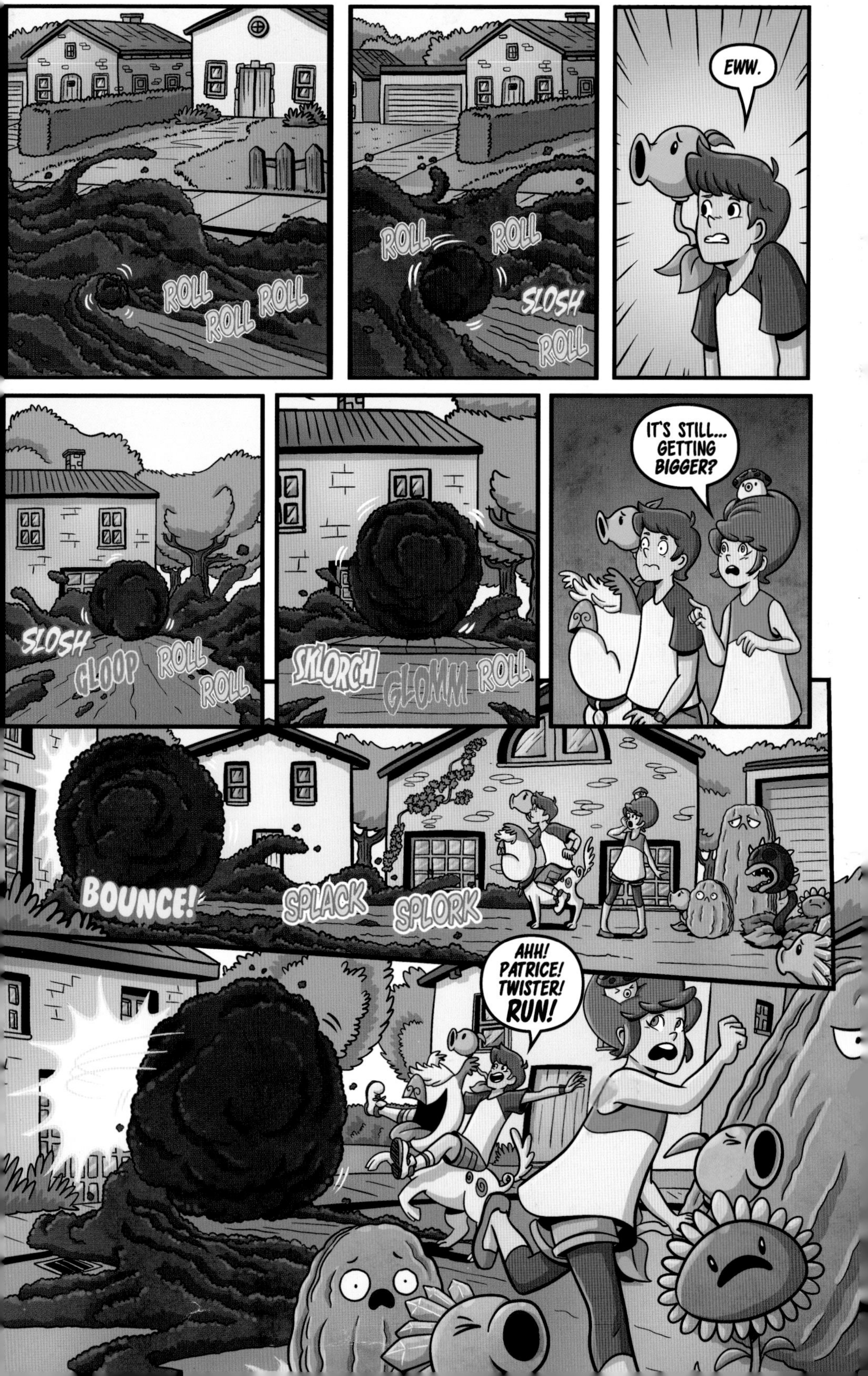

ROLL
ROLL ROLL
ROLL ROLL
SLOSH
ROLL
EWW.
SLOSH
GLOOP ROLL
ROLL
SKLORCH
GLOMM ROLL
IT'S STILL... GETTING BIGGER?
BOUNCE!
SPLACK
SPLORK
AHH! PATRICE! TWISTER! RUN!

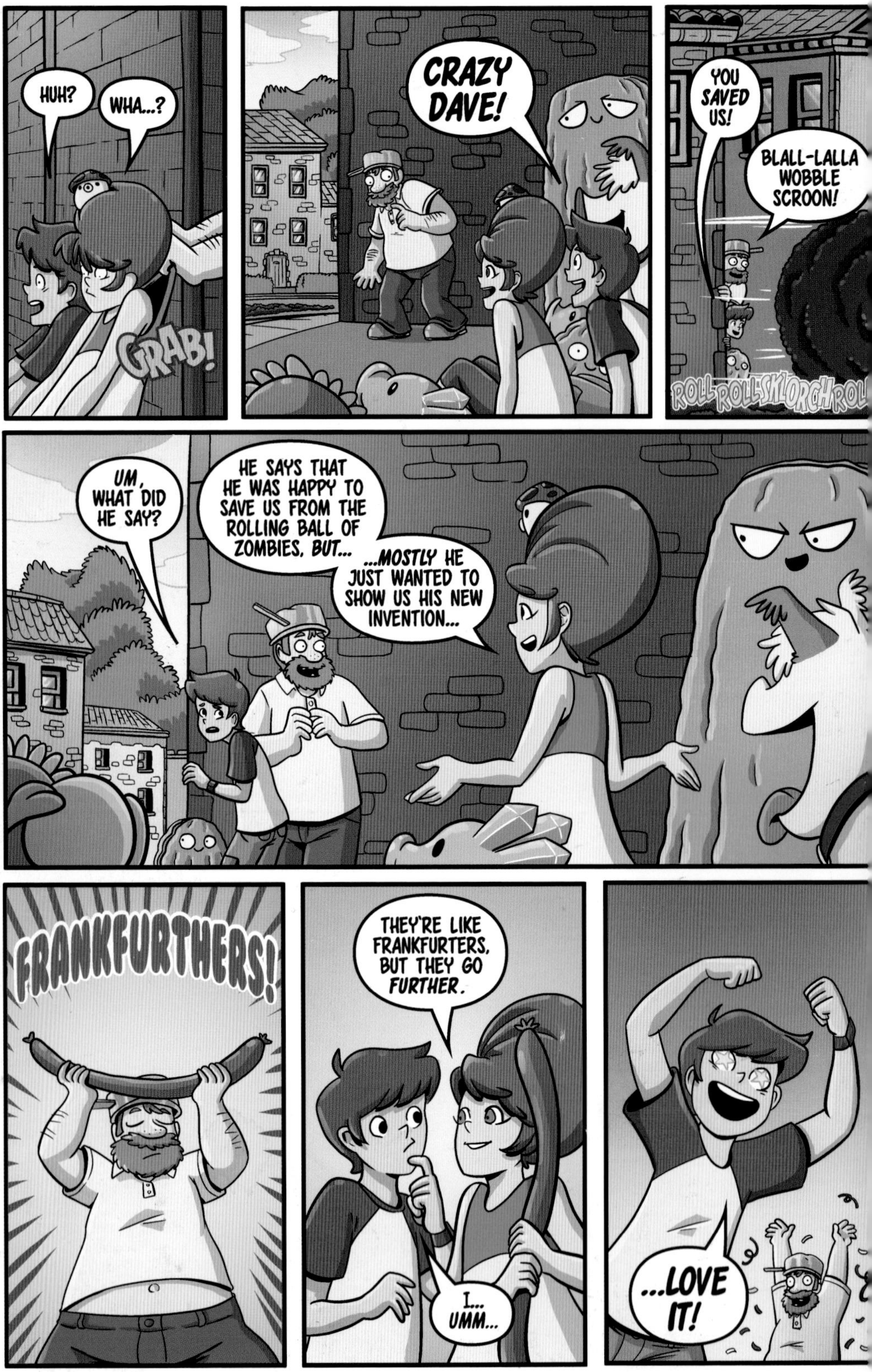
HUH?
WHA...?
GRAB!
CRAZY DAVE!
YOU SAVED US!
BLALL-LALLA WOBBLE SCROON!
ROLL ROLL SKLORCH ROLL
UM, WHAT DID HE SAY?
HE SAYS THAT HE WAS HAPPY TO SAVE US FROM THE ROLLING BALL OF ZOMBIES, BUT...
...MOSTLY HE JUST WANTED TO SHOW US HIS NEW INVENTION...
FRANKFURTHERS!
THEY'RE LIKE FRANKFURTERS, BUT THEY GO FURTHER.
I... UMM...
...LOVE IT!

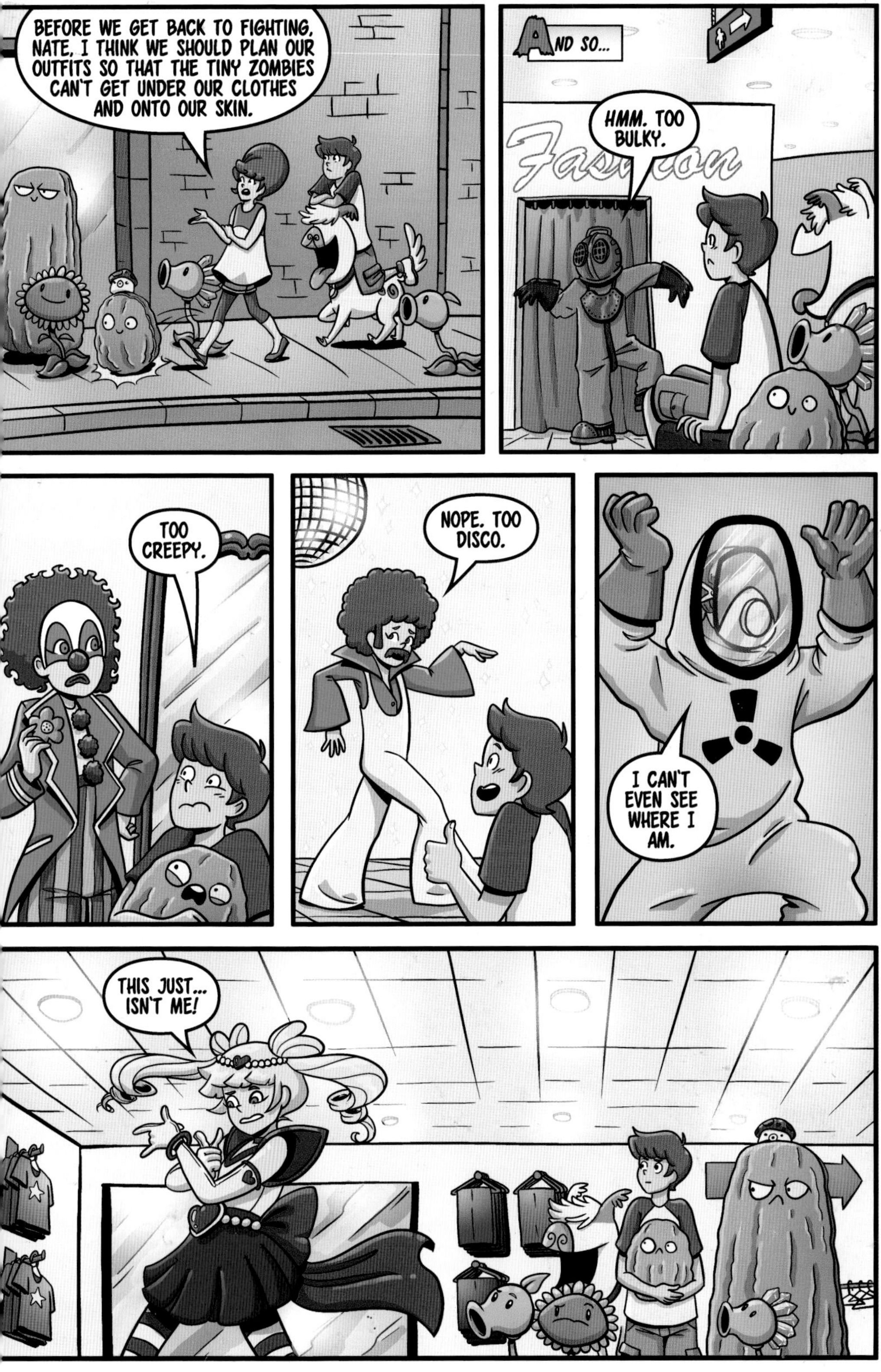
BEFORE WE GET BACK TO FIGHTING, NATE, I THINK WE SHOULD PLAN OUR OUTFITS SO THAT THE TINY ZOMBIES CAN'T GET UNDER OUR CLOTHES AND ONTO OUR SKIN.
AND SO...
HMM. TOO BULKY.
TOO CREEPY.
NOPE. TOO DISCO.
I CAN'T EVEN SEE WHERE I AM.
THIS JUST... ISN'T ME!

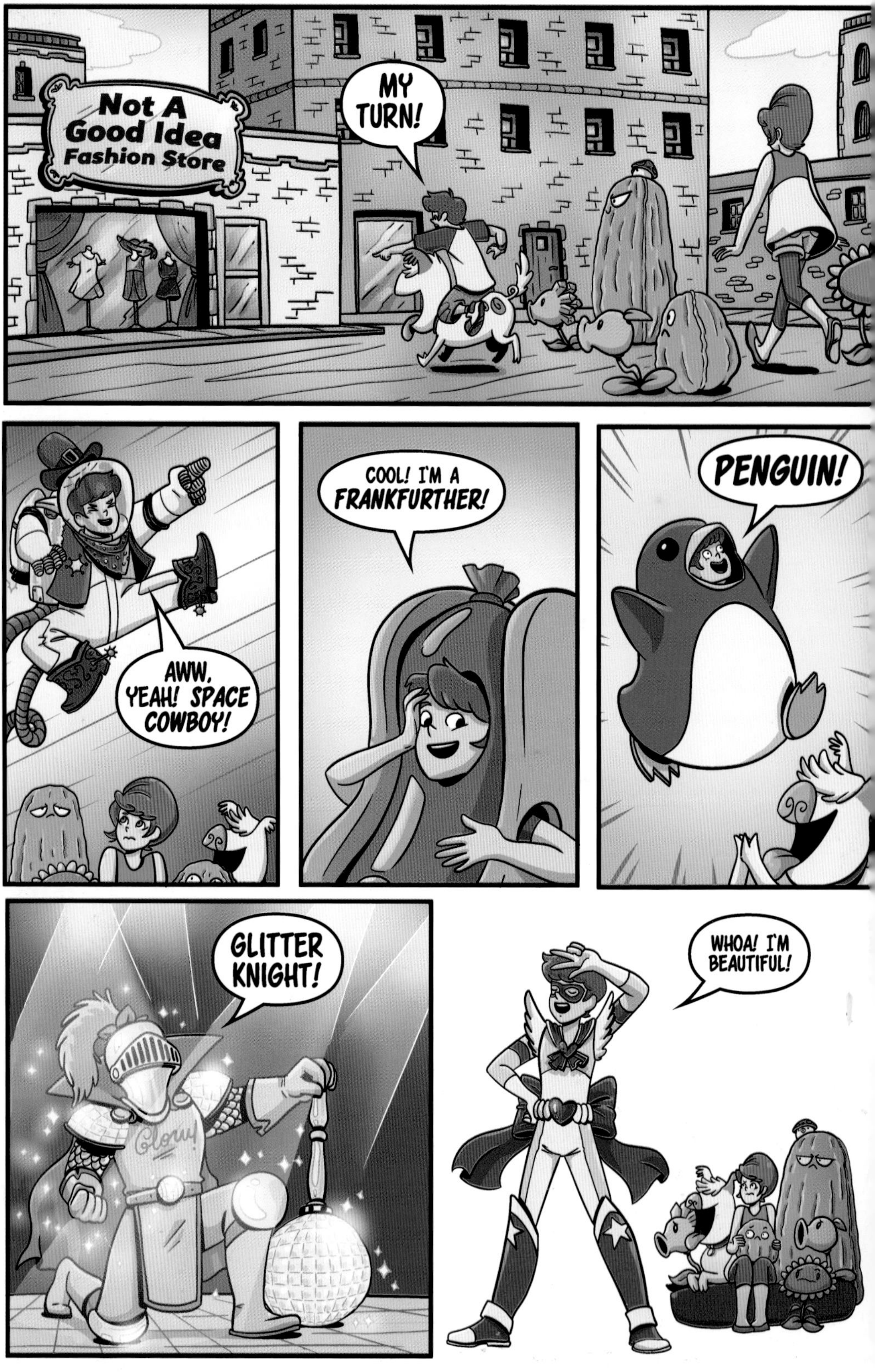
Not A Good Idea Fashion Store
MY TURN!
AWW, YEAH! SPACE COWBOY!
COOL! I'M A FRANKFURTHER!
PENGUIN!
GLITTER KNIGHT!
Glory
WHOA! I'M BEAUTIFUL!

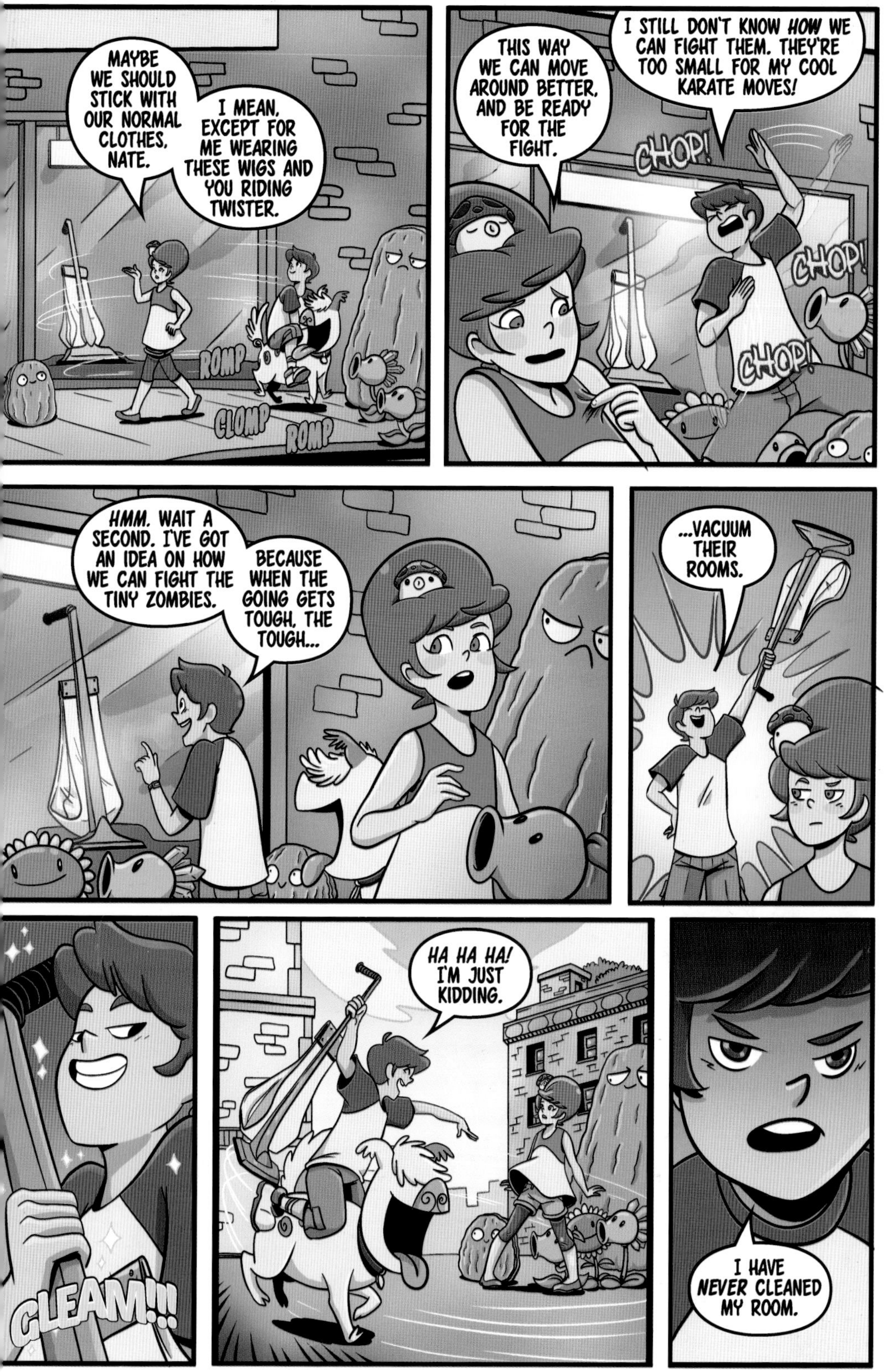
MAYBE WE SHOULD STICK WITH OUR NORMAL CLOTHES, NATE.
I MEAN, EXCEPT FOR ME WEARING THESE WIGS AND YOU RIDING TWISTER.
ROMP
CLOMP
ROMP
THIS WAY WE CAN MOVE AROUND BETTER, AND BE READY FOR THE FIGHT.
I STILL DON'T KNOW *HOW* WE CAN FIGHT THEM. THEY'RE TOO SMALL FOR MY COOL KARATE MOVES!
CHOP!
CHOP!
CHOP!
HMM. WAIT A SECOND. I'VE GOT AN IDEA ON HOW WE CAN FIGHT THE TINY ZOMBIES.
BECAUSE WHEN THE GOING GETS TOUGH, THE TOUGH...
...VACUUM THEIR ROOMS.
GLEAM!!!
HA HA HA! I'M JUST KIDDING.
I HAVE *NEVER* CLEANED MY ROOM.

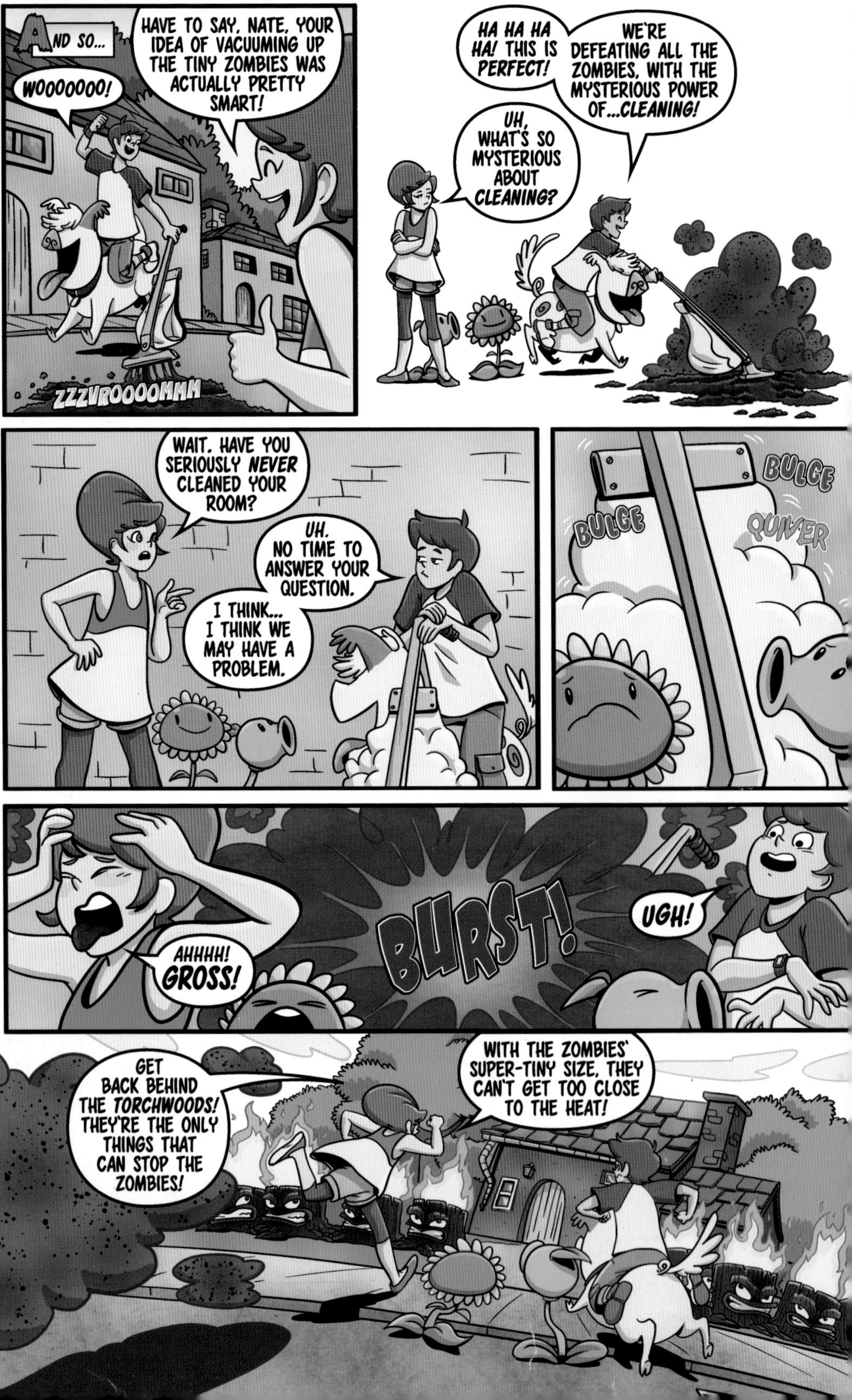
AND SO...
HAVE TO SAY, NATE, YOUR IDEA OF VACUUMING UP THE TINY ZOMBIES WAS ACTUALLY PRETTY SMART!
WOOOOOOO!
ZZZVROOOOMMM
HA HA HA HA! THIS IS PERFECT!
WE'RE DEFEATING ALL THE ZOMBIES, WITH THE MYSTERIOUS POWER OF...CLEANING!
UH, WHAT'S SO MYSTERIOUS ABOUT CLEANING?
WAIT. HAVE YOU SERIOUSLY NEVER CLEANED YOUR ROOM?
UH. NO TIME TO ANSWER YOUR QUESTION.
I THINK... I THINK WE MAY HAVE A PROBLEM.
BULGE
BULGE
QUIVER
BURST!
AHHHH! GROSS!
UGH!
GET BACK BEHIND THE TORCHWOODS! THEY'RE THE ONLY THINGS THAT CAN STOP THE ZOMBIES!
WITH THE ZOMBIES' SUPER-TINY SIZE, THEY CAN'T GET TOO CLOSE TO THE HEAT!

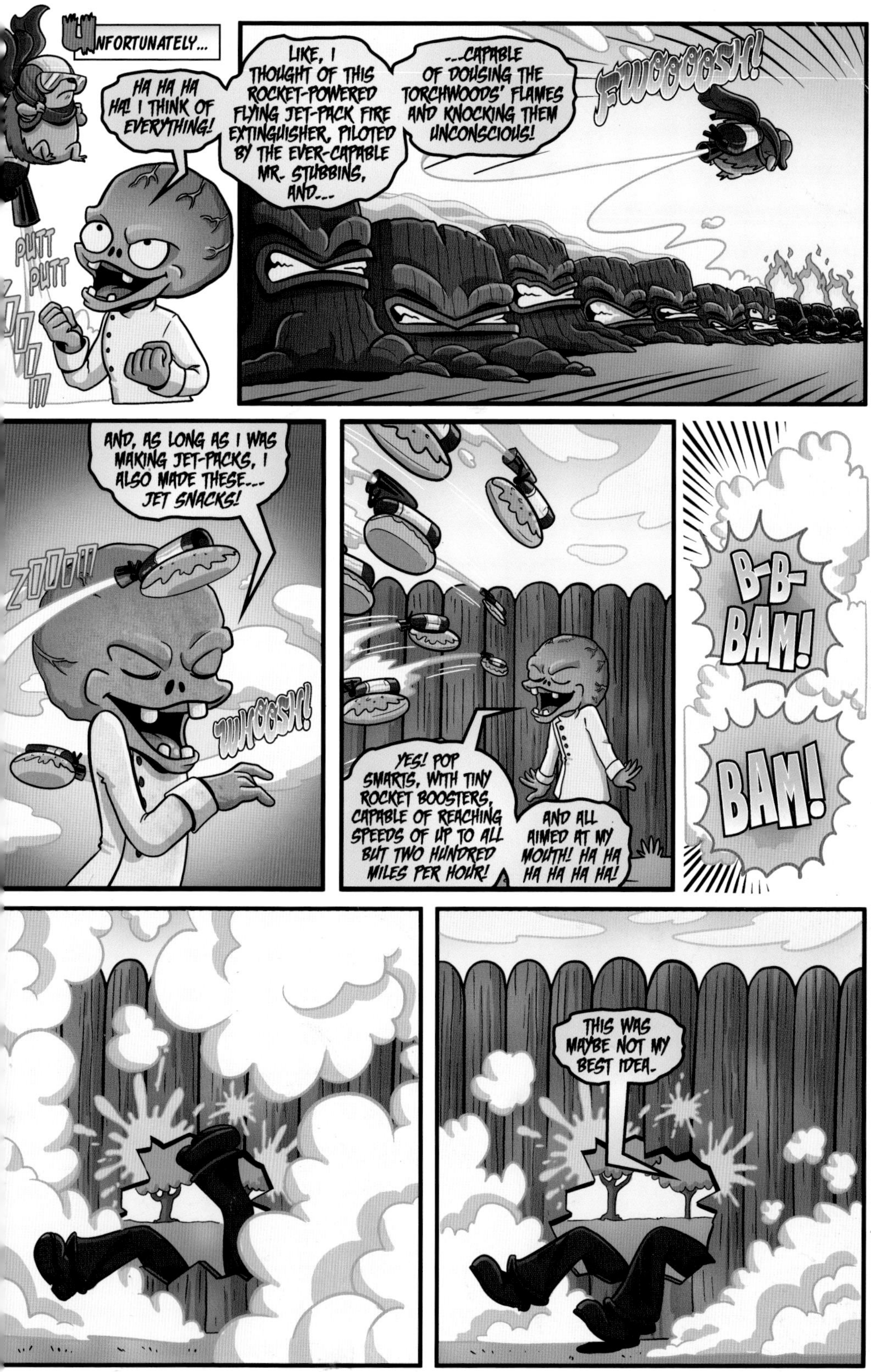
UNFORTUNATELY...
HA HA HA HA! I THINK OF EVERYTHING!
LIKE, I THOUGHT OF THIS ROCKET-POWERED FLYING JET-PACK FIRE EXTINGUISHER, PILOTED BY THE EVER-CAPABLE MR. STUBBINS, AND...
...CAPABLE OF DOUSING THE TORCHWOODS' FLAMES AND KNOCKING THEM UNCONSCIOUS!
FWOOOOOSH!
PUTT PUTT
ZOOOM
AND, AS LONG AS I WAS MAKING JET-PACKS, I ALSO MADE THESE... JET SNACKS!
ZOOOM
WHOOSH!
YES! POP SMARTS, WITH TINY ROCKET BOOSTERS, CAPABLE OF REACHING SPEEDS OF UP TO ALL BUT TWO HUNDRED MILES PER HOUR!
AND ALL AIMED AT MY MOUTH! HA HA HA HA HA HA!
B-B-BAM!
BAM!
THIS WAS MAYBE NOT MY BEST IDEA.

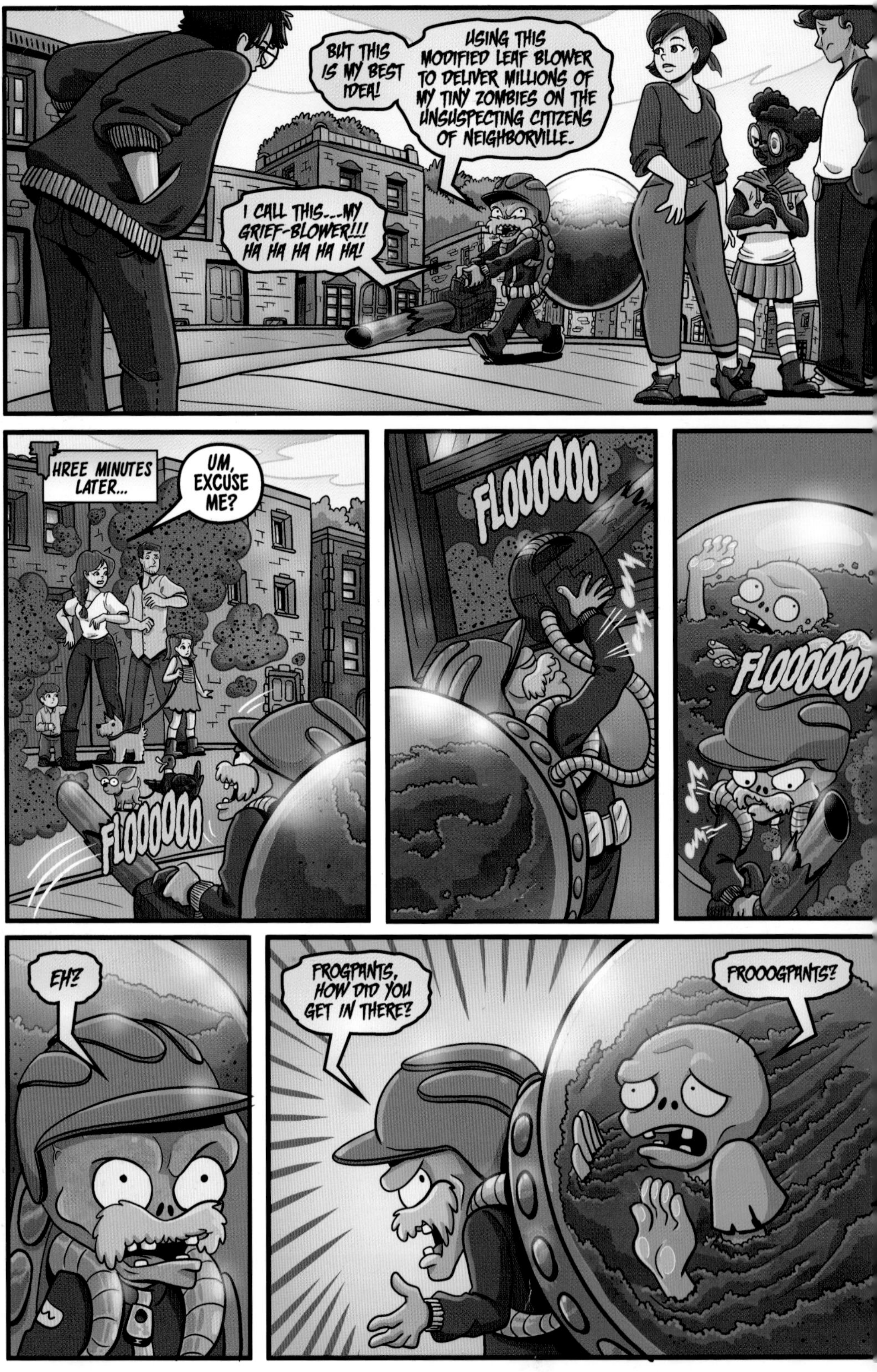
BUT THIS IS MY BEST IDEA!
USING THIS MODIFIED LEAF BLOWER TO DELIVER MILLIONS OF MY TINY ZOMBIES ON THE UNSUSPECTING CITIZENS OF NEIGHBORVILLE.
I CALL THIS...MY GRIEF-BLOWER!!!! HA HA HA HA HA!
THREE MINUTES LATER...
UM, EXCUSE ME?
FLOOOOOO
FLOOOOOO
FLOOOOOO
EH?
FROGPANTS, HOW DID YOU GET IN THERE?
FROOOGPANTS?

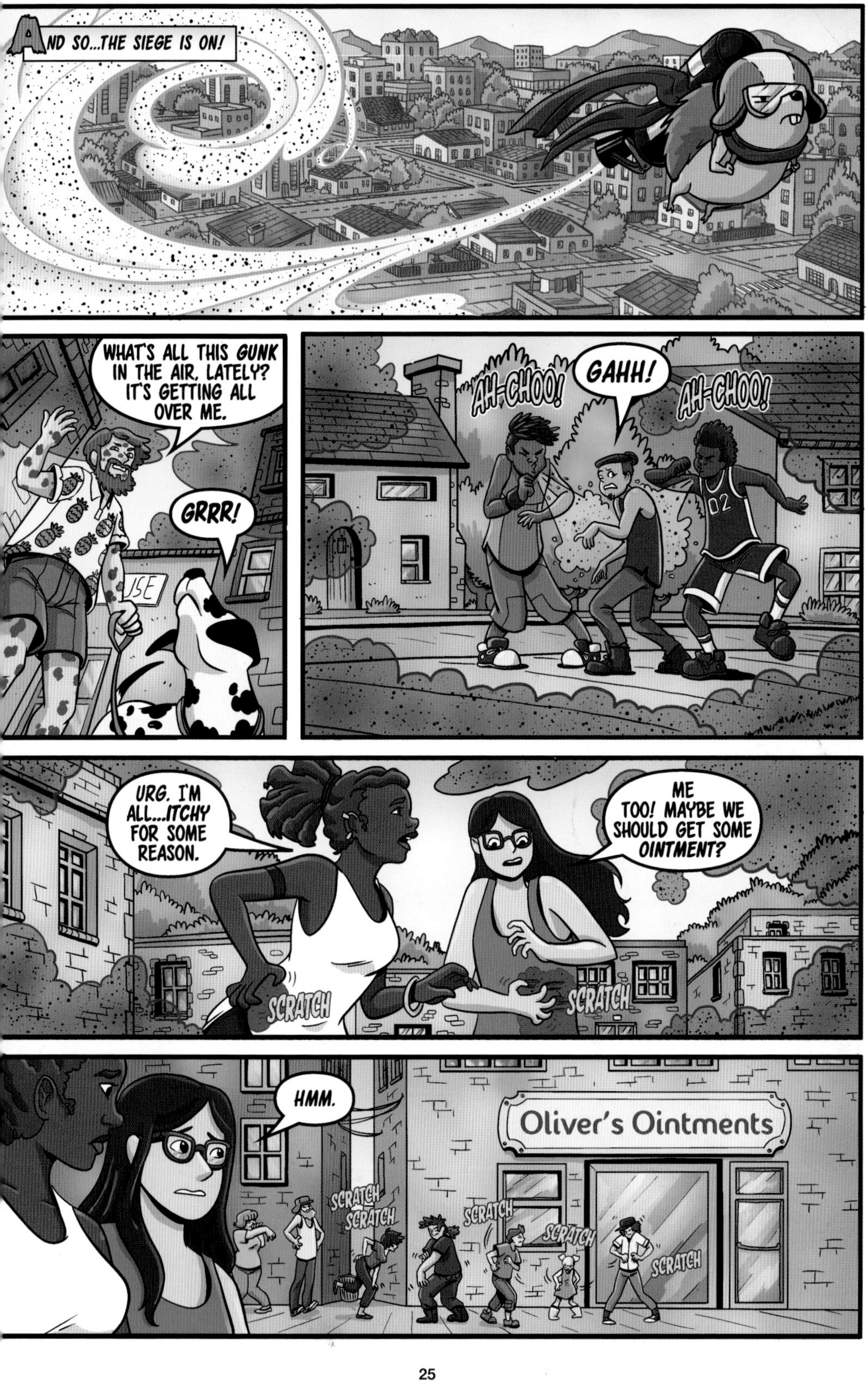
AND SO...THE SIEGE IS ON!
WHAT'S ALL THIS GUNK IN THE AIR, LATELY? IT'S GETTING ALL OVER ME.
GRRR!
AH-CHOO!
GAHH!
AH-CHOO!
URG. I'M ALL...ITCHY FOR SOME REASON.
ME TOO! MAYBE WE SHOULD GET SOME OINTMENT?
SCRATCH
SCRATCH
HMM.
Oliver's Ointments
SCRATCH
SCRATCH
SCRATCH
SCRATCH
SCRATCH

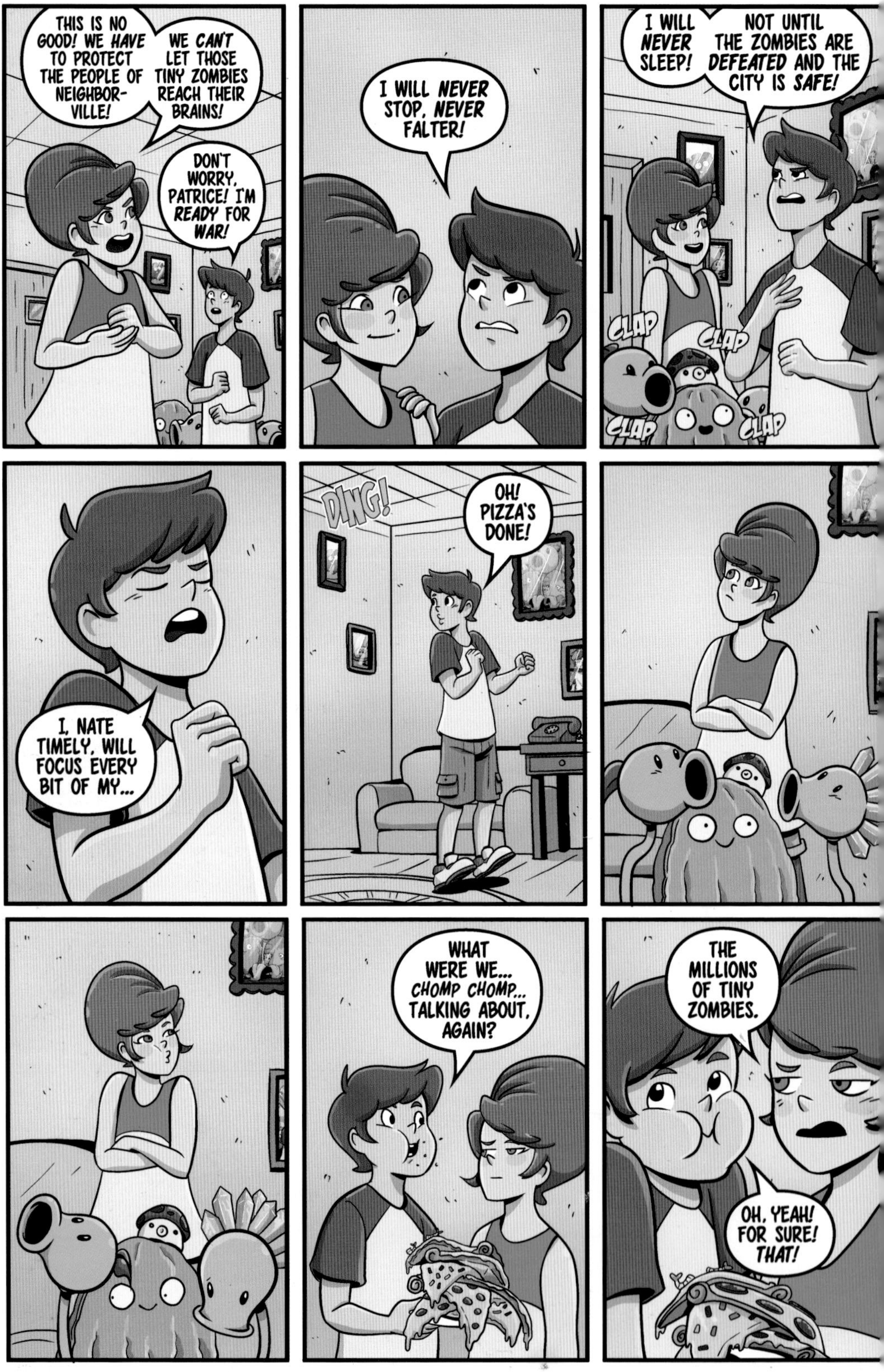
THIS IS NO GOOD! WE HAVE TO PROTECT THE PEOPLE OF NEIGHBOR-VILLE!
WE CAN'T LET THOSE TINY ZOMBIES REACH THEIR BRAINS!
DON'T WORRY, PATRICE! I'M READY FOR WAR!
I WILL NEVER STOP, NEVER FALTER!
I WILL NEVER SLEEP!
NOT UNTIL THE ZOMBIES ARE DEFEATED AND THE CITY IS SAFE!
CLAP
CLAP
CLAP
CLAP
I, NATE TIMELY, WILL FOCUS EVERY BIT OF MY...
DING!
OH! PIZZA'S DONE!
WHAT WERE WE... CHOMP CHOMP... TALKING ABOUT, AGAIN?
THE MILLIONS OF TINY ZOMBIES.
OH, YEAH! FOR SURE! THAT!

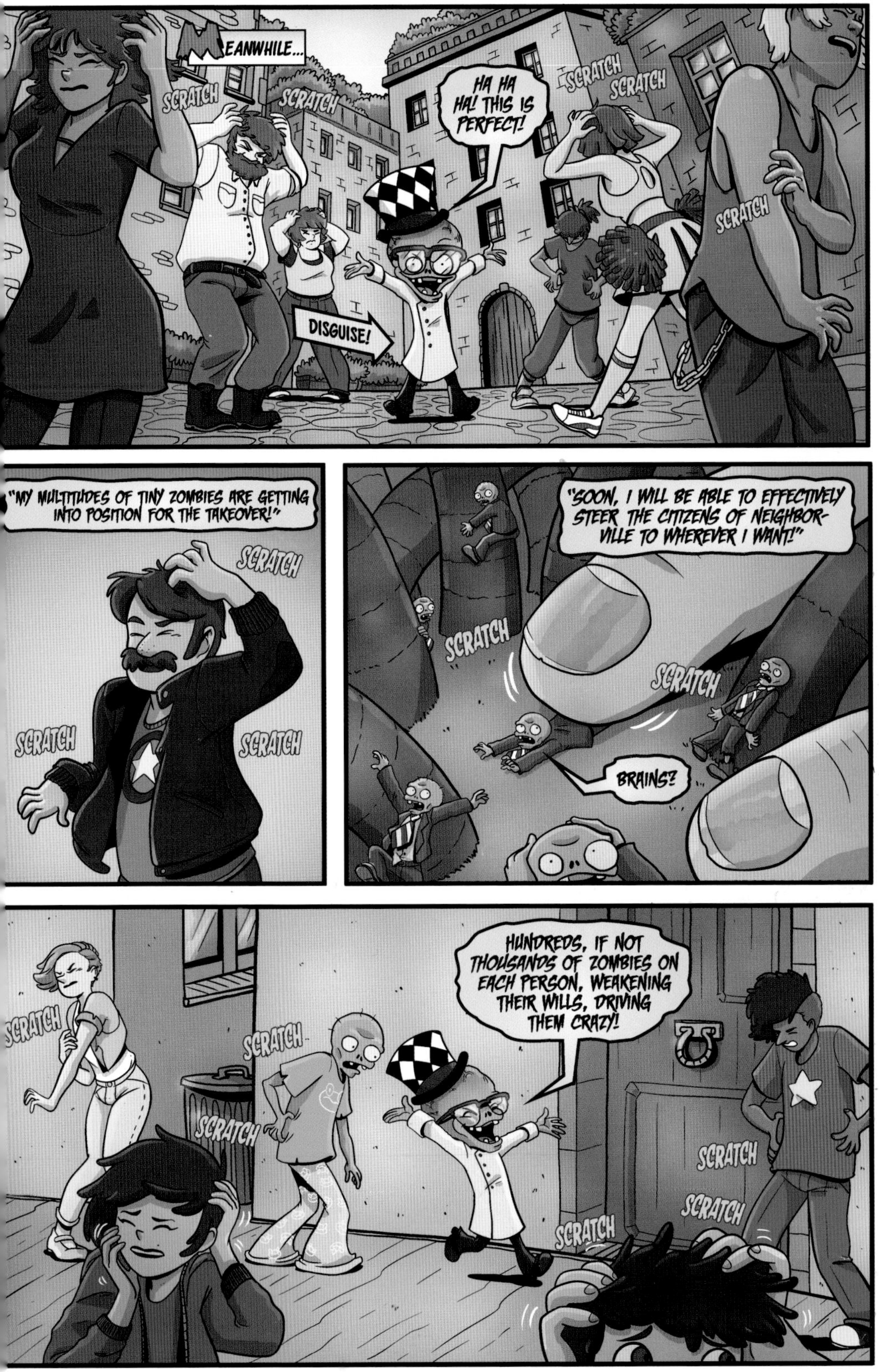
MEANWHILE...
SCRATCH
SCRATCH
HA HA HA! THIS IS PERFECT!
SCRATCH
SCRATCH
SCRATCH
DISGUISE!
"MY MULTITUDES OF TINY ZOMBIES ARE GETTING INTO POSITION FOR THE TAKEOVER!"
SCRATCH
SCRATCH
SCRATCH
"SOON, I WILL BE ABLE TO EFFECTIVELY STEER THE CITIZENS OF NEIGHBOR-VILLE TO WHEREVER I WANT!"
SCRATCH
SCRATCH
BRAINS?
HUNDREDS, IF NOT THOUSANDS OF ZOMBIES ON EACH PERSON, WEAKENING THEIR WILLS, DRIVING THEM CRAZY!
SCRATCH
SCRATCH
SCRATCH
SCRATCH
SCRATCH
SCRATCH

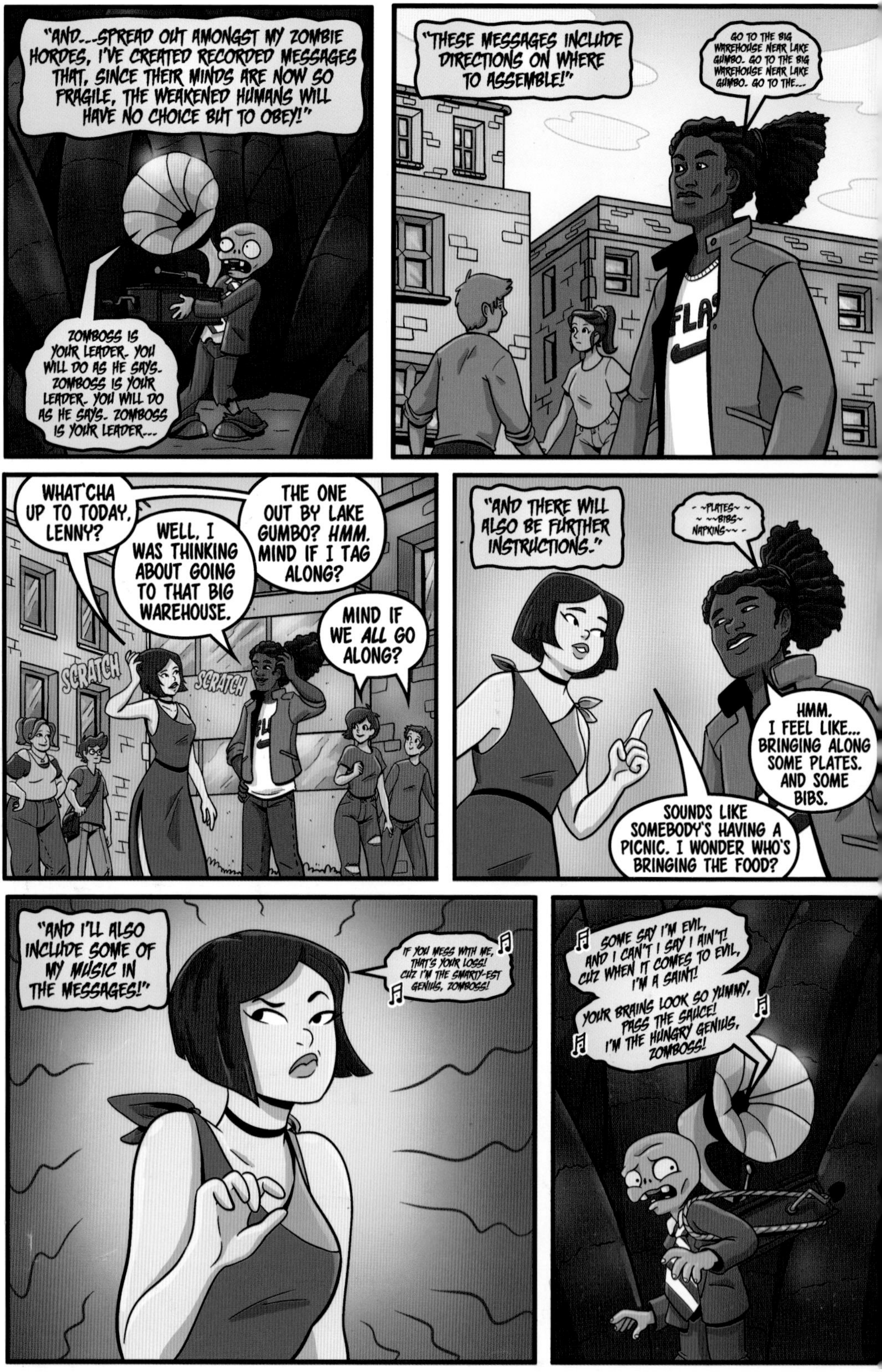
"AND...SPREAD OUT AMONGST MY ZOMBIE HORDES, I'VE CREATED RECORDED MESSAGES THAT, SINCE THEIR MINDS ARE NOW SO FRAGILE, THE WEAKENED HUMANS WILL HAVE NO CHOICE BUT TO OBEY!"
ZOMBOSS IS YOUR LEADER. YOU WILL DO AS HE SAYS. ZOMBOSS IS YOUR LEADER. YOU WILL DO AS HE SAYS. ZOMBOSS IS YOUR LEADER...
"THESE MESSAGES INCLUDE DIRECTIONS ON WHERE TO ASSEMBLE!"
GO TO THE BIG WAREHOUSE NEAR LAKE GUMBO. GO TO THE BIG WAREHOUSE NEAR LAKE GUMBO. GO TO THE...
WHAT'CHA UP TO TODAY, LENNY?
WELL, I WAS THINKING ABOUT GOING TO THAT BIG WAREHOUSE.
THE ONE OUT BY LAKE GUMBO? HMM. MIND IF I TAG ALONG?
MIND IF WE ALL GO ALONG?
SCRATCH
SCRATCH
"AND THERE WILL ALSO BE FURTHER INSTRUCTIONS."
~PLATES~ ~BIBS~ NAPKINS~
HMM. I FEEL LIKE... BRINGING ALONG SOME PLATES. AND SOME BIBS.
SOUNDS LIKE SOMEBODY'S HAVING A PICNIC. I WONDER WHO'S BRINGING THE FOOD?
"AND I'LL ALSO INCLUDE SOME OF MY MUSIC IN THE MESSAGES!"
IF YOU MESS WITH ME, THAT'S YOUR LOSS! CUZ I'M THE SMARTY-EST GENIUS, ZOMBOSS!
SOME SAY I'M EVIL, AND I CAN'T SAY I AIN'T! CUZ WHEN IT COMES TO EVIL, I'M A SAINT!
YOUR BRAINS LOOK SO YUMMY, PASS THE SAUCE! I'M THE HUNGRY GENIUS, ZOMBOSS!

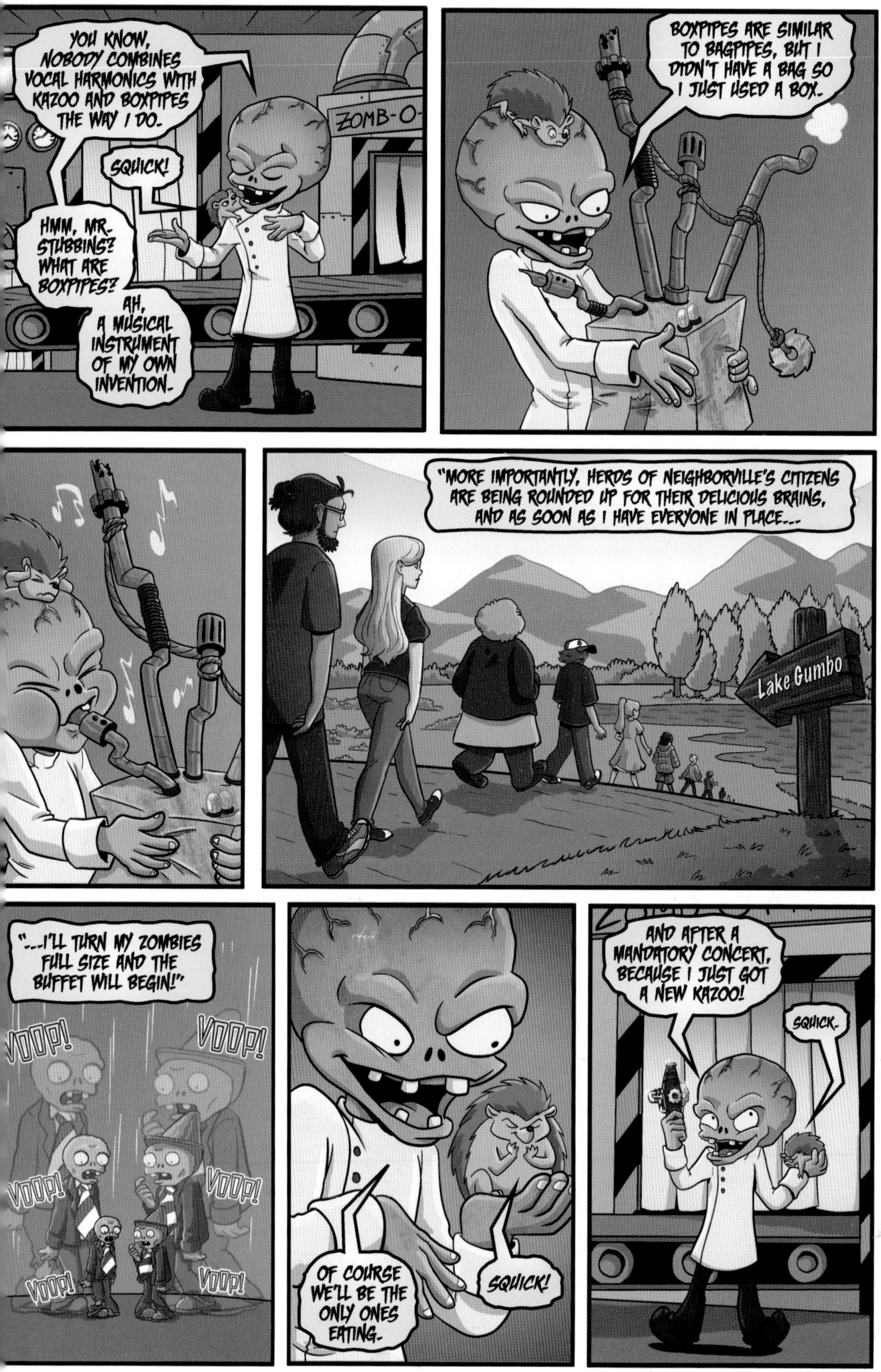
YOU KNOW, NOBODY COMBINES VOCAL HARMONICS WITH KAZOO AND BOXPIPES THE WAY I DO.
ZOMB-O-
SQUICK!
HMM, MR. STUBBINS? WHAT ARE BOXPIPES?
AH, A MUSICAL INSTRUMENT OF MY OWN INVENTION.
BOXPIPES ARE SIMILAR TO BAGPIPES, BUT I DIDN'T HAVE A BAG SO I JUST USED A BOX.
"MORE IMPORTANTLY, HERDS OF NEIGHBORVILLE'S CITIZENS ARE BEING ROUNDED UP FOR THEIR DELICIOUS BRAINS, AND AS SOON AS I HAVE EVERYONE IN PLACE...
Lake Gumbo
"...I'LL TURN MY ZOMBIES FULL SIZE AND THE BUFFET WILL BEGIN!"
VOOP!
VOOP!
VOOP!
VOOP!
VOOP!
VOOP!
OF COURSE WE'LL BE THE ONLY ONES EATING.
SQUICK!
AND AFTER A MANDATORY CONCERT, BECAUSE I JUST GOT A NEW KAZOO!
SQUICK.

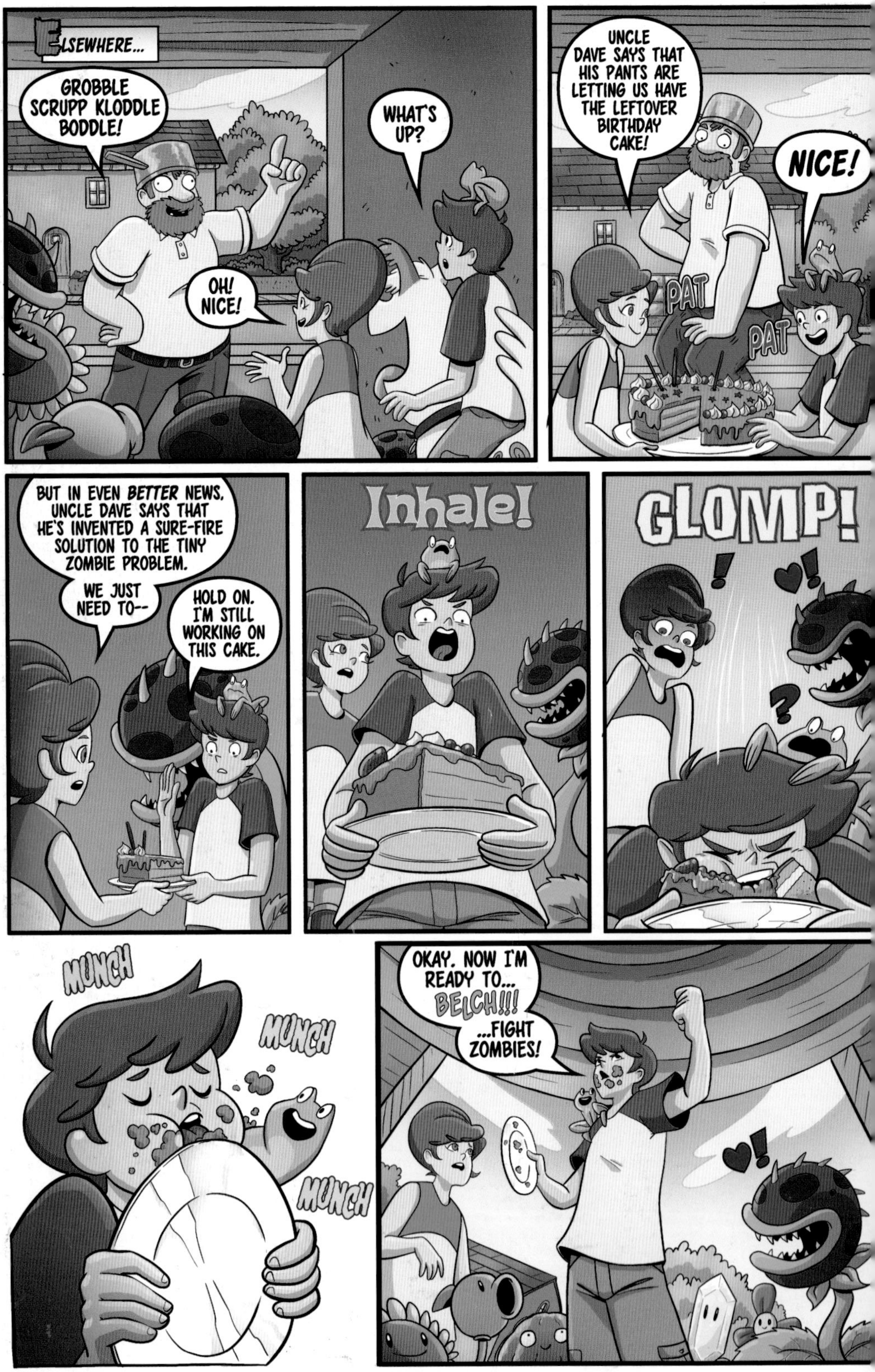
ELSEWHERE...
GROBBLE SCRUPP KLODDLE BODDLE!
WHAT'S UP?
OH! NICE!
UNCLE DAVE SAYS THAT HIS PANTS ARE LETTING US HAVE THE LEFTOVER BIRTHDAY CAKE!
NICE!
PAT
PAT
BUT IN EVEN BETTER NEWS, UNCLE DAVE SAYS THAT HE'S INVENTED A SURE-FIRE SOLUTION TO THE TINY ZOMBIE PROBLEM.
WE JUST NEED TO--
HOLD ON. I'M STILL WORKING ON THIS CAKE.
Inhale!
GLOMP!
MUNCH
MUNCH
MUNCH
OKAY. NOW I'M READY TO... BELCH!!! ...FIGHT ZOMBIES!

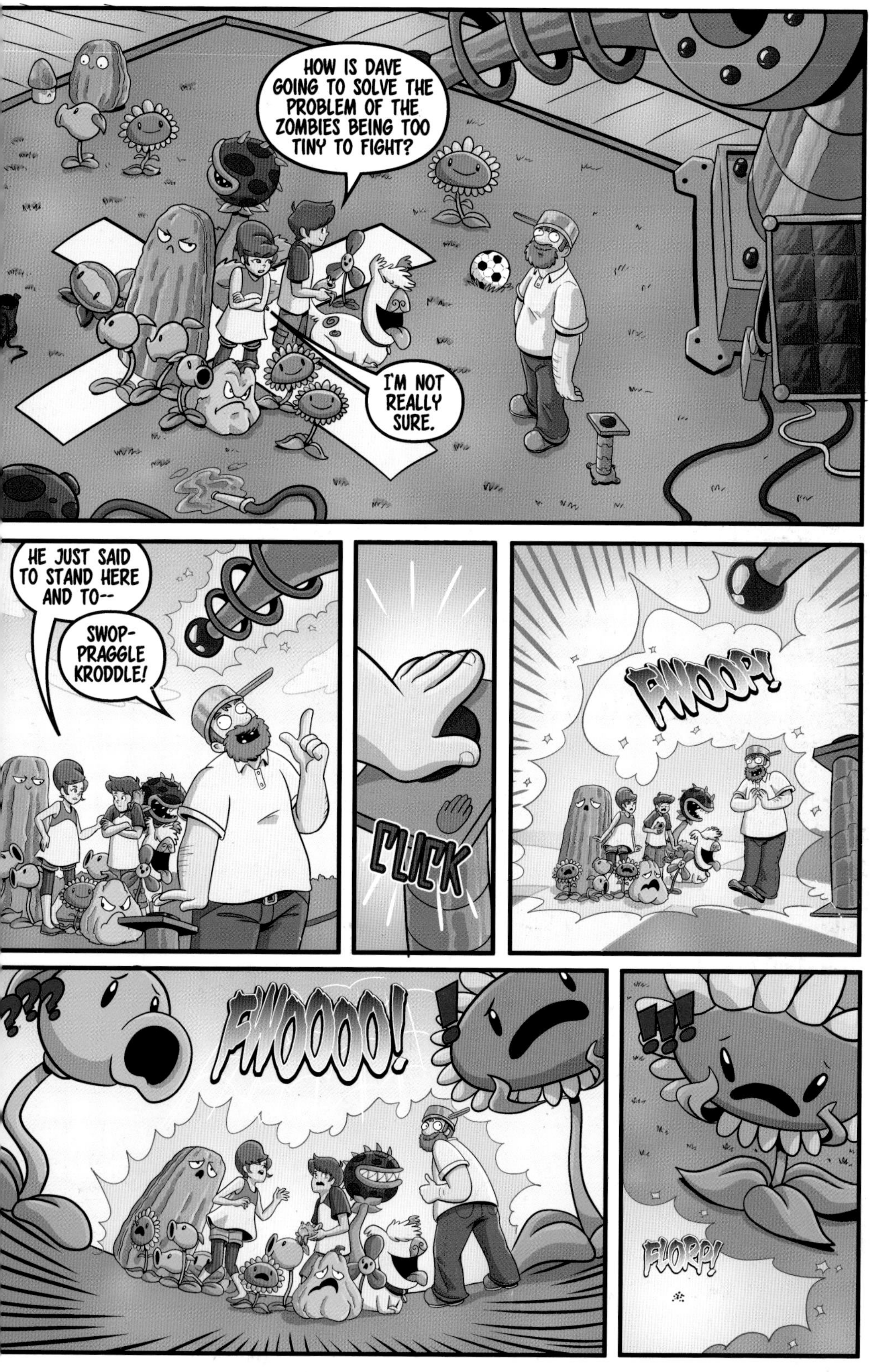
HOW IS DAVE GOING TO SOLVE THE PROBLEM OF THE ZOMBIES BEING TOO TINY TO FIGHT?
I'M NOT REALLY SURE.
HE JUST SAID TO STAND HERE AND TO--
SWOP-PRAGGLE KRODDLE!
CLICK
FWOOP!
???
FWOOOO!
!
!!
FLORP!

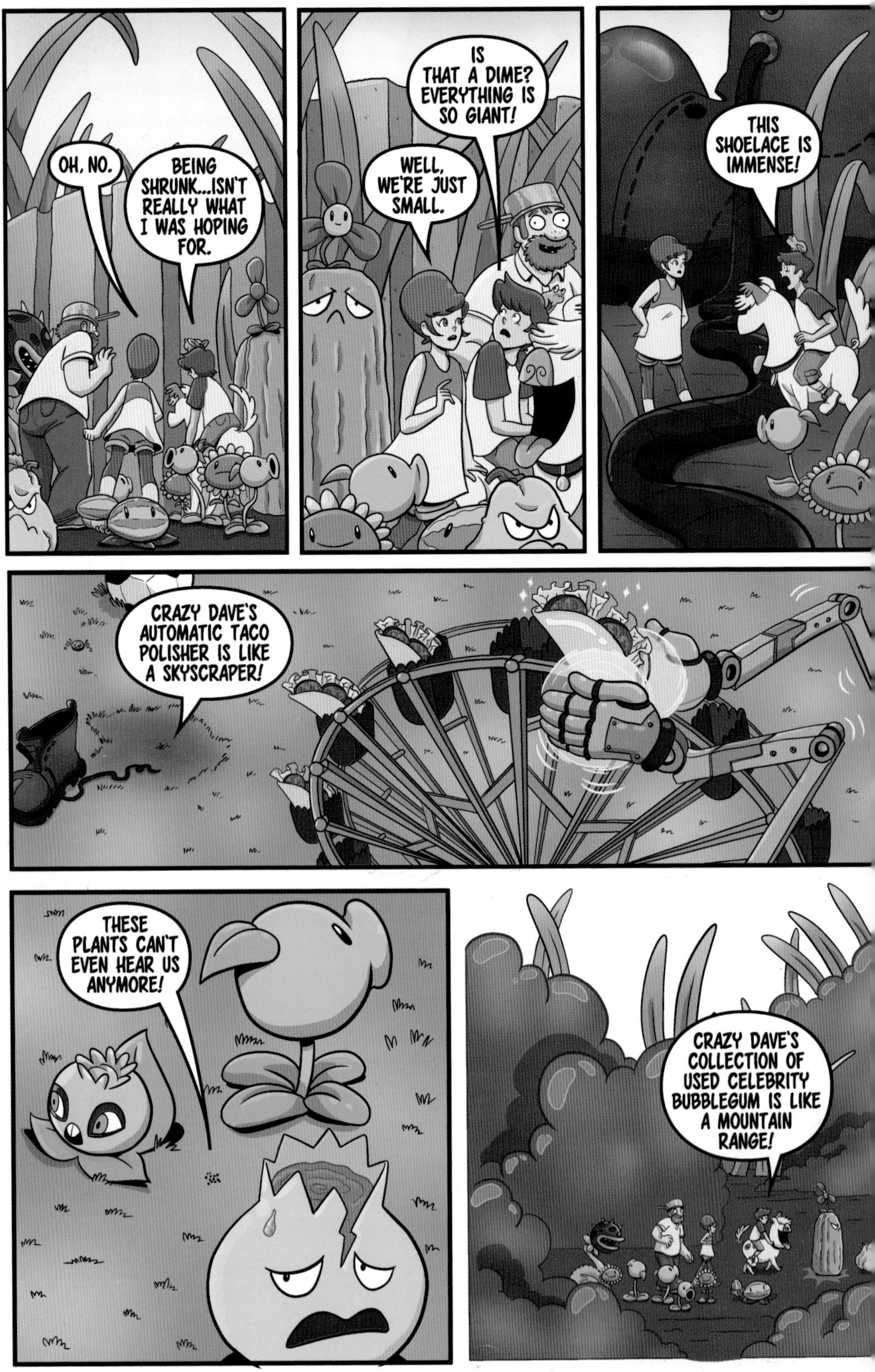
OH, NO.
BEING SHRUNK...ISN'T REALLY WHAT I WAS HOPING FOR.
IS THAT A DIME? EVERYTHING IS SO GIANT!
WELL, WE'RE JUST SMALL.
THIS SHOELACE IS IMMENSE!
CRAZY DAVE'S AUTOMATIC TACO POLISHER IS LIKE A SKYSCRAPER!
THESE PLANTS CAN'T EVEN HEAR US ANYMORE!
CRAZY DAVE'S COLLECTION OF USED CELEBRITY BUBBLEGUM IS LIKE A MOUNTAIN RANGE!

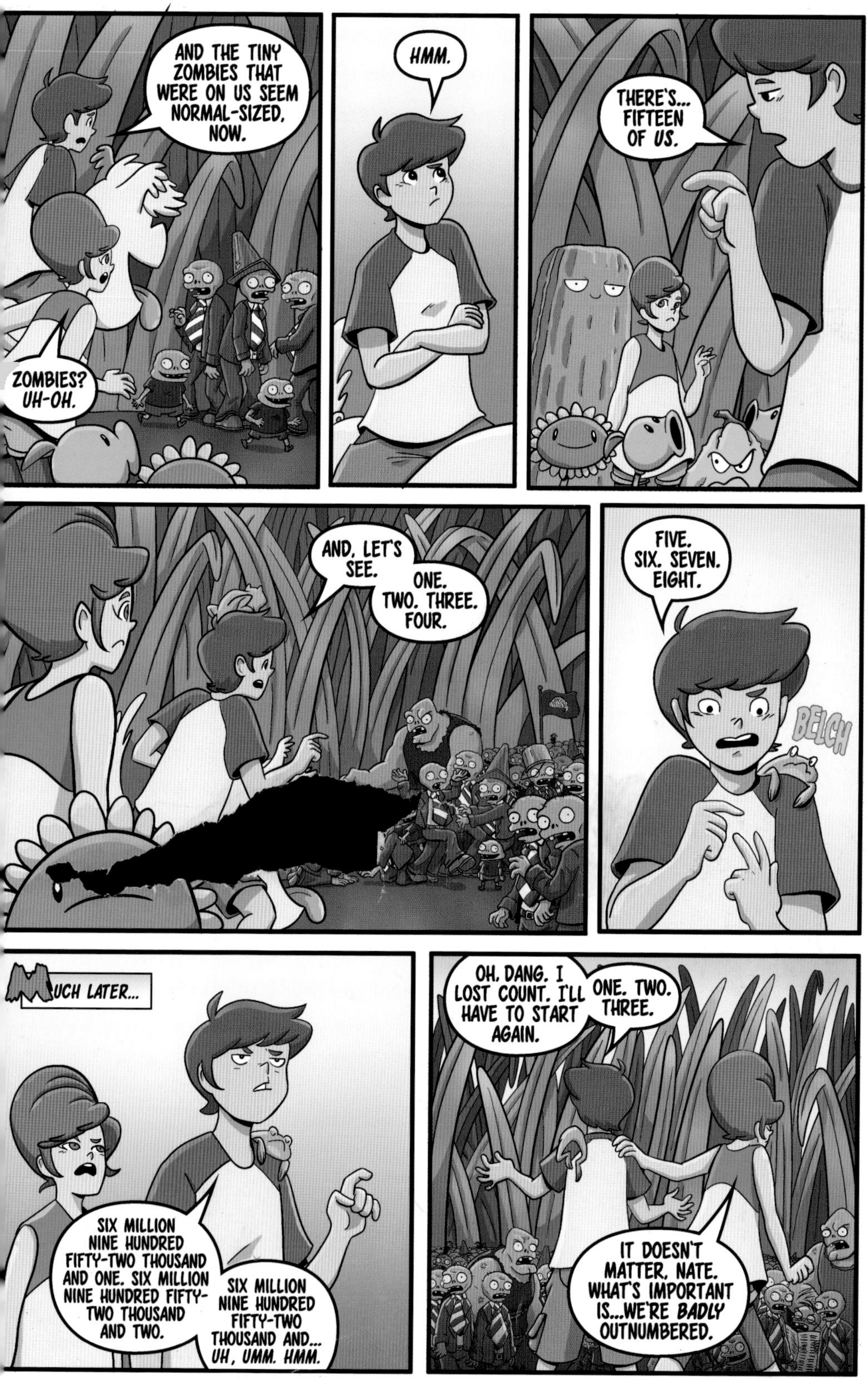
AND THE TINY ZOMBIES THAT WERE ON US SEEM NORMAL-SIZED, NOW.
ZOMBIES? UH-OH.
HMM.
THERE'S... FIFTEEN OF US.
AND, LET'S SEE.
ONE. TWO. THREE. FOUR.
FIVE. SIX. SEVEN. EIGHT.
BELCH
MUCH LATER...
SIX MILLION NINE HUNDRED FIFTY-TWO THOUSAND AND ONE. SIX MILLION NINE HUNDRED FIFTY-TWO THOUSAND AND TWO.
SIX MILLION NINE HUNDRED FIFTY-TWO THOUSAND AND... UH, UMM. HMM.
OH, DANG. I LOST COUNT. I'LL HAVE TO START AGAIN.
ONE. TWO. THREE.
IT DOESN'T MATTER, NATE. WHAT'S IMPORTANT IS...WE'RE BADLY OUTNUMBERED.

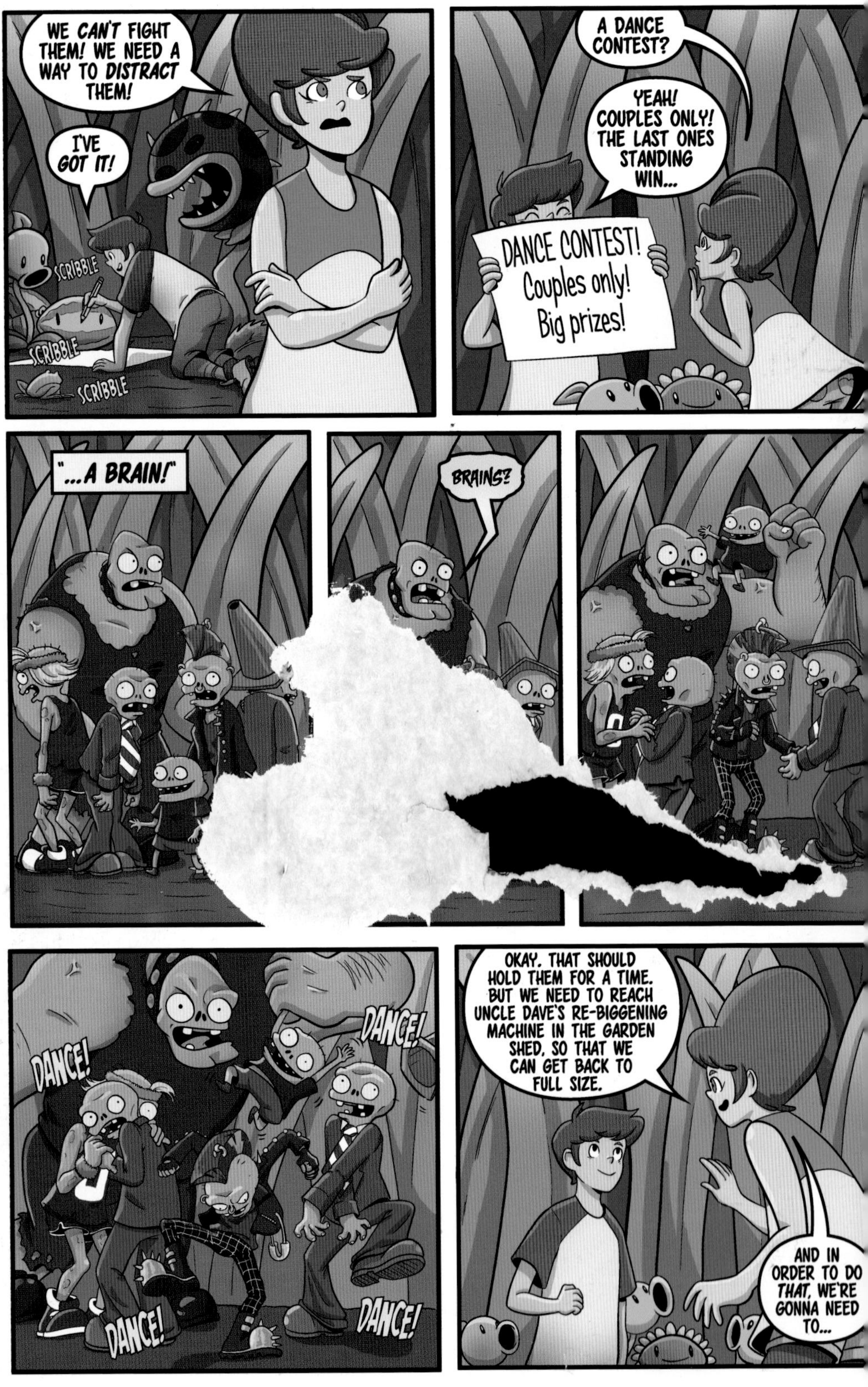
WE CAN'T FIGHT THEM! WE NEED A WAY TO DISTRACT THEM!
I'VE GOT IT!
SCRIBBLE
SCRIBBLE
SCRIBBLE
A DANCE CONTEST?
YEAH! COUPLES ONLY! THE LAST ONES STANDING WIN...
DANCE CONTEST! Couples only! Big prizes!
"...A BRAIN!"
BRAINS?
DANCE!
DANCE!
DANCE!
DANCE!
OKAY. THAT SHOULD HOLD THEM FOR A TIME. BUT WE NEED TO REACH UNCLE DAVE'S RE-BIGGENING MACHINE IN THE GARDEN SHED, SO THAT WE CAN GET BACK TO FULL SIZE.
AND IN ORDER TO DO THAT, WE'RE GONNA NEED TO...

"...CROSS THE YARD."

THIS *ISN'T* GOING TO BE EASY. IT'S LIKE A THICK *CITY OF GRASS.*

OOH! A CITY!

...ARE ...RANTS? ...OSE SOME ...IZZA!

THERE ARE NO RESTAURANTS, NATE. ONLY... OBSTACLES.

"LIKE YOUR SKATEBOARD. WE'LL HAVE TO GO AROUND IT.

"AND THOSE PIZZA BOXES. WE'LL HAVE TO CLIMB OVER THEM."

SUNSHINE PIZZA

PIZZA

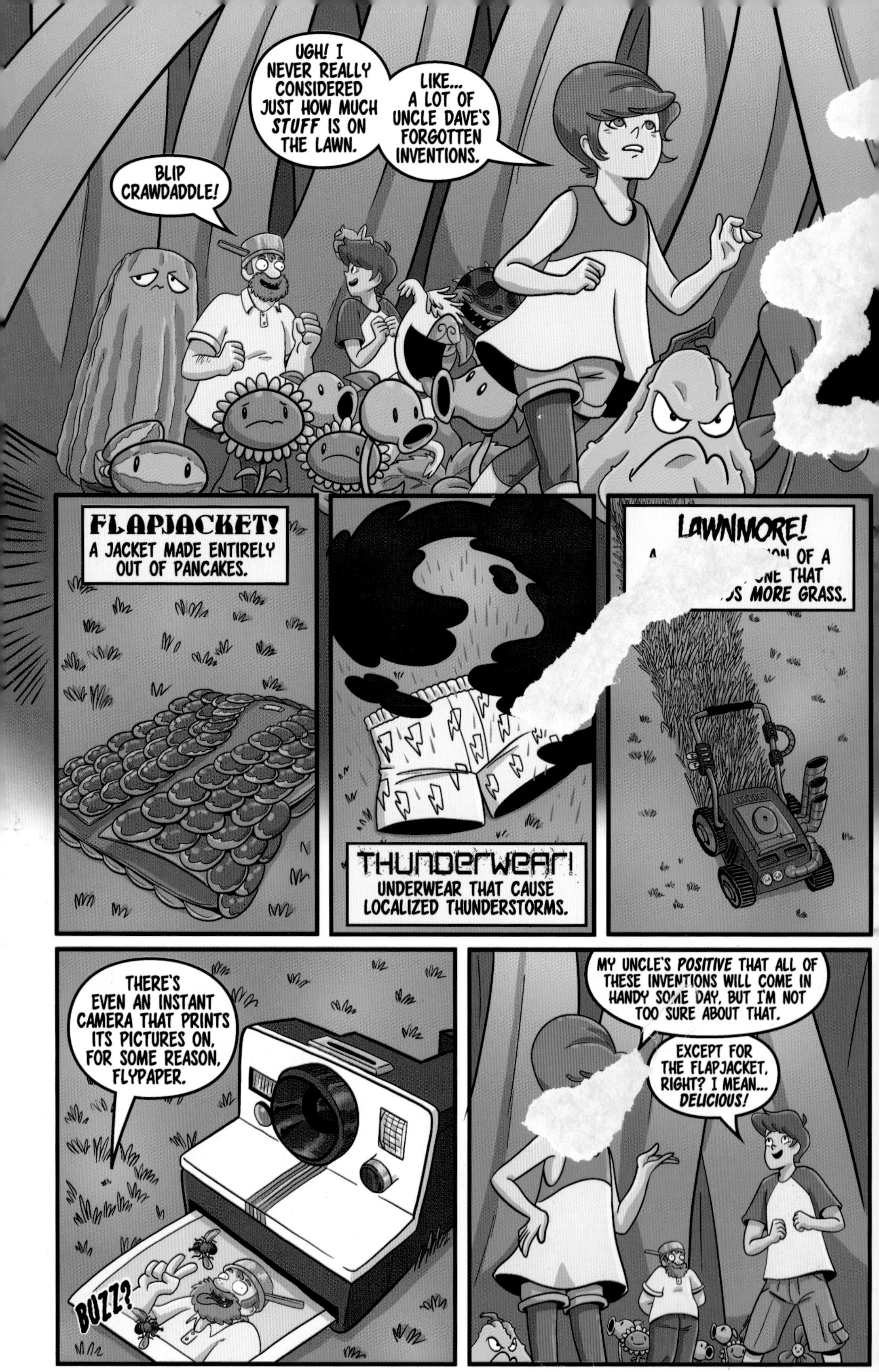
UGH! I NEVER REALLY CONSIDERED JUST HOW MUCH STUFF IS ON THE LAWN.
LIKE... A LOT OF UNCLE DAVE'S FORGOTTEN INVENTIONS.
BLIP CRAWDADDLE!
FLAPJACKET!
A JACKET MADE ENTIRELY OUT OF PANCAKES.
THUNDERWEAR!
UNDERWEAR THAT CAUSE LOCALIZED THUNDERSTORMS.
LAWNMORE!
MORE GRASS.
THERE'S EVEN AN INSTANT CAMERA THAT PRINTS ITS PICTURES ON, FOR SOME REASON, FLYPAPER.
BUZZ?
MY UNCLE'S POSITIVE THAT ALL OF THESE INVENTIONS WILL COME IN HANDY SOME DAY, BUT I'M NOT TOO SURE ABOUT THAT.
EXCEPT FOR THE FLAPJACKET, RIGHT? I MEAN... DELICIOUS!

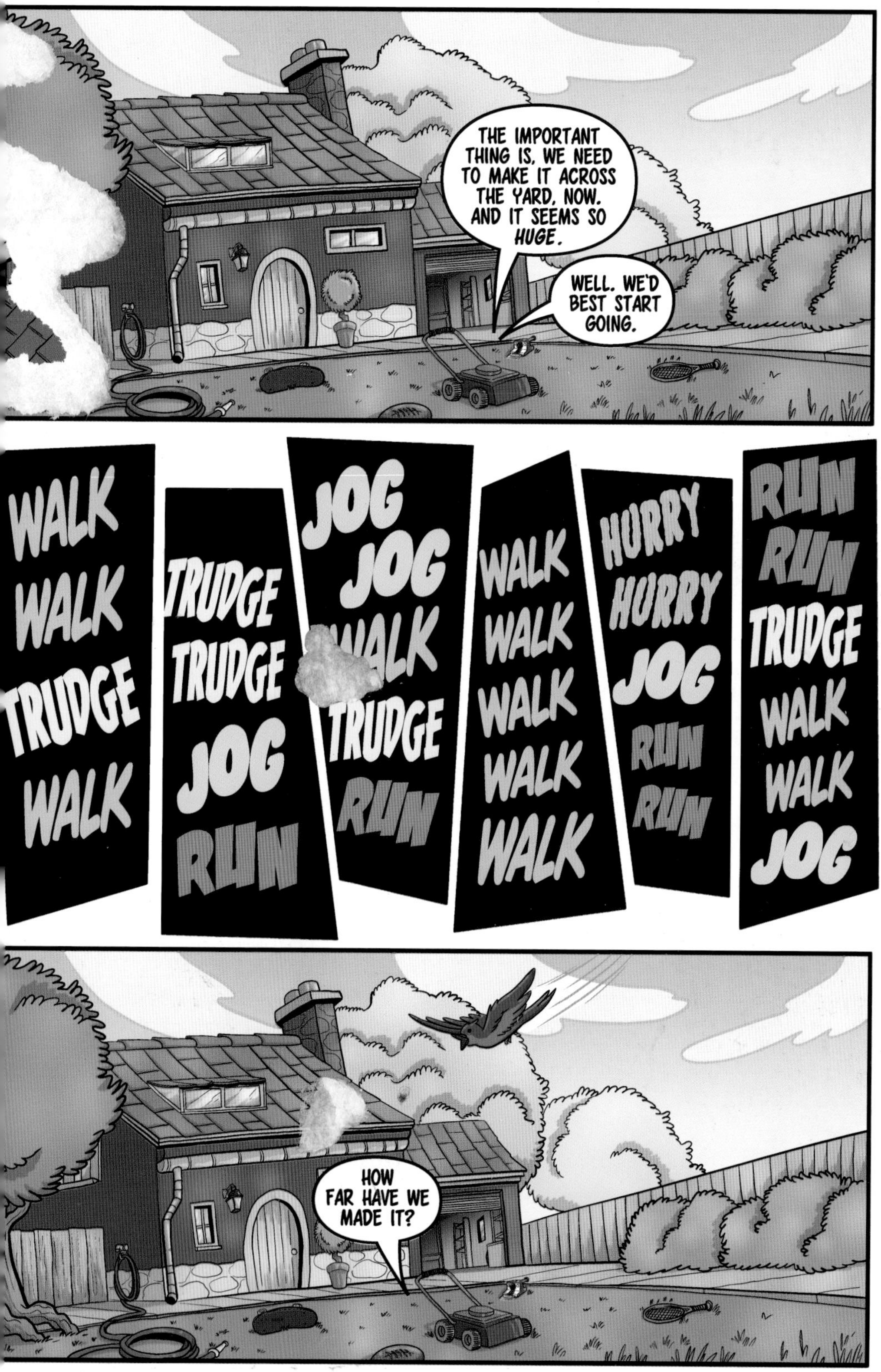
THE IMPORTANT THING IS, WE NEED TO MAKE IT ACROSS THE YARD, NOW. AND IT SEEMS SO *HUGE*.
WELL. WE'D BEST START GOING.
WALK WALK TRUDGE WALK
TRUDGE TRUDGE JOG RUN
JOG JOG WALK TRUDGE RUN
WALK WALK WALK WALK WALK
HURRY HURRY JOG RUN RUN
RUN RUN TRUDGE WALK WALK JOG
HOW FAR HAVE WE MADE IT?

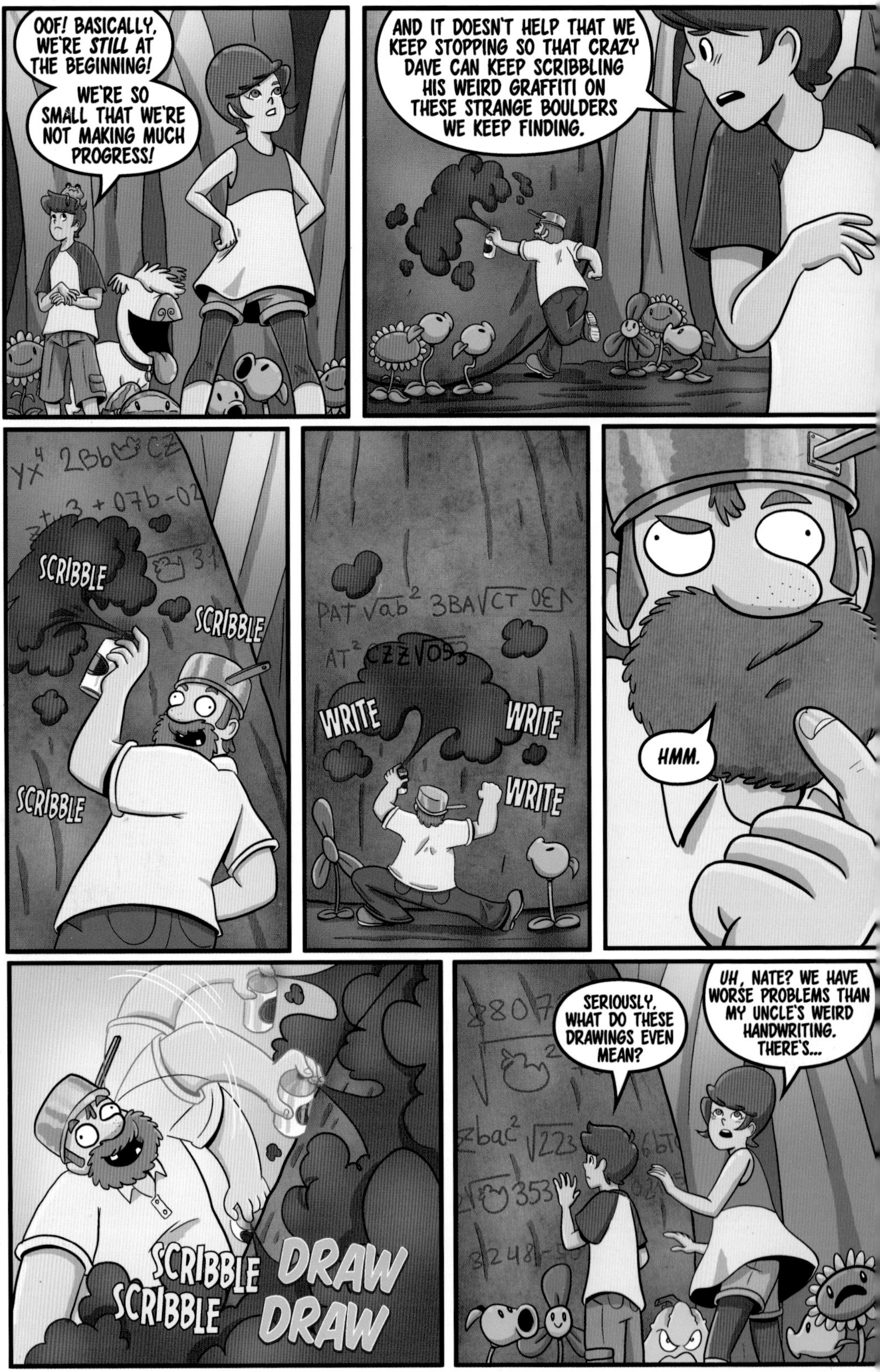
OOF! BASICALLY, WE'RE *STILL* AT THE BEGINNING!
WE'RE SO SMALL THAT WE'RE NOT MAKING MUCH PROGRESS!
AND IT DOESN'T HELP THAT WE KEEP STOPPING SO THAT CRAZY DAVE CAN KEEP SCRIBBLING HIS WEIRD GRAFFITI ON THESE STRANGE BOULDERS WE KEEP FINDING.
SCRIBBLE
SCRIBBLE
SCRIBBLE
WRITE
WRITE
WRITE
HMM.
SCRIBBLE
SCRIBBLE
DRAW
DRAW
SERIOUSLY, WHAT DO THESE DRAWINGS EVEN MEAN?
UH, NATE? WE HAVE WORSE PROBLEMS THAN MY UNCLE'S WEIRD HANDWRITING. THERE'S...

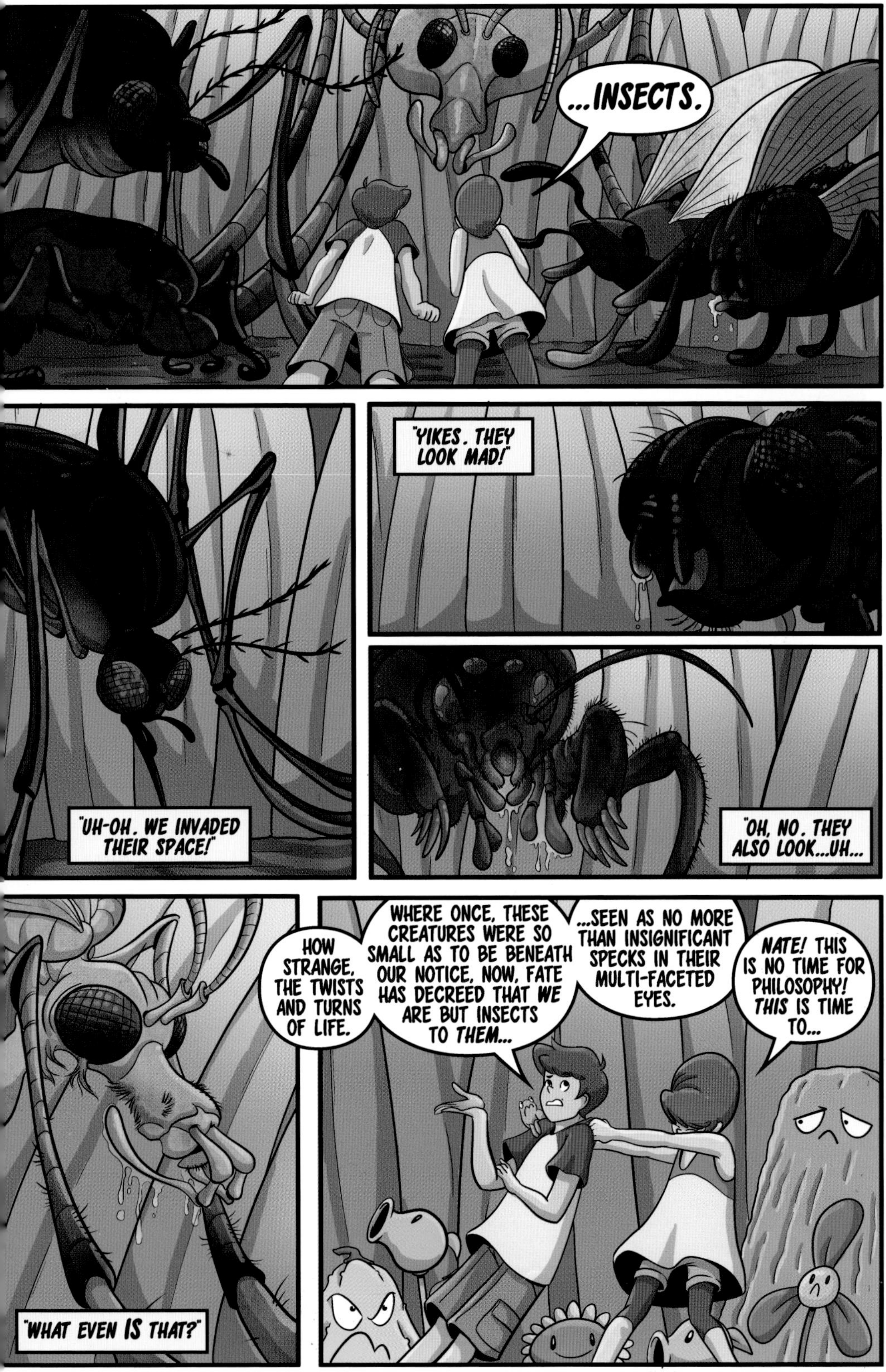
...INSECTS.
"YIKES. THEY LOOK MAD!"
"UH-OH. WE INVADED THEIR SPACE!"
"OH, NO. THEY ALSO LOOK...UH...
"WHAT EVEN IS THAT?"
HOW STRANGE, THE TWISTS AND TURNS OF LIFE.
WHERE ONCE, THESE CREATURES WERE SO SMALL AS TO BE BENEATH OUR NOTICE, NOW, FATE HAS DECREED THAT WE ARE BUT INSECTS TO THEM...
...SEEN AS NO MORE THAN INSIGNIFICANT SPECKS IN THEIR MULTI-FACETED EYES.
NATE! THIS IS NO TIME FOR PHILOSOPHY! THIS IS TIME TO...

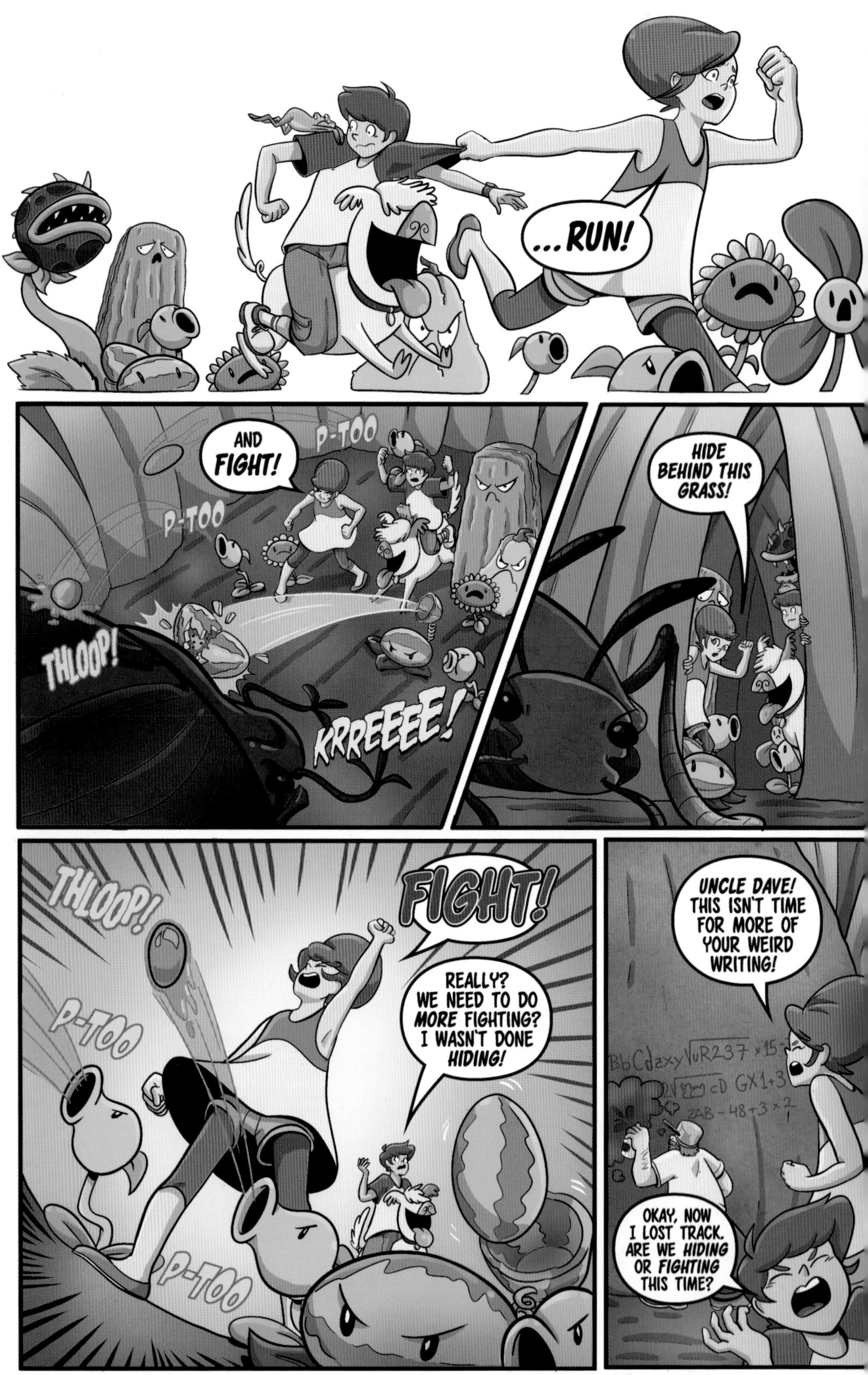
...RUN!
AND FIGHT!
P-TOO
P-TOO
THLOOP!
KRREEEE!
HIDE BEHIND THIS GRASS!
THLOOP!
P-TOO
FIGHT!
REALLY? WE NEED TO DO MORE FIGHTING? I WASN'T DONE HIDING!
P-TOO
UNCLE DAVE! THIS ISN'T TIME FOR MORE OF YOUR WEIRD WRITING!
OKAY, NOW I LOST TRACK. ARE WE HIDING OR FIGHTING THIS TIME?

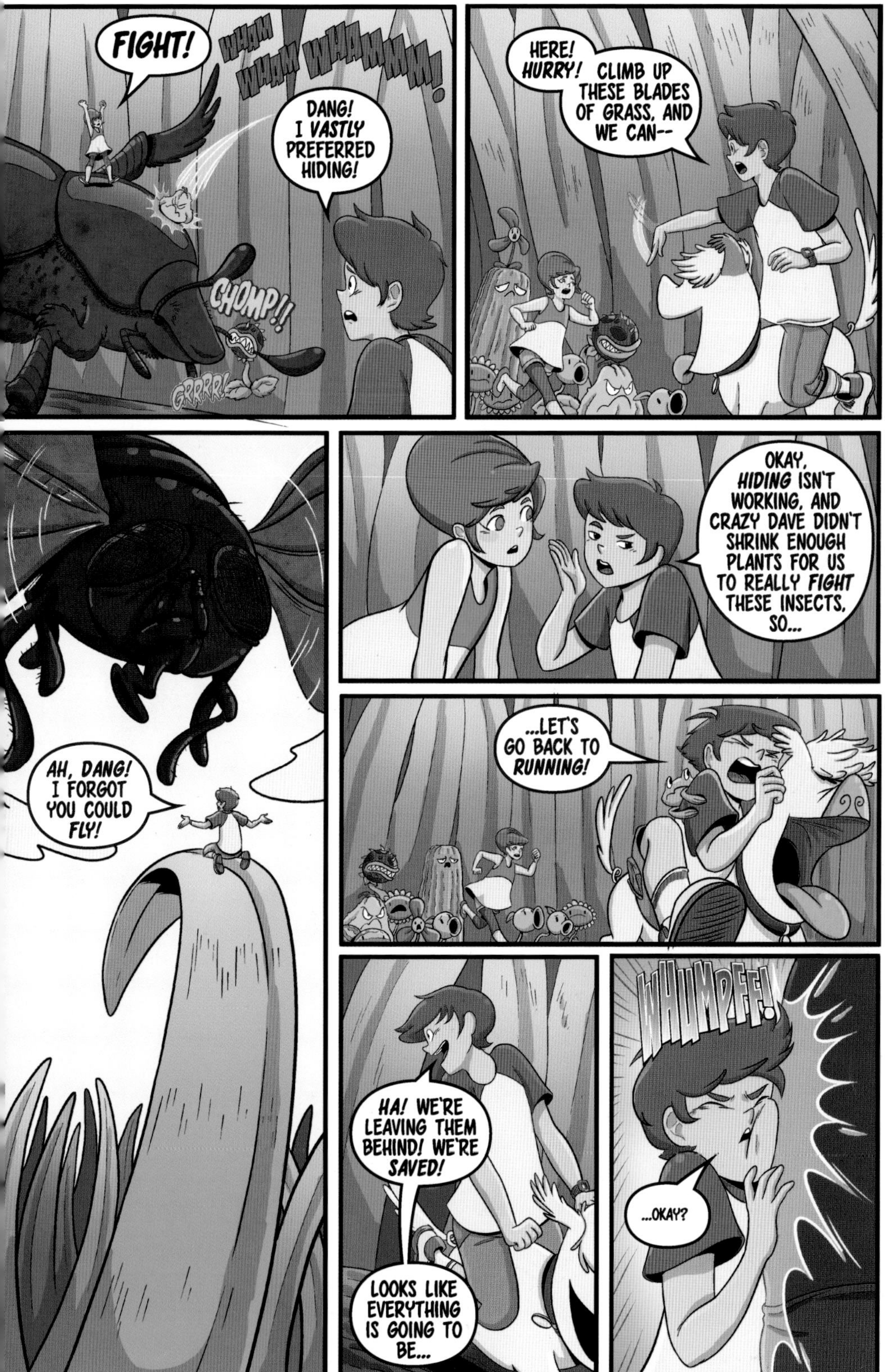
FIGHT!
WHAM WHAM WHAMMM!
DANG! I VASTLY PREFERRED HIDING!
CHOMP!!
GRRRR!
HERE! HURRY!
CLIMB UP THESE BLADES OF GRASS, AND WE CAN--
AH, DANG! I FORGOT YOU COULD FLY!
OKAY, HIDING ISN'T WORKING, AND CRAZY DAVE DIDN'T SHRINK ENOUGH PLANTS FOR US TO REALLY FIGHT THESE INSECTS, SO...
...LET'S GO BACK TO RUNNING!
HA! WE'RE LEAVING THEM BEHIND! WE'RE SAVED!
LOOKS LIKE EVERYTHING IS GOING TO BE...
WHUMPFF!
...OKAY?

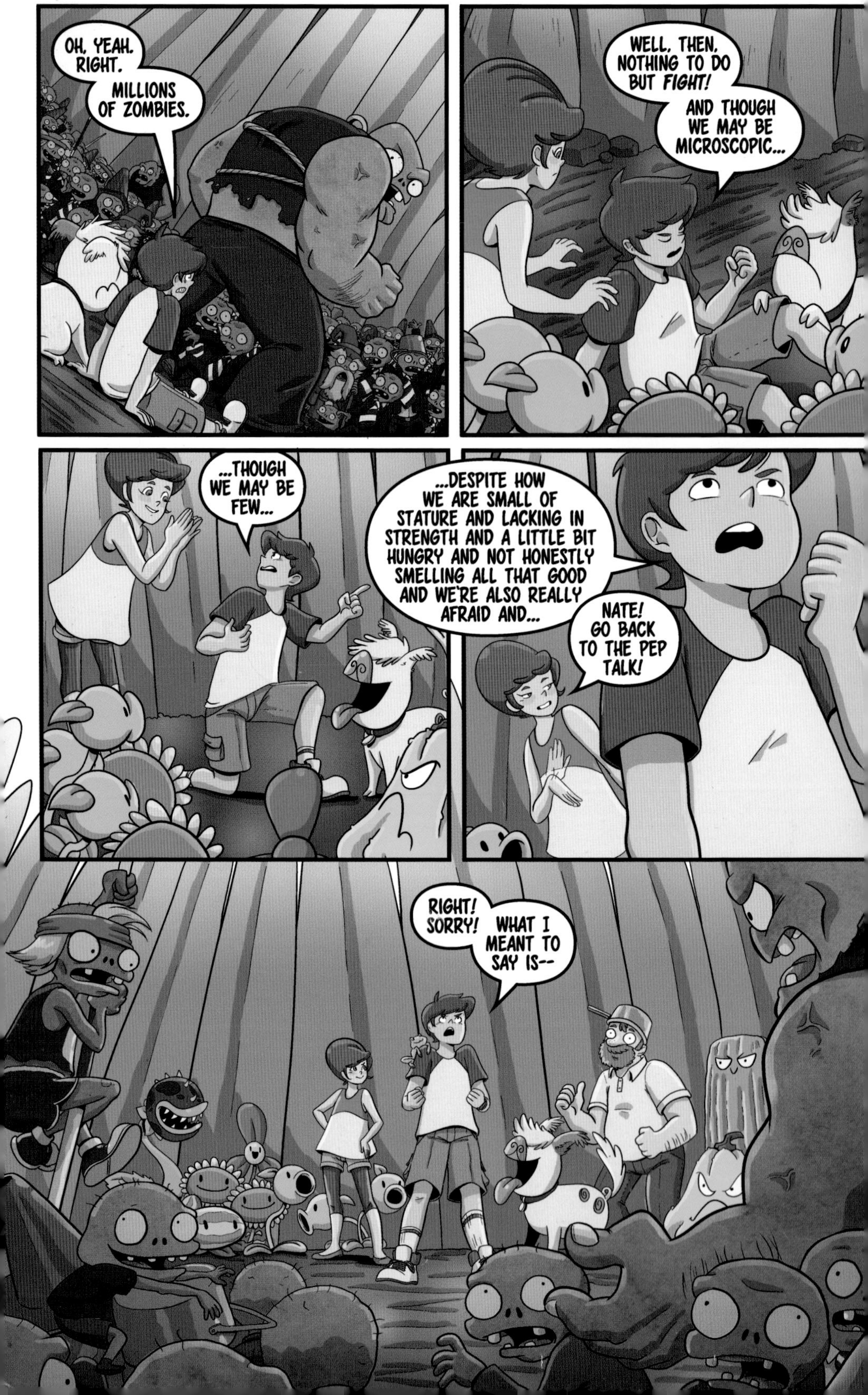
OH, YEAH. RIGHT.
MILLIONS OF ZOMBIES.
WELL, THEN, NOTHING TO DO BUT FIGHT!
AND THOUGH WE MAY BE MICROSCOPIC...
...THOUGH WE MAY BE FEW...
...DESPITE HOW WE ARE SMALL OF STATURE AND LACKING IN STRENGTH AND A LITTLE BIT HUNGRY AND NOT HONESTLY SMELLING ALL THAT GOOD AND WE'RE ALSO REALLY AFRAID AND...
NATE! GO BACK TO THE PEP TALK!
RIGHT! SORRY!
WHAT I MEANT TO SAY IS--

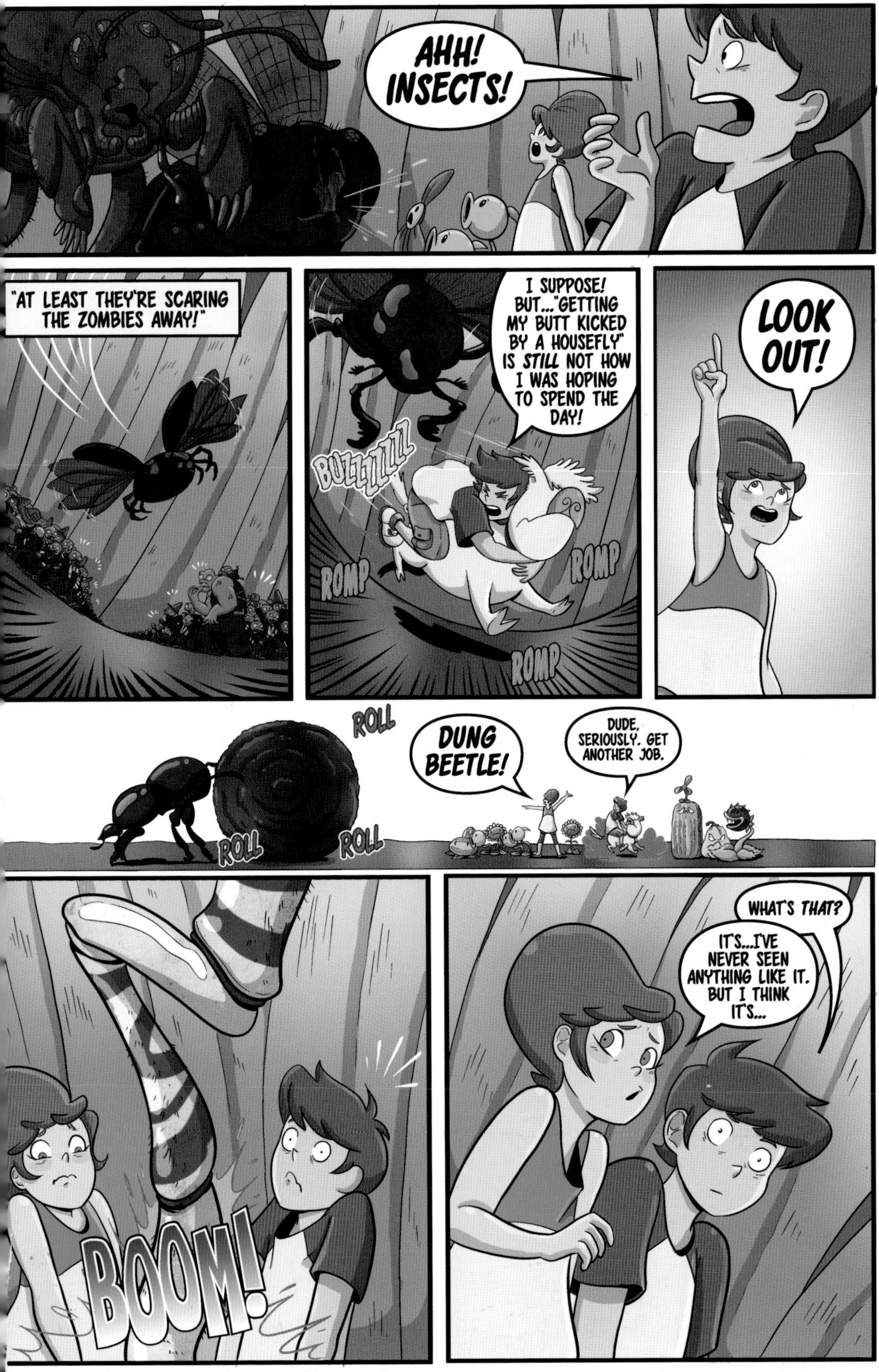
AHH! INSECTS!
"AT LEAST THEY'RE SCARING THE ZOMBIES AWAY!"
I SUPPOSE! BUT..."GETTING MY BUTT KICKED BY A HOUSEFLY" IS STILL NOT HOW I WAS HOPING TO SPEND THE DAY!
BUZZZZZZ
ROMP
ROMP
ROMP
LOOK OUT!
ROLL
ROLL
ROLL
DUNG BEETLE!
DUDE, SERIOUSLY. GET ANOTHER JOB.
BOOM!
WHAT'S THAT?
IT'S...I'VE NEVER SEEN ANYTHING LIKE IT. BUT I THINK IT'S...

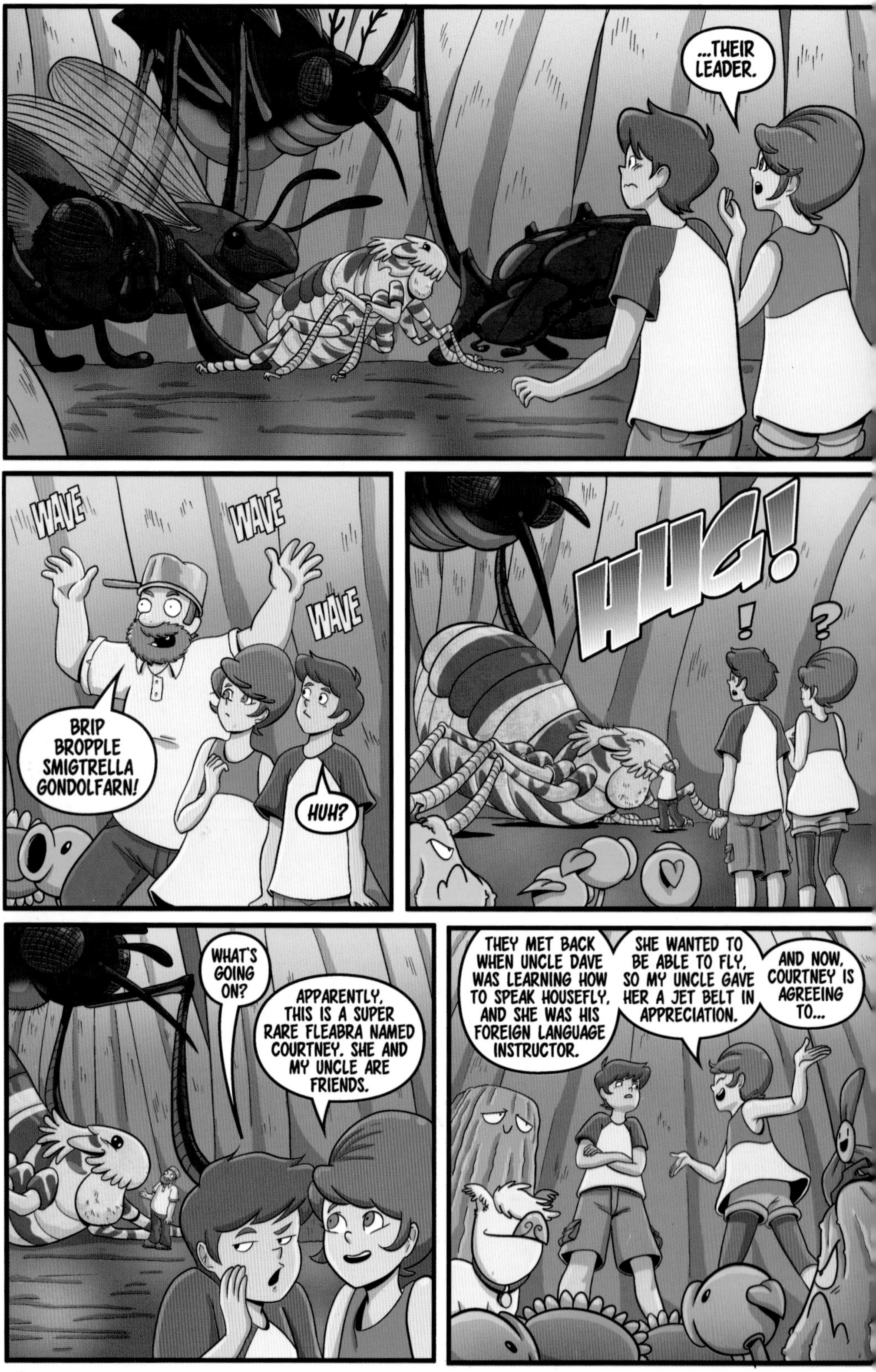
...THEIR LEADER.
WAVE
WAVE
WAVE
BRIP BROPPLE SMIGTRELLA GONDOLFARN!
HUH?
HUG!
!
?
WHAT'S GOING ON?
APPARENTLY, THIS IS A SUPER RARE FLEABRA NAMED COURTNEY. SHE AND MY UNCLE ARE FRIENDS.
THEY MET BACK WHEN UNCLE DAVE WAS LEARNING HOW TO SPEAK HOUSEFLY, AND SHE WAS HIS FOREIGN LANGUAGE INSTRUCTOR.
SHE WANTED TO BE ABLE TO FLY, SO MY UNCLE GAVE HER A JET BELT IN APPRECIATION.
AND NOW, COURTNEY IS AGREEING TO...

"...SEND OUT A VAST ARMY OF VARIOUS INSECTS..."

RRRR!
BUZZ
BUZZ
BUZZ
BUZZ
BUZZ
WHOOOSH
RRRR!

"...TO EVERY SINGLE PERSON IN NEIGHBORVILLE THAT'S BEING PLAGUED BY THE TINY ZOMBIES PLAYING MESSAGES IN THEIR HAIR."

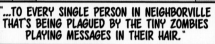

ASSEMBLE AT THE WAREHOUSE! NEAR LAKE GUMBO!

OOH! I JUST THOUGHT OF A SONG!

ALSO, AS LONG AS I HAVE YOUR ATTENTION, LET ME TELL YOU A FEW CHARMING STORIES FROM MY CHILDHOOD.

SCRATCH

SCRATCH

I SHALL NOW COMMENCE READING PAGE 12,746 OF MY MEMOIRS.

"THE INSECTS WILL BUZZ AROUND EACH AND EVERY PERSON'S EARS, DROWNING OUT THE 'BRAINWASHING' OF ZOMBOSS' EVIL MESSAGES, AND...EVEN MORE THANKFULLY..."

BUZZ BUZZ
BUZZ BUZZ
BUZZ BUZZ
BUZZ

BUZZ BUZZ
BUZZ BUZZ BUZZ
BUZZZ
BUZZZ

"...HIS SUPER EVILLY BAD MUSIC!"

NOOOOO!

45

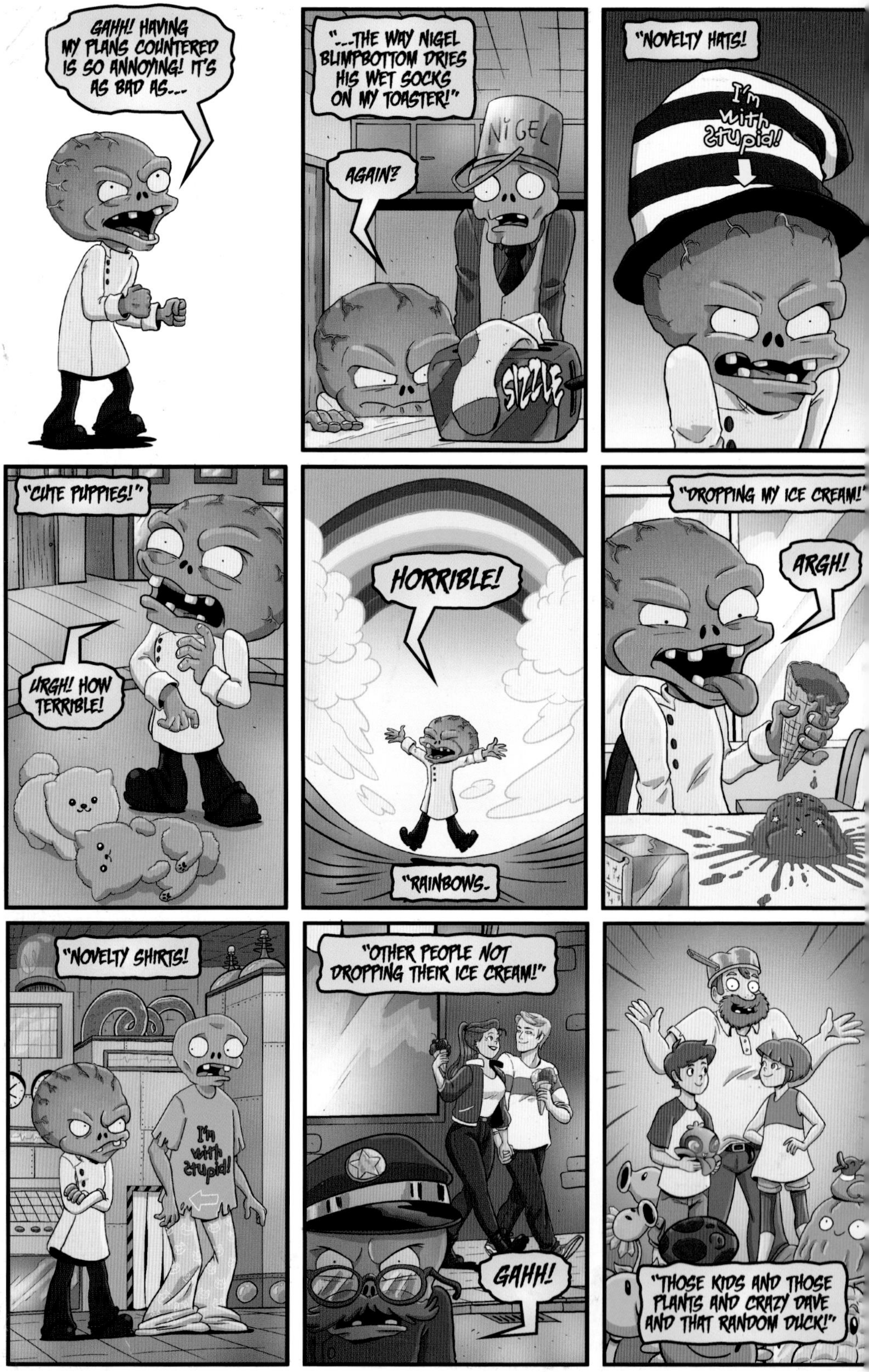
GAHH! HAVING MY PLANS COUNTERED IS SO ANNOYING! IT'S AS BAD AS...
"...THE WAY NIGEL BLIMPBOTTOM DRIES HIS WET SOCKS ON MY TOASTER!"
NIGEL
AGAIN?
SIZZLE
"NOVELTY HATS!
I'm with Stupid!
"CUTE PUPPIES!"
URGH! HOW TERRIBLE!
HORRIBLE!
"RAINBOWS.
"DROPPING MY ICE CREAM!"
ARGH!
"NOVELTY SHIRTS!
I'm with Stupid!
"OTHER PEOPLE NOT DROPPING THEIR ICE CREAM!"
GAHH!
"THOSE KIDS AND THOSE PLANTS AND CRAZY DAVE AND THAT RANDOM DUCK!"

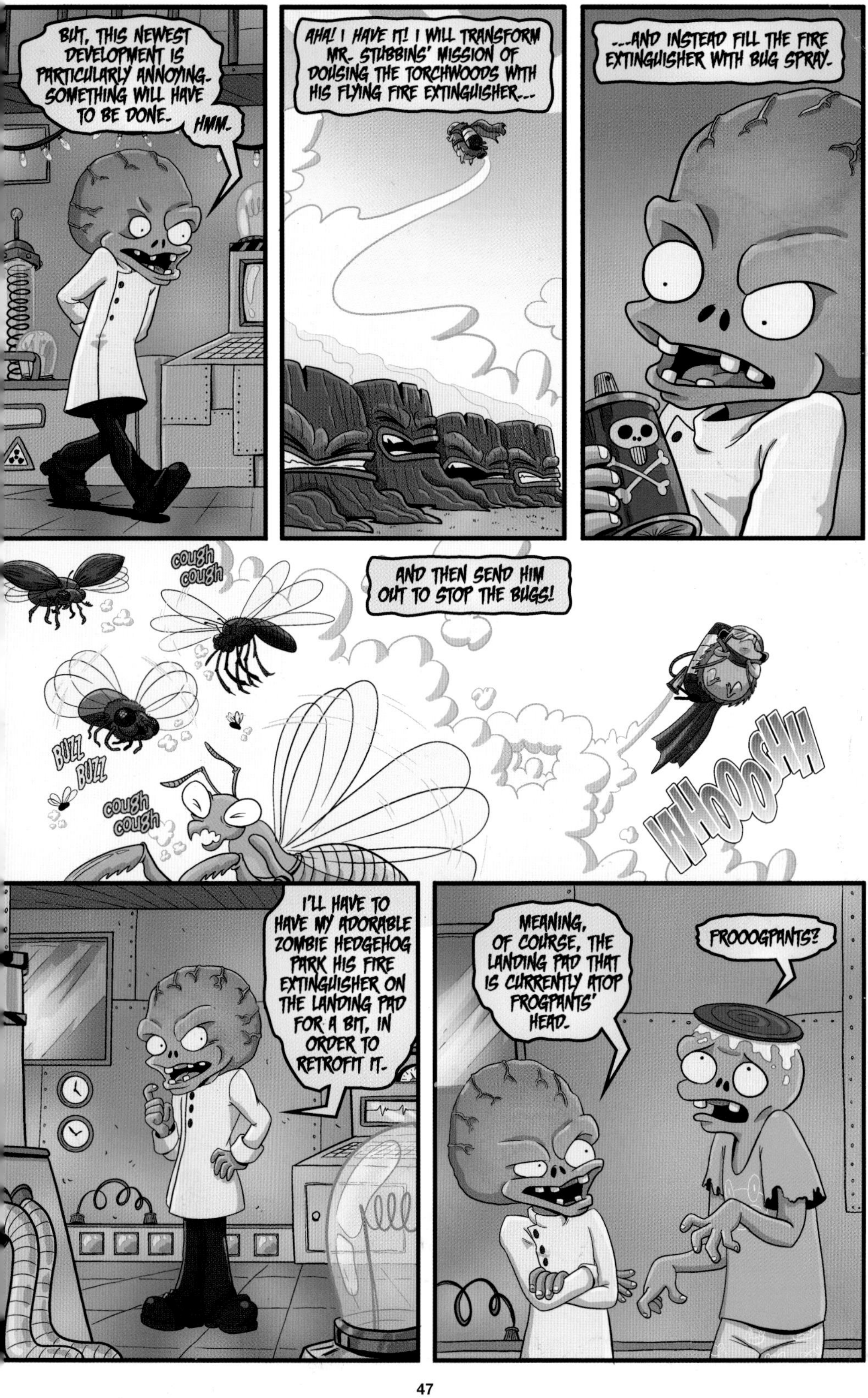
BUT, THIS NEWEST DEVELOPMENT IS PARTICULARLY ANNOYING. SOMETHING WILL HAVE TO BE DONE.
HMM.
AHA! I HAVE IT! I WILL TRANSFORM MR. STUBBINS' MISSION OF DOUSING THE TORCHWOODS WITH HIS FLYING FIRE EXTINGUISHER...
...AND INSTEAD FILL THE FIRE EXTINGUISHER WITH BUG SPRAY.
cough cough
AND THEN SEND HIM OUT TO STOP THE BUGS!
BUZZ BUZZ
cough cough
WHOOOSHH
I'LL HAVE TO HAVE MY ADORABLE ZOMBIE HEDGEHOG PARK HIS FIRE EXTINGUISHER ON THE LANDING PAD FOR A BIT, IN ORDER TO RETROFIT IT.
MEANING, OF COURSE, THE LANDING PAD THAT IS CURRENTLY ATOP PROGPANTS' HEAD.
PROOOGPANTS?

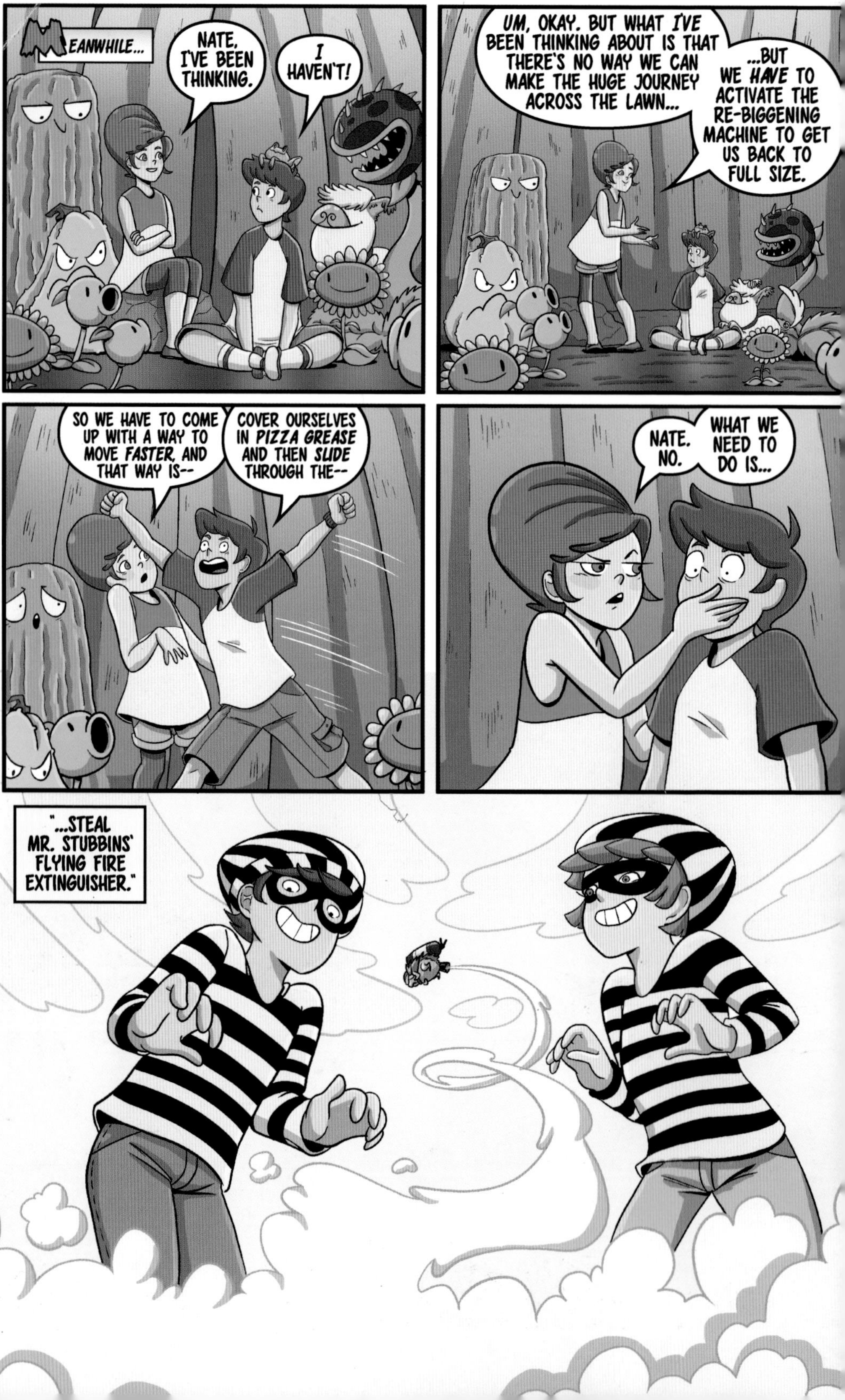
MEANWHILE...
NATE, I'VE BEEN THINKING.
I HAVEN'T!
UM, OKAY. BUT WHAT I'VE BEEN THINKING ABOUT IS THAT THERE'S NO WAY WE CAN MAKE THE HUGE JOURNEY ACROSS THE LAWN...
...BUT WE HAVE TO ACTIVATE THE RE-BIGGENING MACHINE TO GET US BACK TO FULL SIZE.
SO WE HAVE TO COME UP WITH A WAY TO MOVE FASTER, AND THAT WAY IS--
COVER OURSELVES IN PIZZA GREASE AND THEN SLIDE THROUGH THE--
NATE. NO.
WHAT WE NEED TO DO IS...
"...STEAL MR. STUBBINS' FLYING FIRE EXTINGUISHER."

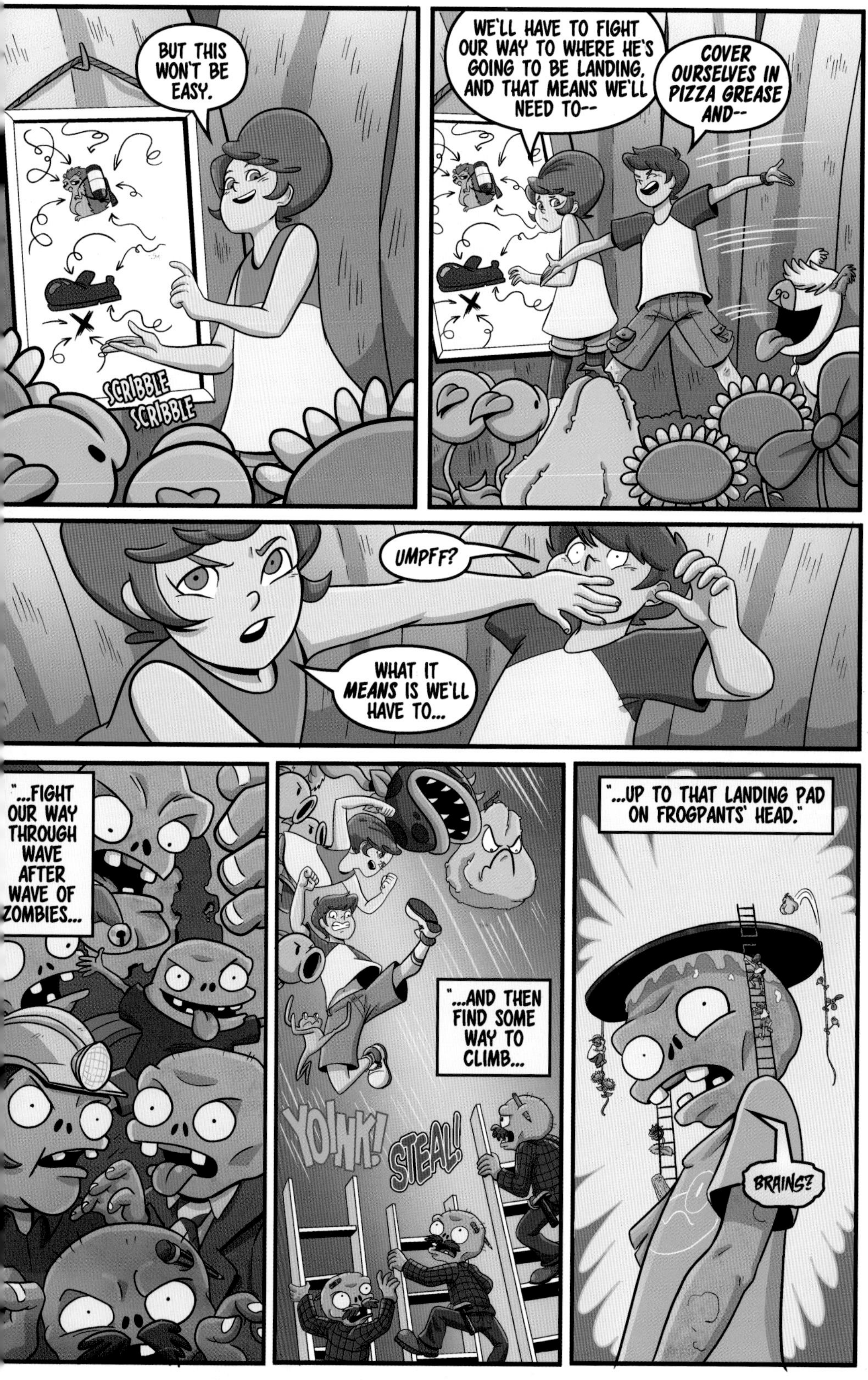
BUT THIS WON'T BE EASY.
SCRIBBLE SCRIBBLE
WE'LL HAVE TO FIGHT OUR WAY TO WHERE HE'S GOING TO BE LANDING, AND THAT MEANS WE'LL NEED TO--
COVER OURSELVES IN PIZZA GREASE AND--
UMPFF?
WHAT IT MEANS IS WE'LL HAVE TO...
"...FIGHT OUR WAY THROUGH WAVE AFTER WAVE OF ZOMBIES...
"...AND THEN FIND SOME WAY TO CLIMB...
YOINK!
STEAL!
"...UP TO THAT LANDING PAD ON FROGPANTS' HEAD."
BRAINS?

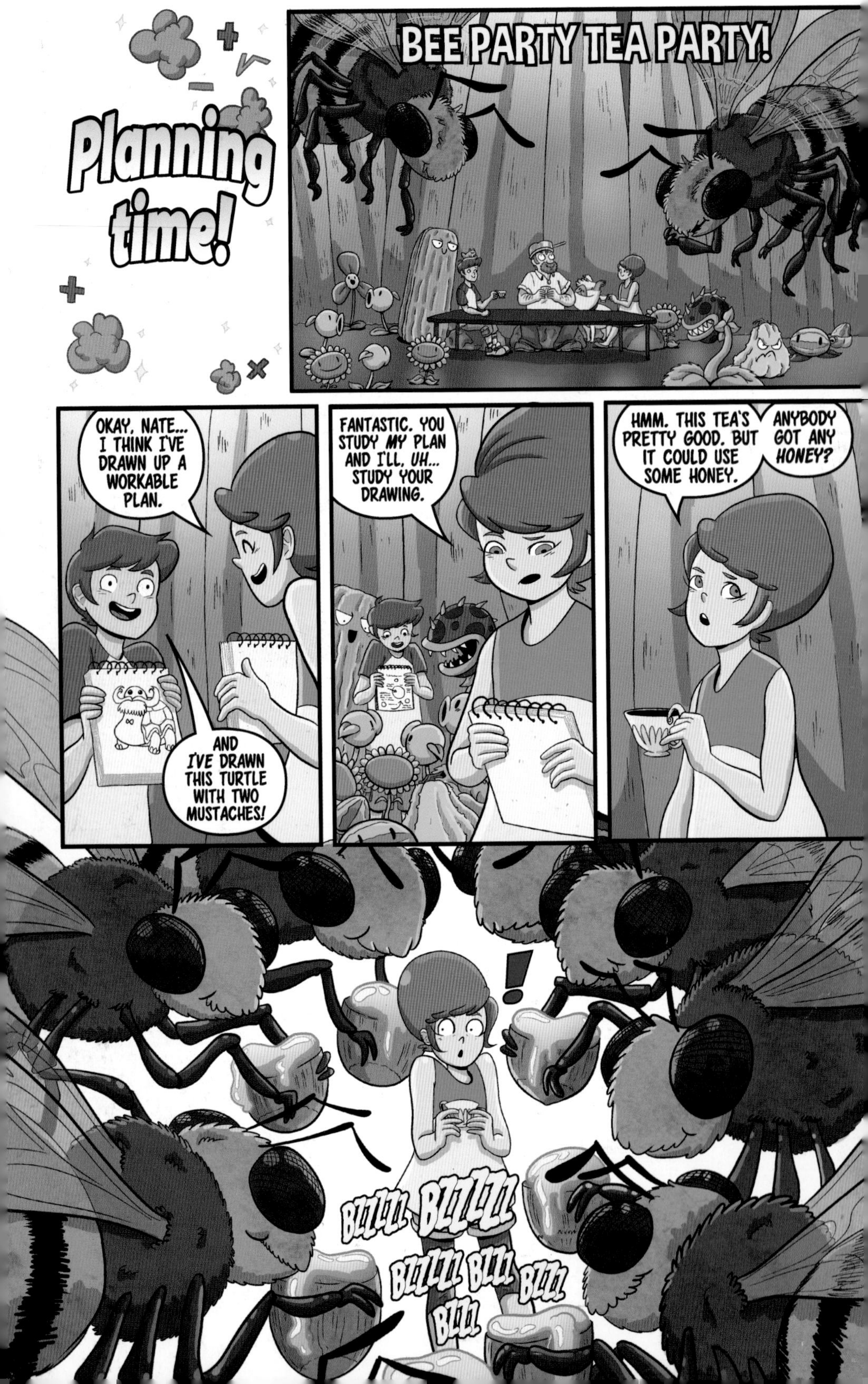
Planning time!
BEE PARTY TEA PARTY!
OKAY, NATE... I THINK I'VE DRAWN UP A WORKABLE PLAN.
AND I'VE DRAWN THIS TURTLE WITH TWO MUSTACHES!
FANTASTIC. YOU STUDY MY PLAN AND I'LL, UH... STUDY YOUR DRAWING.
HMM. THIS TEA'S PRETTY GOOD. BUT IT COULD USE SOME HONEY.
ANYBODY GOT ANY HONEY?
!
BZZZZZ BZZZZZ
BZZZZZ BZZZ BZZZ
BZZZ

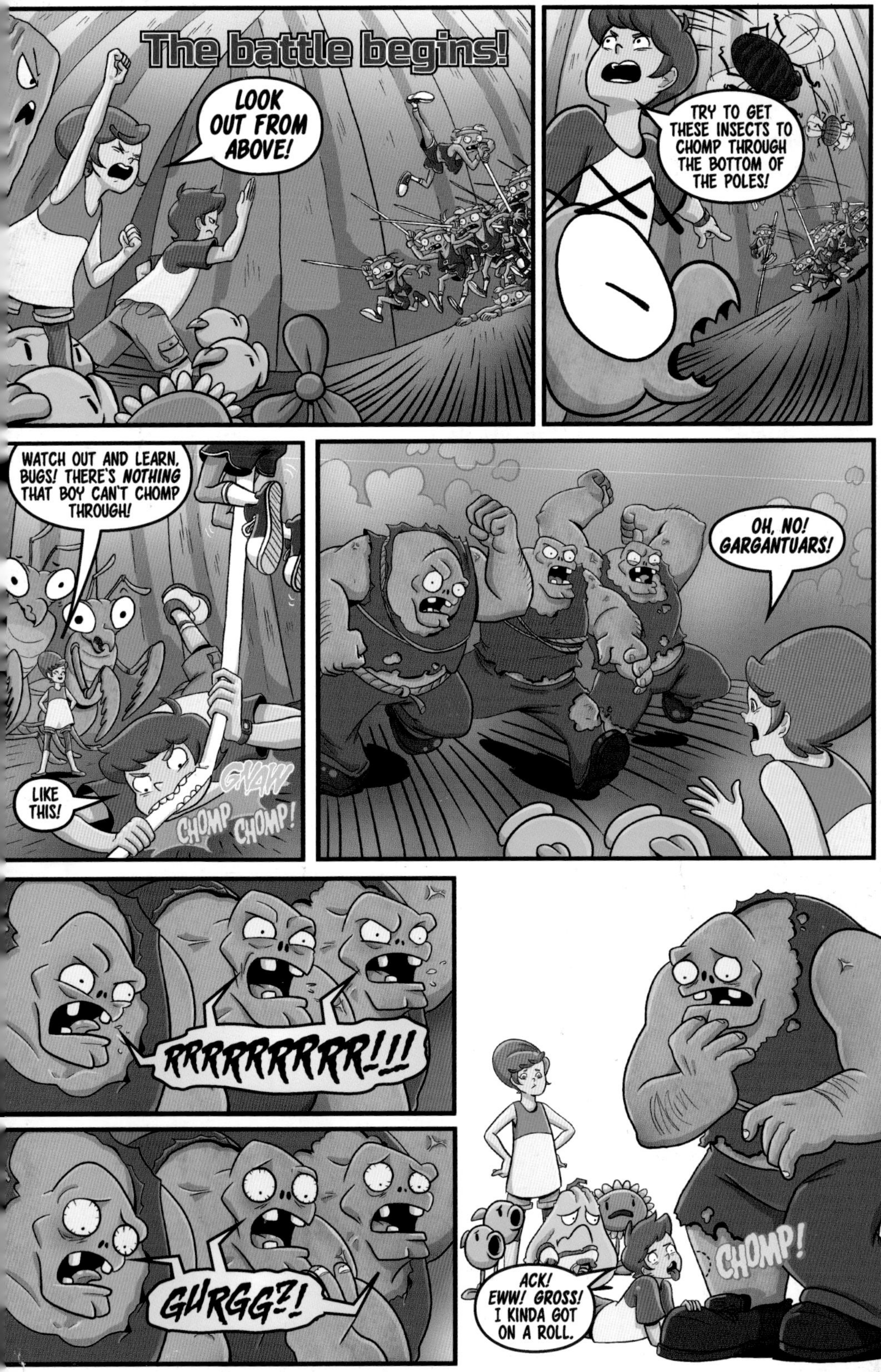
The battle begins!
LOOK OUT FROM ABOVE!
TRY TO GET THESE INSECTS TO CHOMP THROUGH THE BOTTOM OF THE POLES!
WATCH OUT AND LEARN, BUGS! THERE'S *NOTHING* THAT BOY CAN'T CHOMP THROUGH!
LIKE THIS!
GNAW
CHOMP CHOMP!
OH, NO! GARGANTUARS!
RRRRRRRRR!!!
GURGG?!
CHOMP!
ACK! EWW! GROSS! I KINDA GOT ON A ROLL.

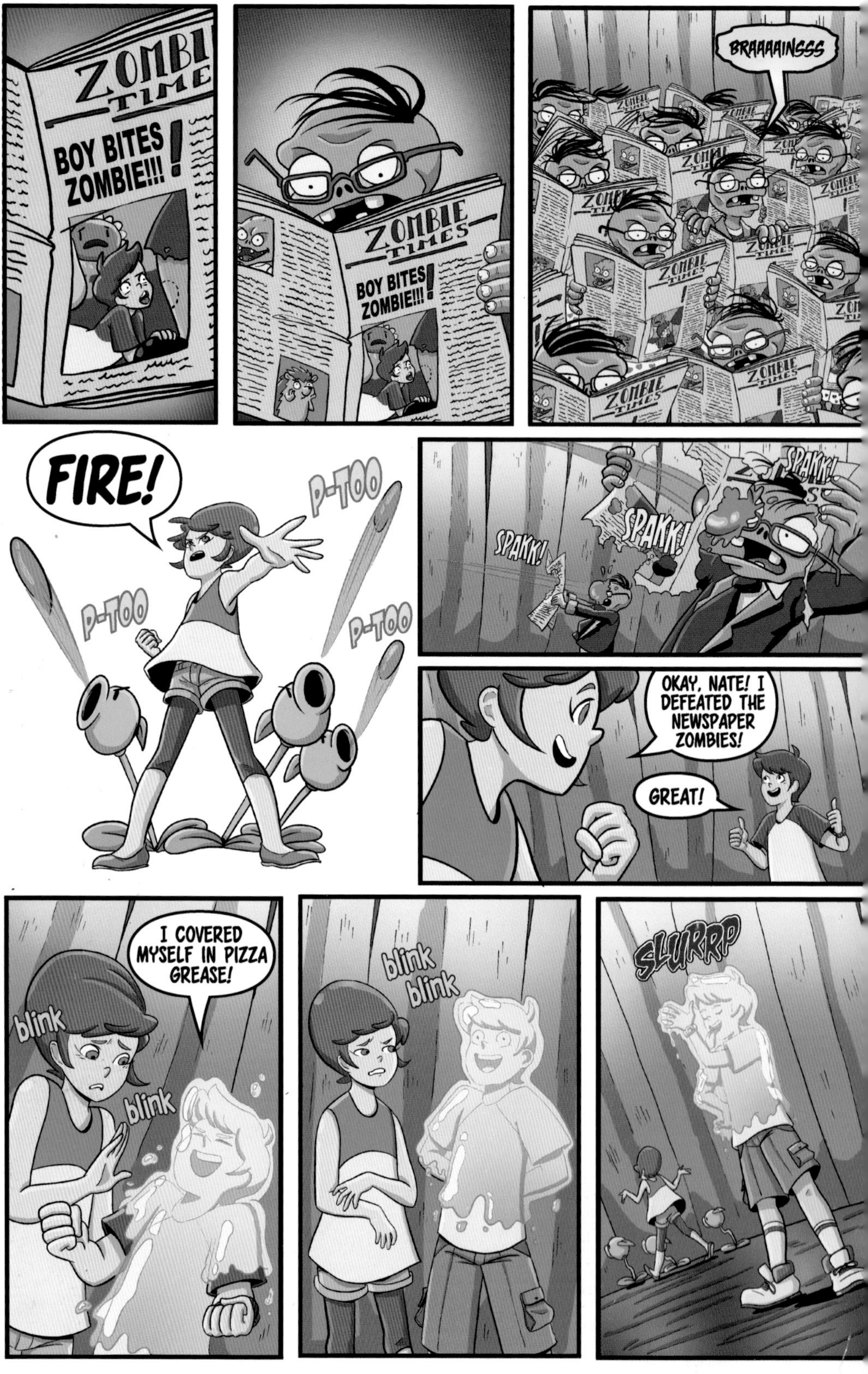
BOY BITES ZOMBIE!!!
ZOMBIE TIMES
BOY BITES ZOMBIE!!!
BRAAAAINSSS
FIRE!
P-TOO
P-TOO
P-TOO
SPAKK!
SPAKK!
SPAKK!
OKAY, NATE! I DEFEATED THE NEWSPAPER ZOMBIES!
GREAT!
I COVERED MYSELF IN PIZZA GREASE!
blink
blink
blink blink
SLURRP

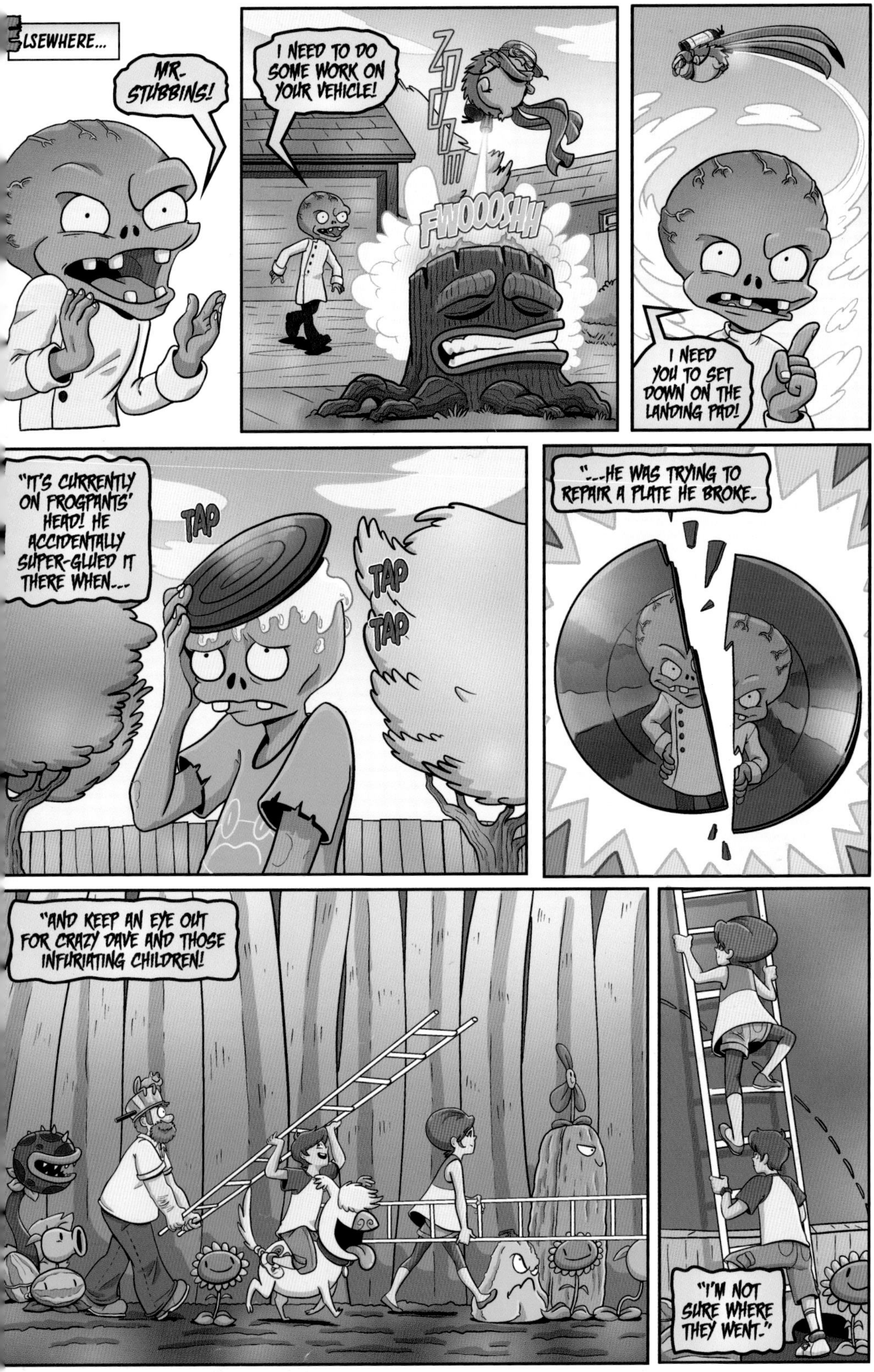
LSEWHERE...
MR. STUBBINS!
I NEED TO DO SOME WORK ON YOUR VEHICLE!
ZOOOM!!!
FWOOOSHH
I NEED YOU TO SET DOWN ON THE LANDING PAD!
"IT'S CURRENTLY ON FROGPANTS' HEAD! HE ACCIDENTALLY SUPER-GLUED IT THERE WHEN...
TAP
TAP
TAP
"...HE WAS TRYING TO REPAIR A PLATE HE BROKE.
"AND KEEP AN EYE OUT FOR CRAZY DAVE AND THOSE INFURIATING CHILDREN!
"I'M NOT SURE WHERE THEY WENT."

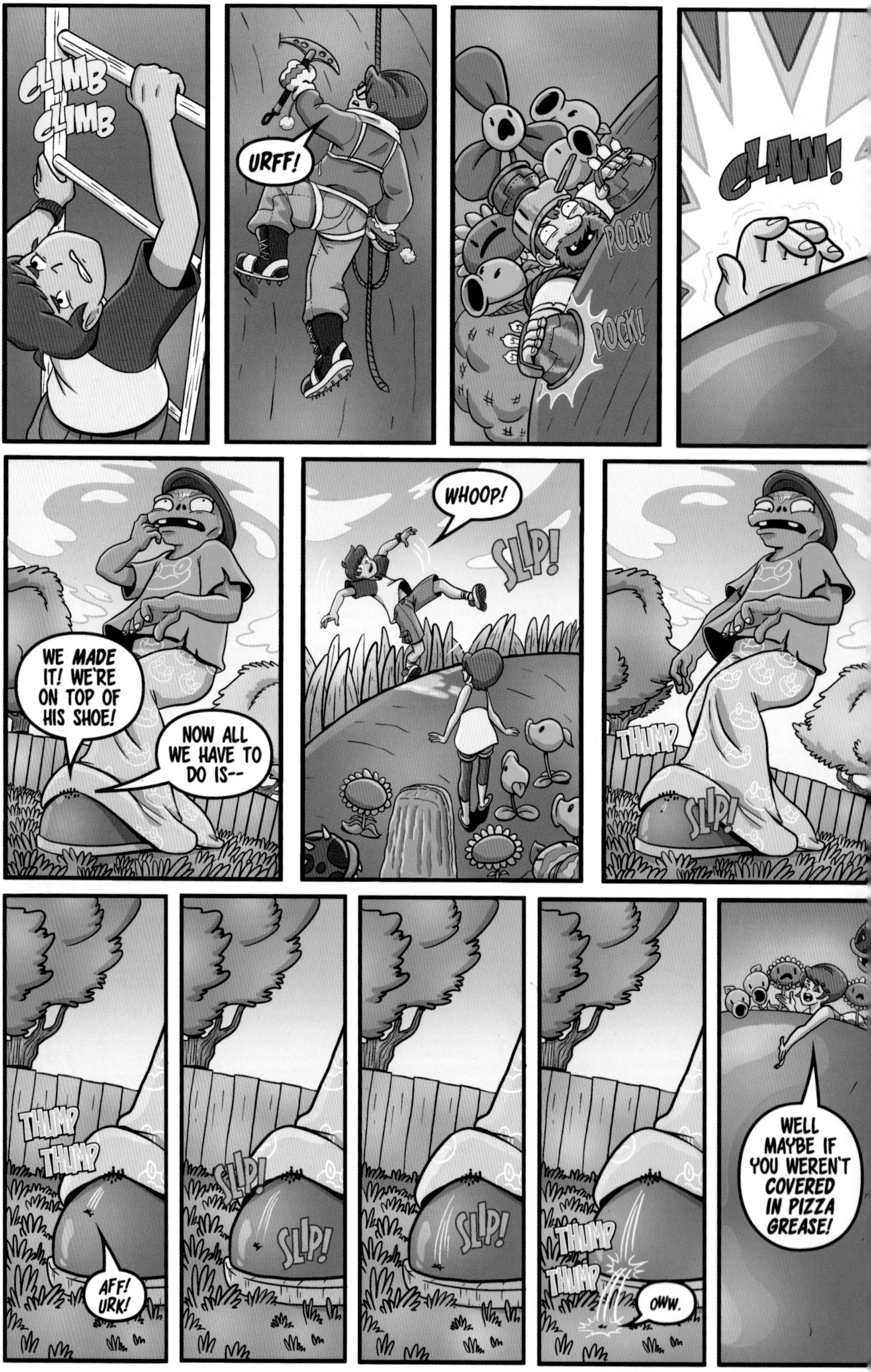
CLIMB
CLIMB
URFF!
POCK!
POCK!
CLAW!
WE MADE IT! WE'RE ON TOP OF HIS SHOE!
NOW ALL WE HAVE TO DO IS--
WHOOP!
SLIP!
THUMP
SLIP!
THUMP
THUMP
AFF! URK!
SLIP!
SLIP!
SLIP!
THUMP
THUMP
OWW.
WELL MAYBE IF YOU WEREN'T COVERED IN PIZZA GREASE!

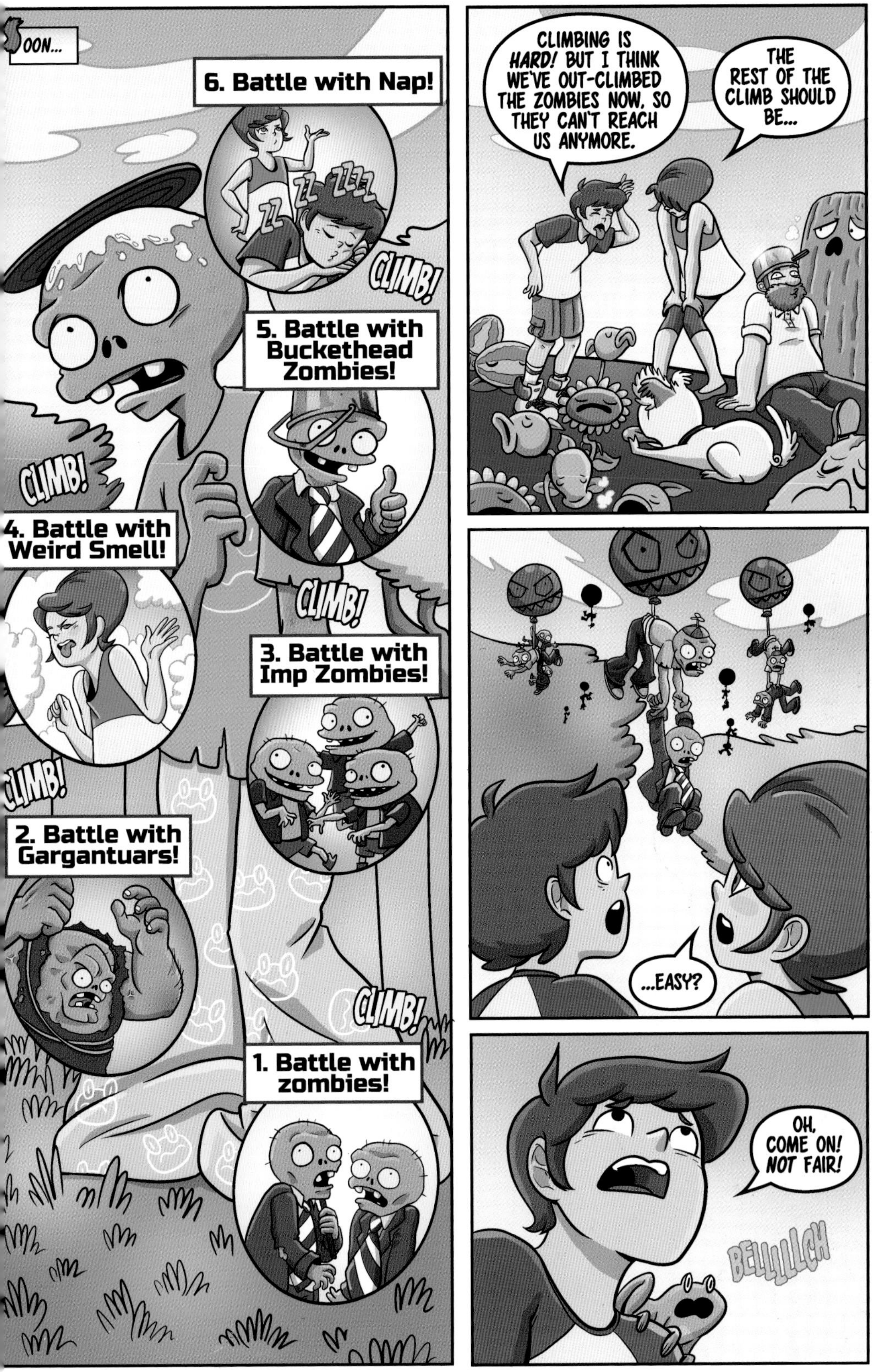
SOON...
6. Battle with Nap!
CLIMB!
5. Battle with Buckethead Zombies!
CLIMB!
4. Battle with Weird Smell!
CLIMB!
3. Battle with Imp Zombies!
CLIMB!
2. Battle with Gargantuars!
CLIMB!
1. Battle with zombies!
CLIMBING IS HARD! BUT I THINK WE'VE OUT-CLIMBED THE ZOMBIES NOW, SO THEY CAN'T REACH US ANYMORE.
THE REST OF THE CLIMB SHOULD BE...
...EASY?
OH, COME ON! NOT FAIR!
BELLLLLCH

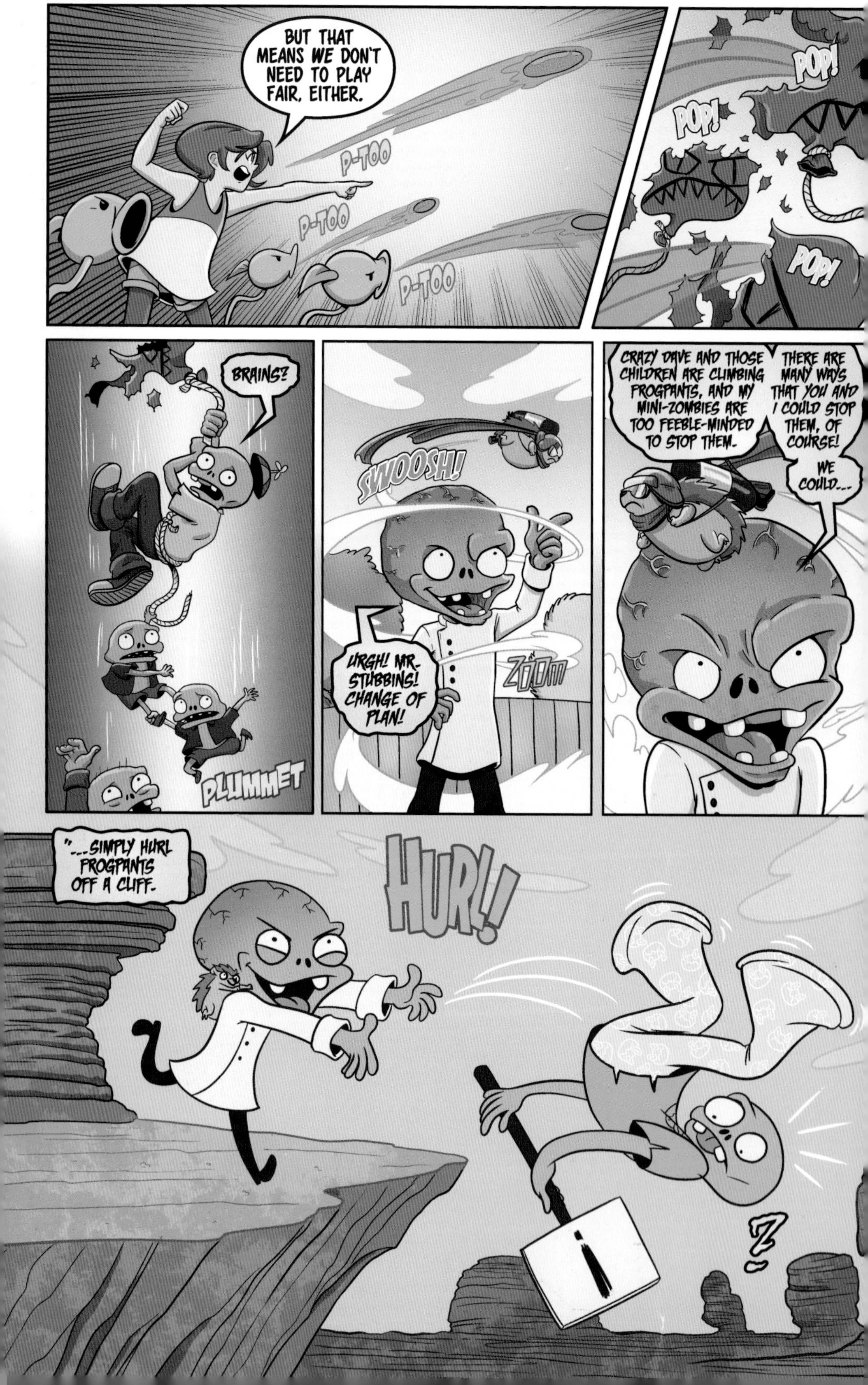
BUT THAT MEANS WE DON'T NEED TO PLAY FAIR, EITHER.
P-TOO
P-TOO
P-TOO
POP!
POP!
POP!
BRAINS?
PLUMMET
SWOOSH!
URGH! MR. STUBBINS! CHANGE OF PLAN!
ZOOM
CRAZY DAVE AND THOSE CHILDREN ARE CLIMBING FROGPANTS, AND MY MINI-ZOMBIES ARE TOO FEEBLE-MINDED TO STOP THEM.
THERE ARE MANY WAYS THAT YOU AND I COULD STOP THEM, OF COURSE!
WE COULD...
"...SIMPLY HURL FROGPANTS OFF A CLIFF.
HURL!
Z

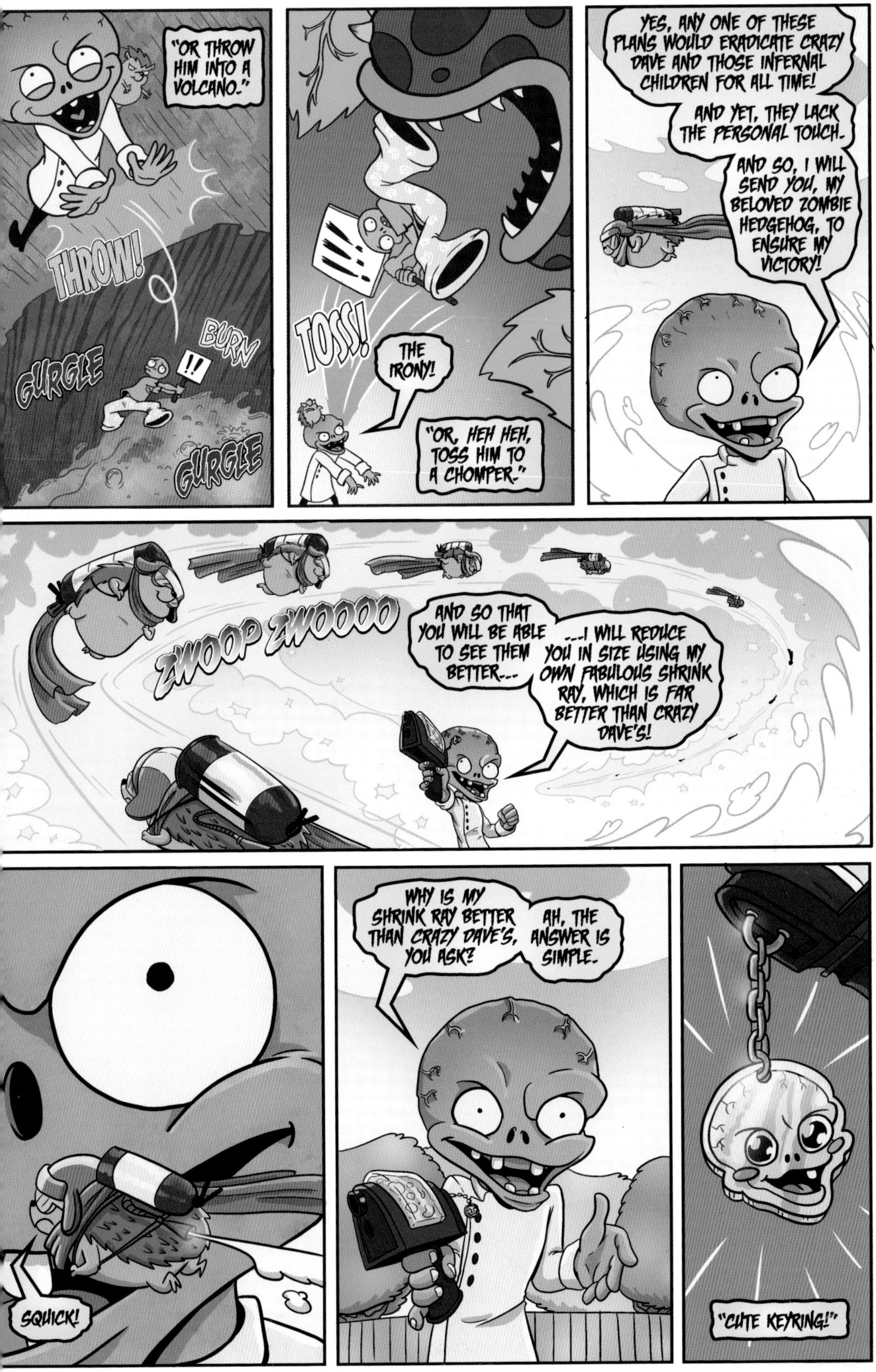
"OR THROW HIM INTO A VOLCANO."
THROW!
BURN
!!
GURGLE
GURGLE
TOSS!
THE IRONY!
"OR, HEH HEH, TOSS HIM TO A CHOMPER."
YES, ANY ONE OF THESE PLANS WOULD ERADICATE CRAZY DAVE AND THOSE INFERNAL CHILDREN FOR ALL TIME!
AND YET, THEY LACK THE PERSONAL TOUCH.
AND SO, I WILL SEND YOU, MY BELOVED ZOMBIE HEDGEHOG, TO ENSURE MY VICTORY!
ZWOOP ZWOOOO
AND SO THAT YOU WILL BE ABLE TO SEE THEM BETTER...
...I WILL REDUCE YOU IN SIZE USING MY OWN FABULOUS SHRINK RAY, WHICH IS FAR BETTER THAN CRAZY DAVE'S!
SQUICK!
WHY IS MY SHRINK RAY BETTER THAN CRAZY DAVE'S, YOU ASK?
AH, THE ANSWER IS SIMPLE.
"CUTE KEYRING!"

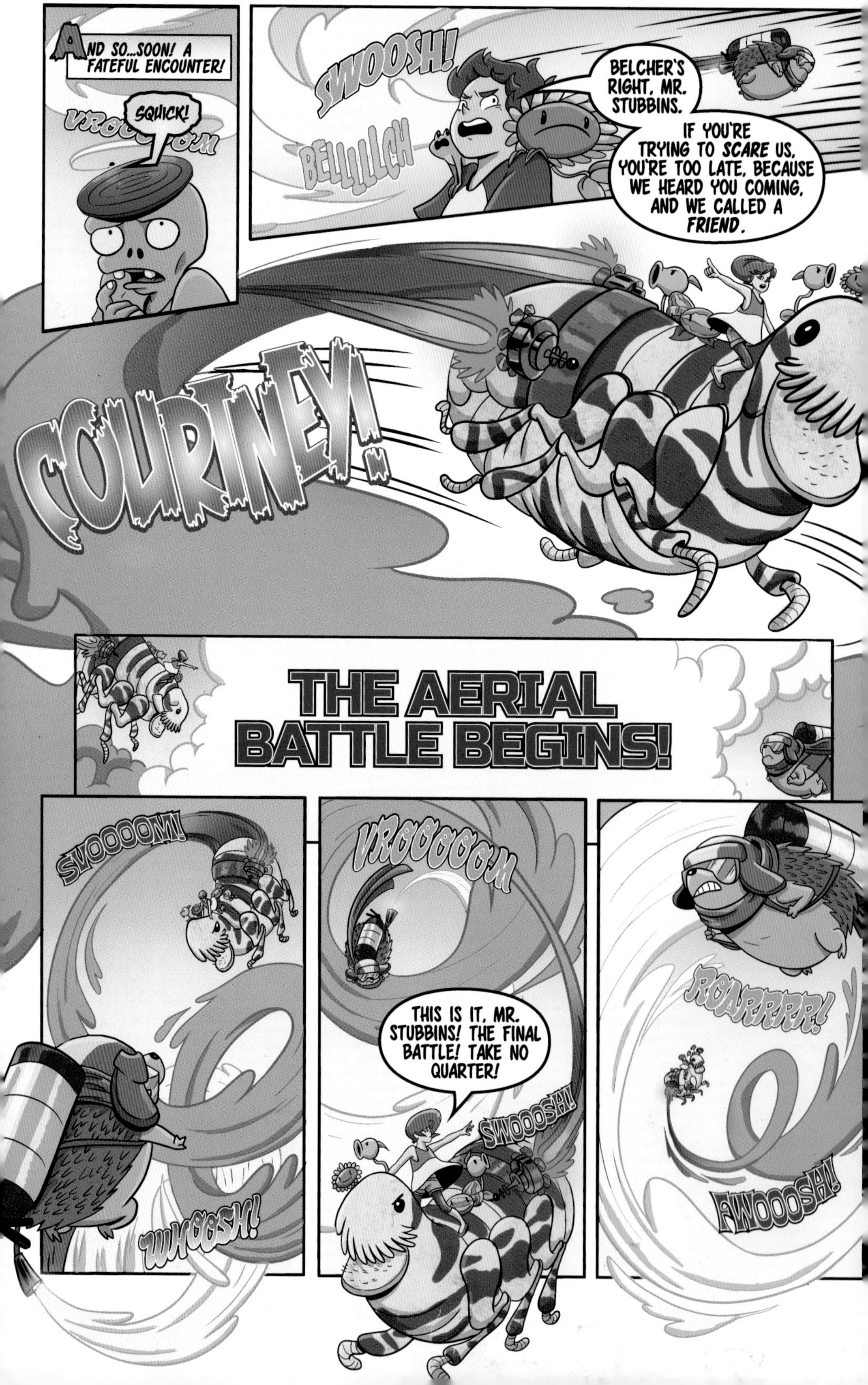

AND SO...SOON! A FATEFUL ENCOUNTER!
VROOOOOOM
SQUICK!
SWOOSH!
BELLLLLCH
BELCHER'S RIGHT, MR. STUBBINS.
IF YOU'RE TRYING TO SCARE US, YOU'RE TOO LATE, BECAUSE WE HEARD YOU COMING, AND WE CALLED A FRIEND.
COURTNEY!
THE AERIAL BATTLE BEGINS!
SVOOOOOM!
WHOOSH!
VROOOOOOM
THIS IS IT, MR. STUBBINS! THE FINAL BATTLE! TAKE NO QUARTER!
SWOOOSH!
ROARRRRR!
FWOOOSH!

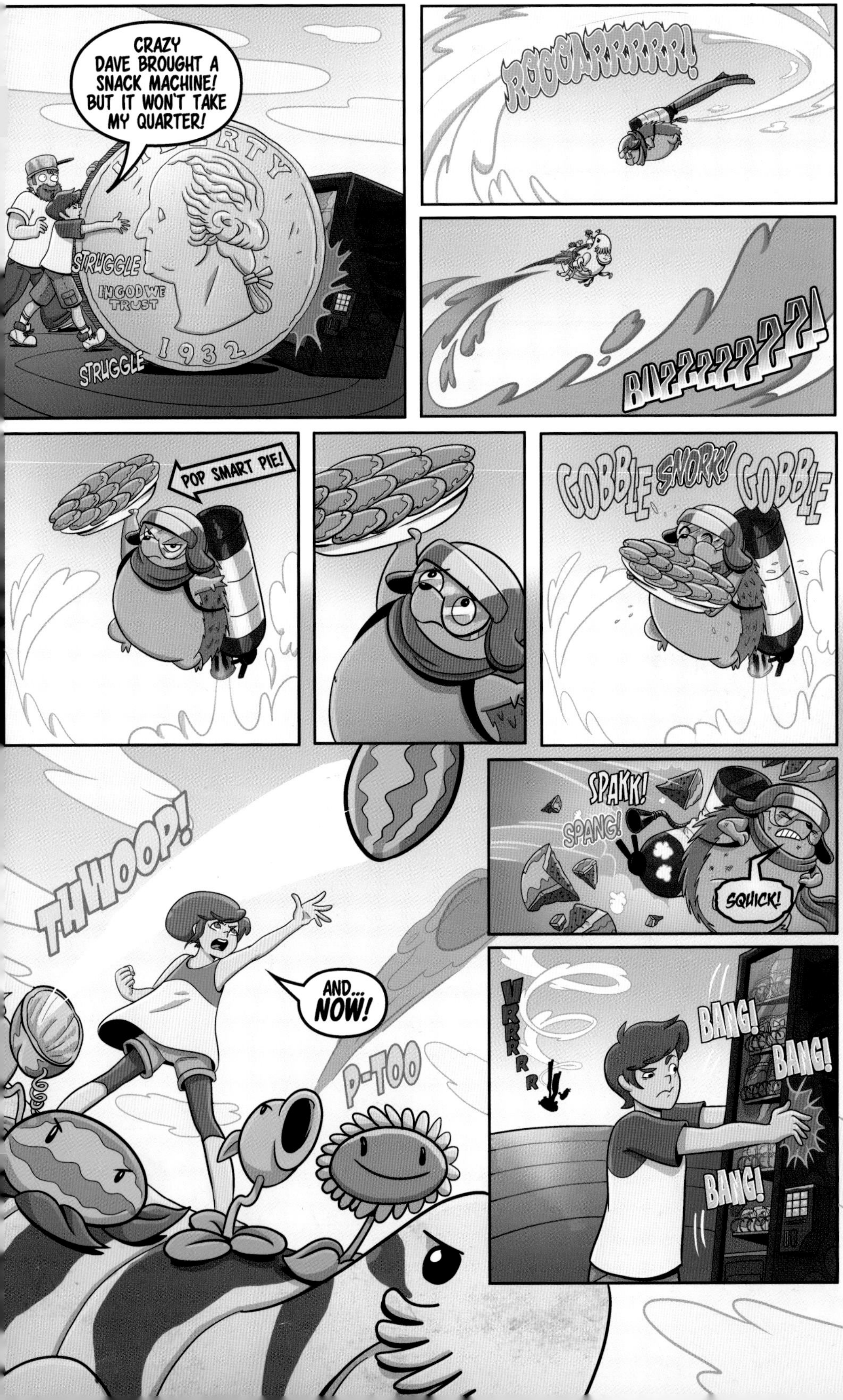
CRAZY DAVE BROUGHT A SNACK MACHINE! BUT IT WON'T TAKE MY QUARTER!
LIBERTY
IN GOD WE TRUST
1932
STRUGGLE
STRUGGLE
ROOOARRRRRR!
BUZZZZZZZZZ!
POP SMART PIE!
GOBBLE SNORK! GOBBLE
THWOOP!
SPAKK!
SPANG!
SQUICK!
AND... NOW!
P-TOO
VRRRRR
BANG!
BANG!
BANG!

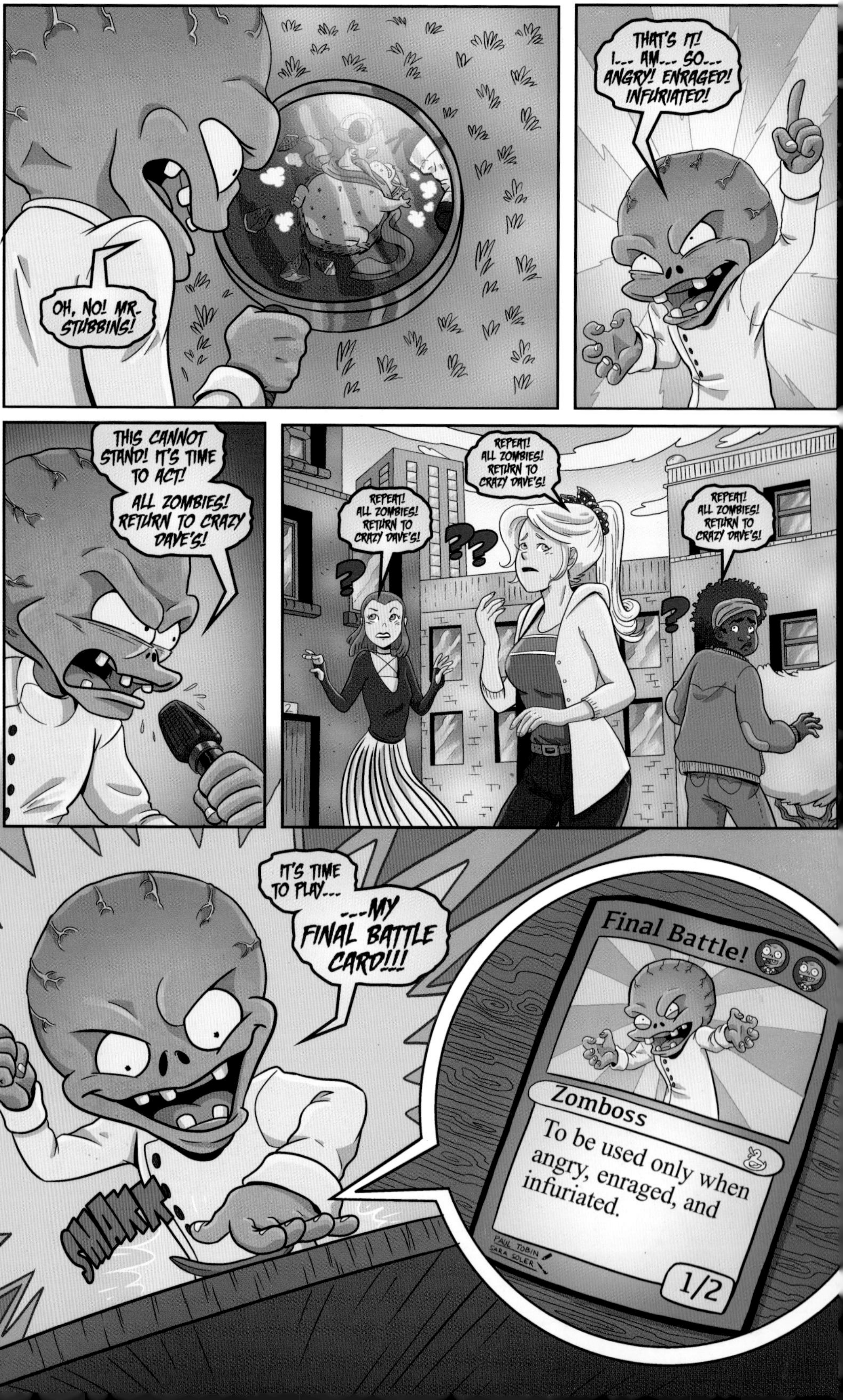
OH, NO! MR. STUBBINS!
THAT'S IT! I... AM... SO... ANGRY! ENRAGED! INFURIATED!
THIS CANNOT STAND! IT'S TIME TO ACT!
ALL ZOMBIES! RETURN TO CRAZY DAVE'S!
REPEAT! ALL ZOMBIES! RETURN TO CRAZY DAVE'S!
REPEAT! ALL ZOMBIES! RETURN TO CRAZY DAVE'S!
REPEAT! ALL ZOMBIES! RETURN TO CRAZY DAVE'S!
IT'S TIME TO PLAY...
...MY FINAL BATTLE CARD!!!
SMAKK
Final Battle!
Zomboss
To be used only when angry, enraged, and infuriated.
PAUL TOBIN
SARA SOLER
1/2

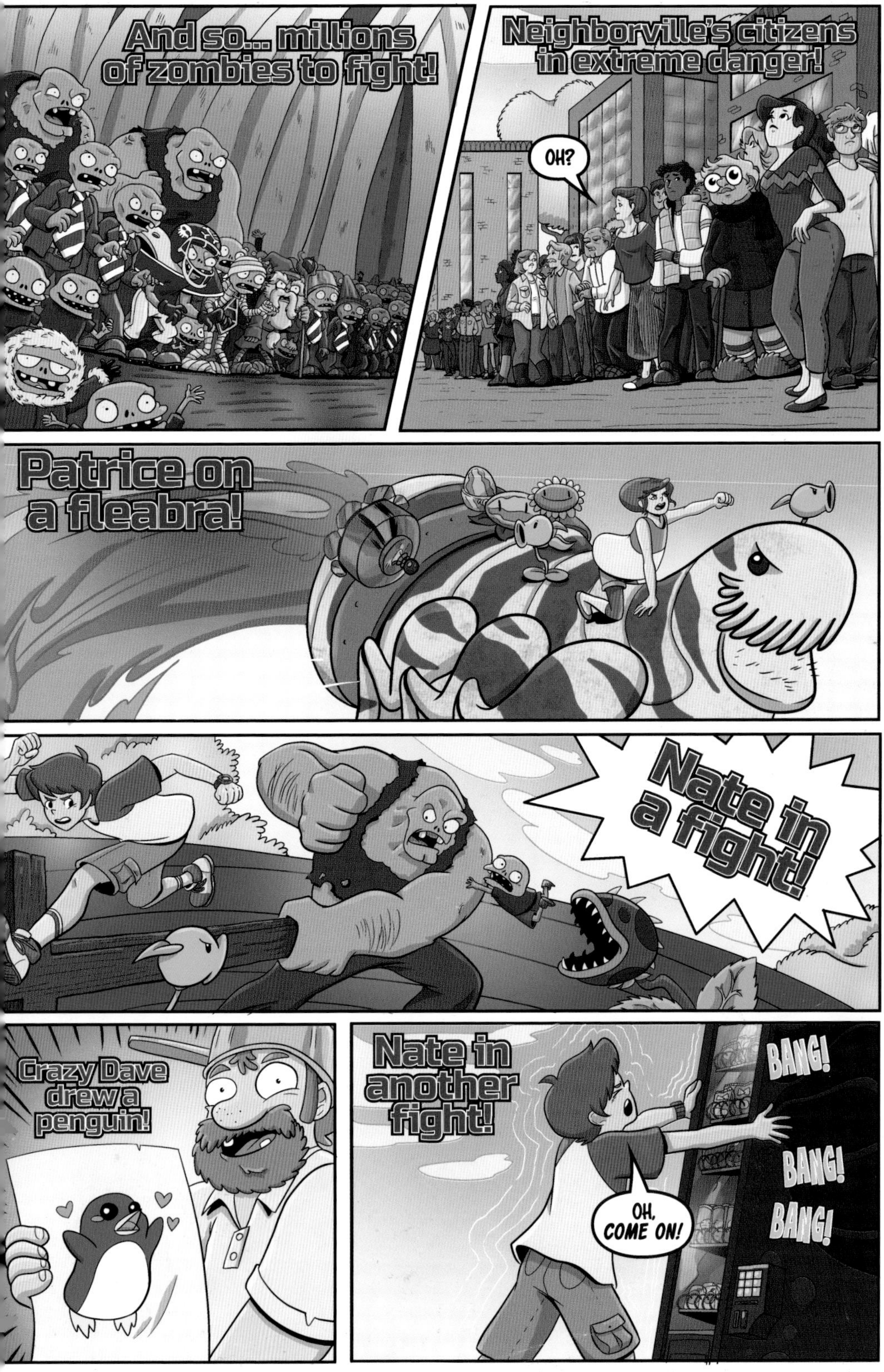
And so... millions of zombies to fight!
Neighborville's citizens in extreme danger!
OH?
Patrice on a fleabra!
Nate in a fight!
Crazy Dave drew a penguin!
Nate in another fight!
BANG!
BANG!
BANG!
OH, COME ON!

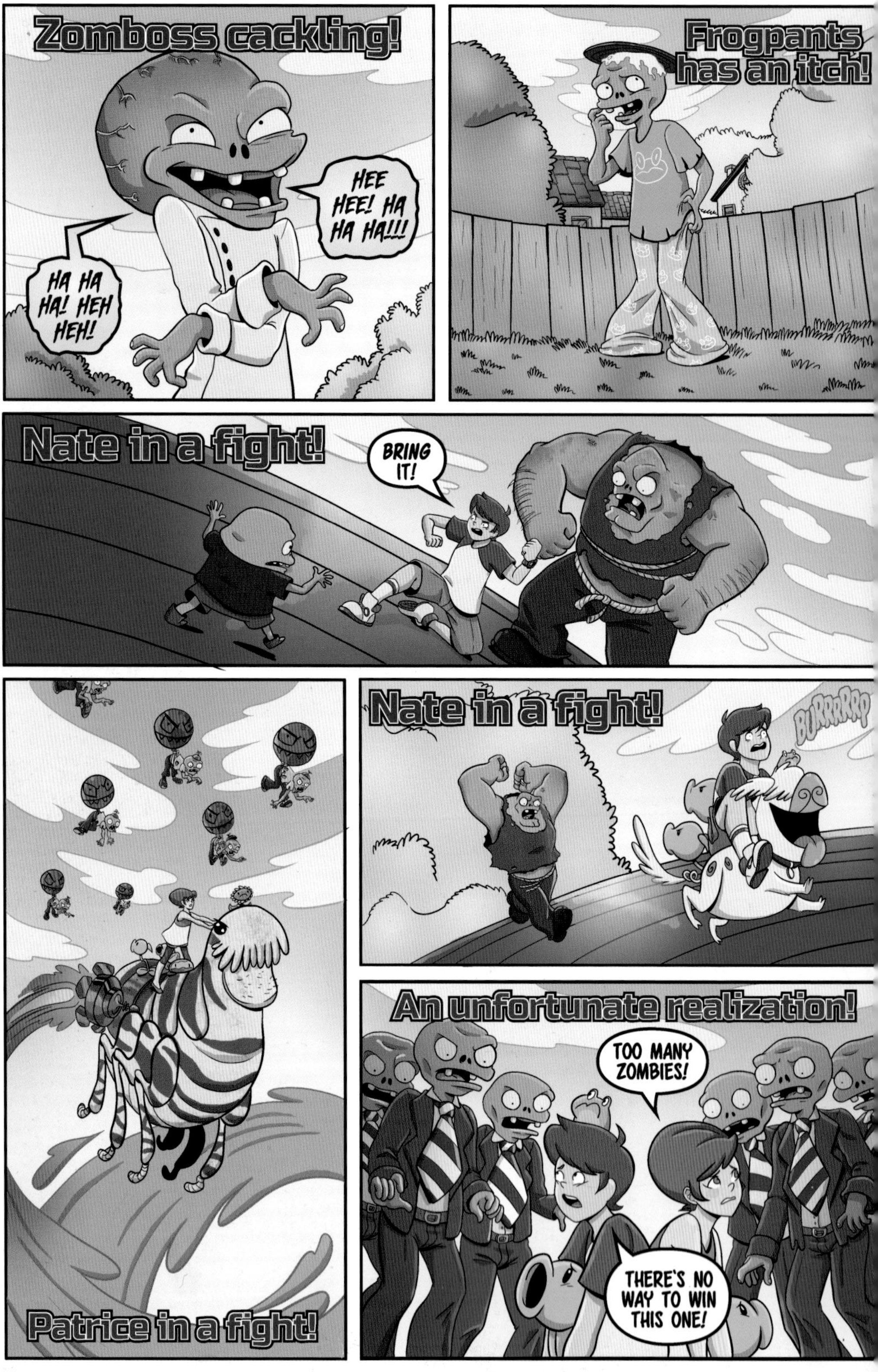
Zomboss cackling!
HEE HEE! HA HA HA!!!
HA HA HA! HEH HEH!
Frogpants has an itch!
Nate in a fight!
BRING IT!
Patrice in a fight!
Nate in a fight!
BURRRRRP
An unfortunate realization!
TOO MANY ZOMBIES!
THERE'S NO WAY TO WIN THIS ONE!

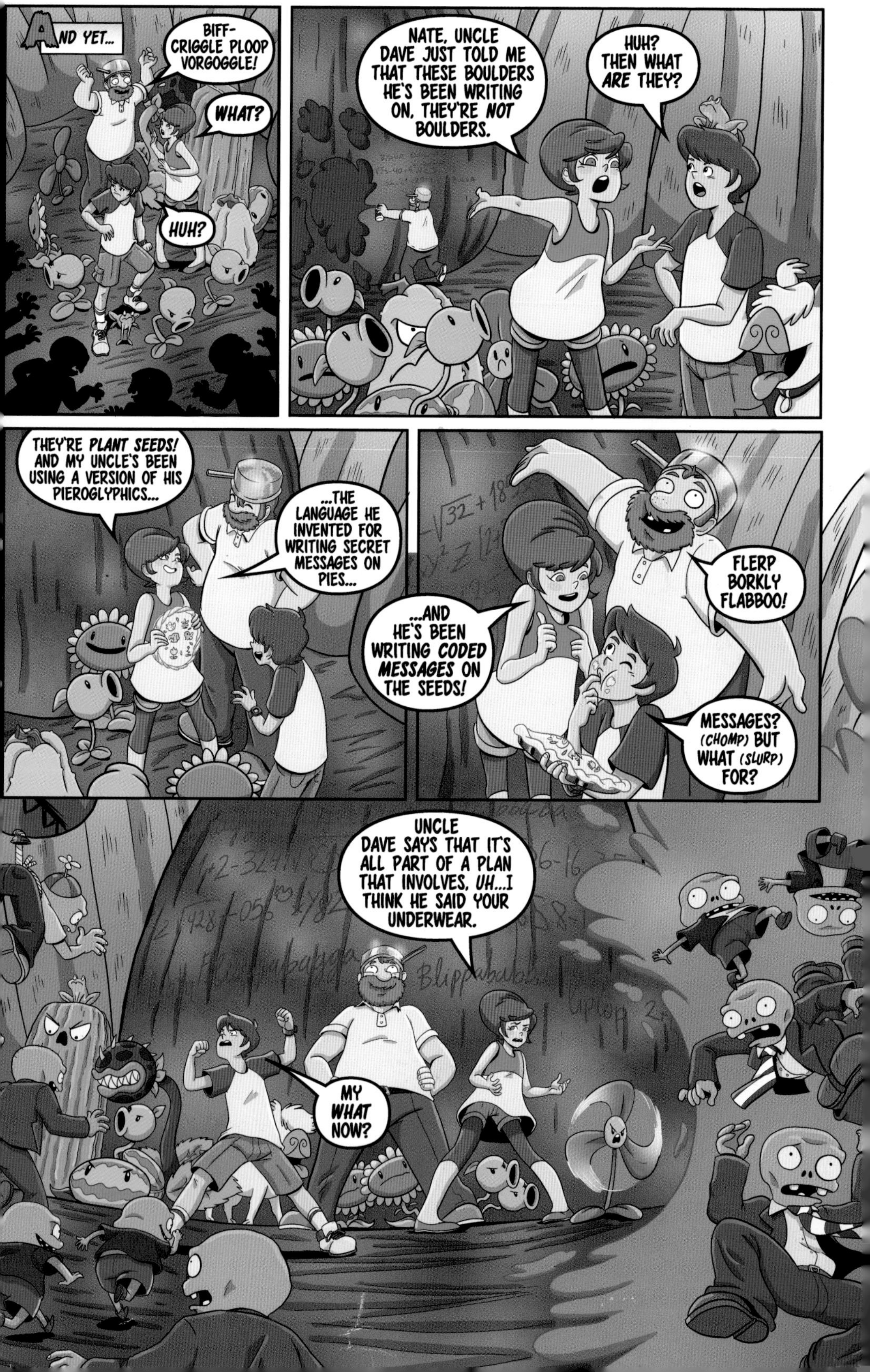
AND YET...
BIFF-CRIGGLE PLOOP VORGOGGLE!
WHAT?
HUH?
NATE, UNCLE DAVE JUST TOLD ME THAT THESE BOULDERS HE'S BEEN WRITING ON, THEY'RE *NOT* BOULDERS.
HUH? THEN WHAT *ARE* THEY?
THEY'RE *PLANT SEEDS!* AND MY UNCLE'S BEEN USING A VERSION OF HIS PIEROGLYPHICS...
...THE LANGUAGE HE INVENTED FOR WRITING SECRET MESSAGES ON PIES...
...AND HE'S BEEN WRITING *CODED MESSAGES* ON THE SEEDS!
FLERP BORKLY FLABBOO!
MESSAGES? (CHOMP) BUT WHAT (SLURP) FOR?
UNCLE DAVE SAYS THAT IT'S ALL PART OF A PLAN THAT INVOLVES, *UH*...I THINK HE SAID YOUR UNDERWEAR.
MY *WHAT* NOW?

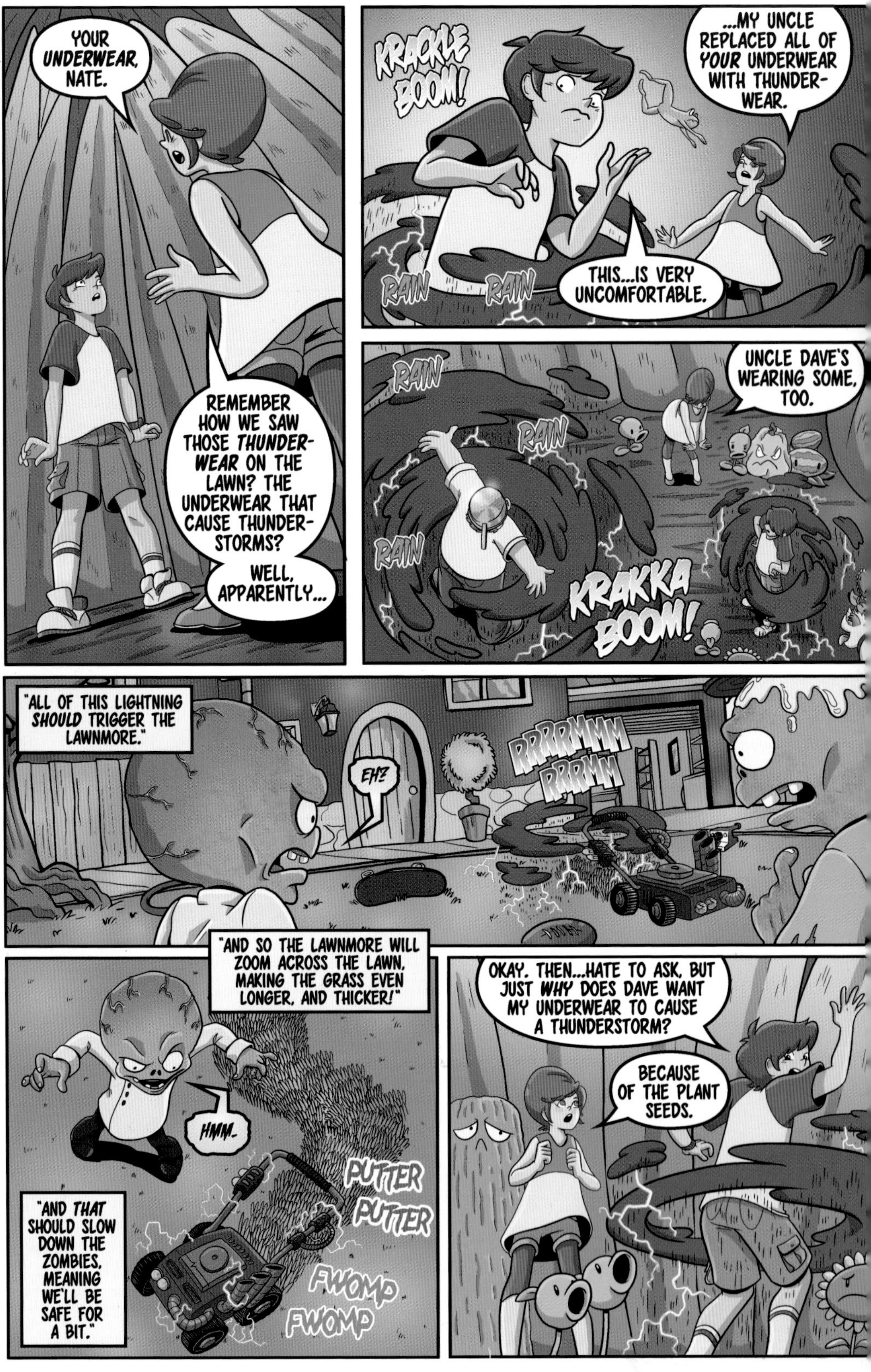
YOUR UNDERWEAR, NATE.
REMEMBER HOW WE SAW THOSE THUNDER-WEAR ON THE LAWN? THE UNDERWEAR THAT CAUSE THUNDER-STORMS?
WELL, APPARENTLY...
KRACKLE BOOM!
...MY UNCLE REPLACED ALL OF YOUR UNDERWEAR WITH THUNDER-WEAR.
RAIN RAIN
THIS...IS VERY UNCOMFORTABLE.
RAIN
UNCLE DAVE'S WEARING SOME, TOO.
RAIN
RAIN
KRAKKA BOOM!
"ALL OF THIS LIGHTNING SHOULD TRIGGER THE LAWNMORE."
EH?
RRRRMMM RRRMM
"AND SO THE LAWNMORE WILL ZOOM ACROSS THE LAWN, MAKING THE GRASS EVEN LONGER, AND THICKER!"
HMM.
PUTTER PUTTER
FWOMP FWOMP
"AND THAT SHOULD SLOW DOWN THE ZOMBIES, MEANING WE'LL BE SAFE FOR A BIT."
OKAY. THEN...HATE TO ASK, BUT JUST WHY DOES DAVE WANT MY UNDERWEAR TO CAUSE A THUNDERSTORM?
BECAUSE OF THE PLANT SEEDS.

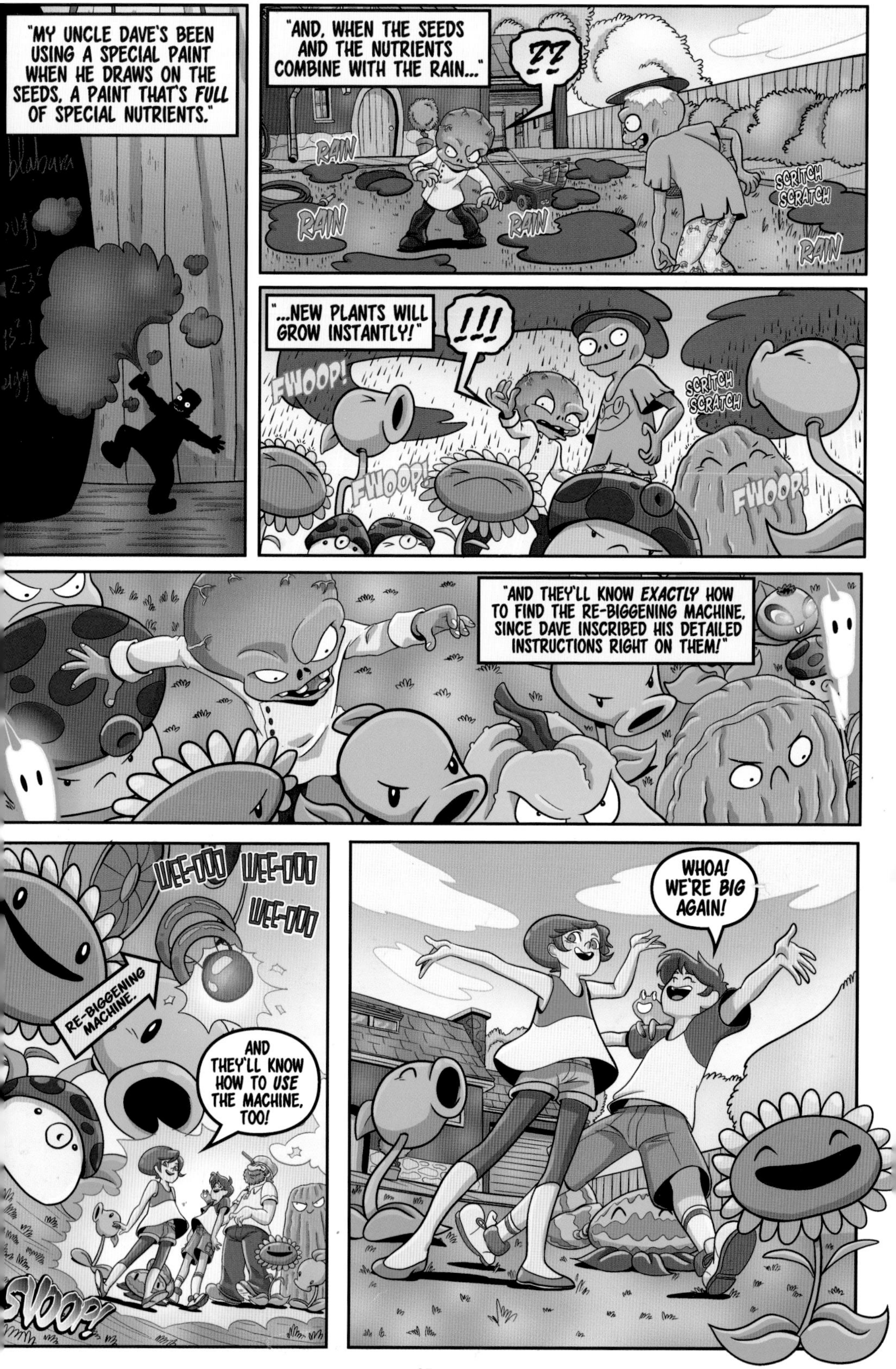
"MY UNCLE DAVE'S BEEN USING A SPECIAL PAINT WHEN HE DRAWS ON THE SEEDS, A PAINT THAT'S *FULL* OF SPECIAL NUTRIENTS."
"AND, WHEN THE SEEDS AND THE NUTRIENTS COMBINE WITH THE RAIN..."
??
RAIN
RAIN
RAIN
SCRITCH SCRATCH
RAIN
"...NEW PLANTS WILL GROW INSTANTLY!"
!!!
FWOOP!
SCRITCH SCRATCH
FWOOP!
FWOOP!
"AND THEY'LL KNOW *EXACTLY* HOW TO FIND THE RE-BIGGENING MACHINE, SINCE DAVE INSCRIBED HIS DETAILED INSTRUCTIONS RIGHT ON THEM!"
WEE-OOO
WEE-OOO
WEE-OOO
RE-BIGGENING MACHINE.
AND THEY'LL KNOW HOW TO *USE* THE MACHINE, TOO!
SVOOP!
WHOA! WE'RE BIG AGAIN!

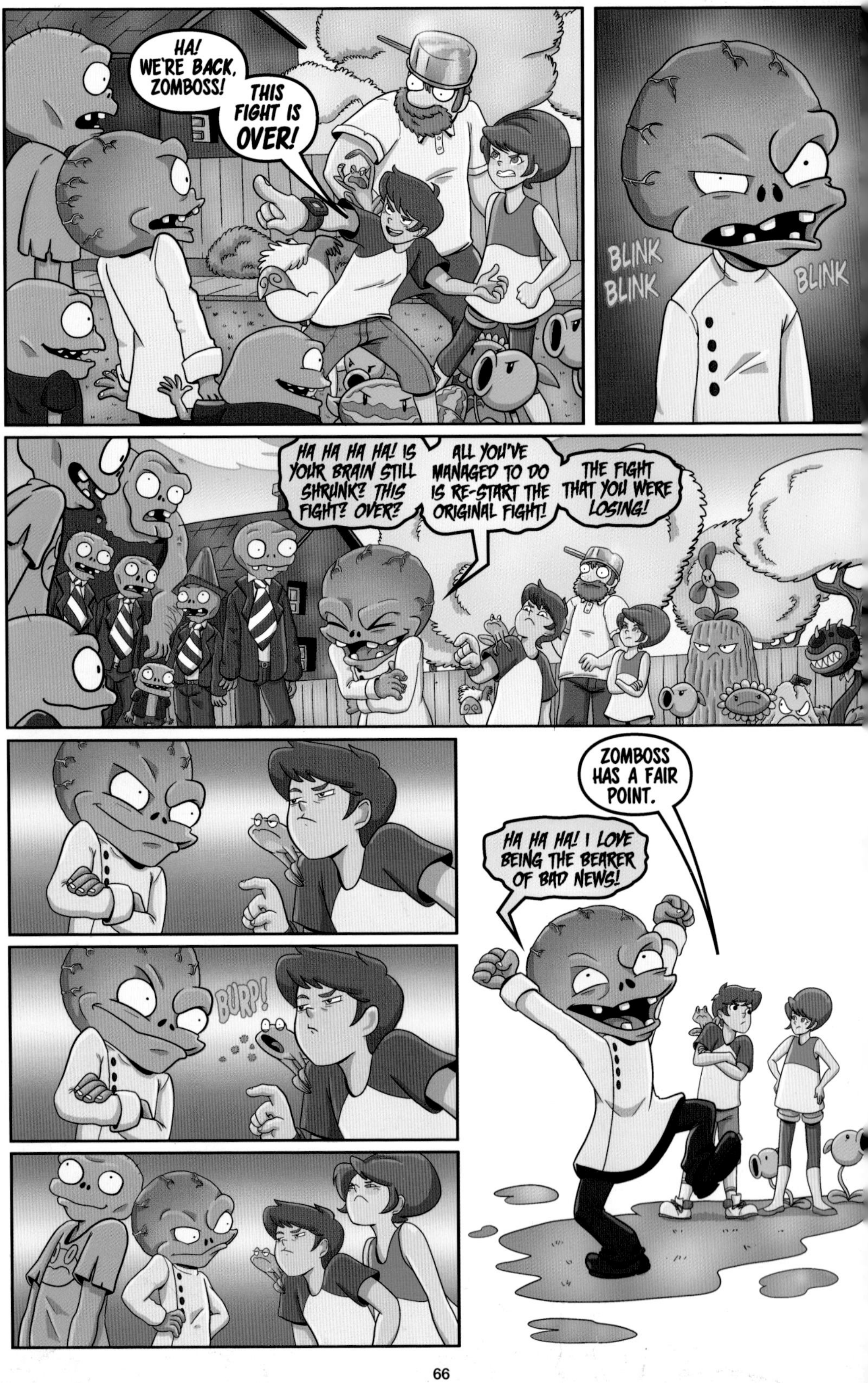
HA! WE'RE BACK, ZOMBOSS!
THIS FIGHT IS OVER!
BLINK
BLINK
BLINK
HA HA HA HA! IS YOUR BRAIN STILL SHRUNK? THIS FIGHT? OVER?
ALL YOU'VE MANAGED TO DO IS RE-START THE ORIGINAL FIGHT!
THE FIGHT THAT YOU WERE LOSING!
BURP!
ZOMBOSS HAS A FAIR POINT.
HA HA HA! I LOVE BEING THE BEARER OF BAD NEWS!

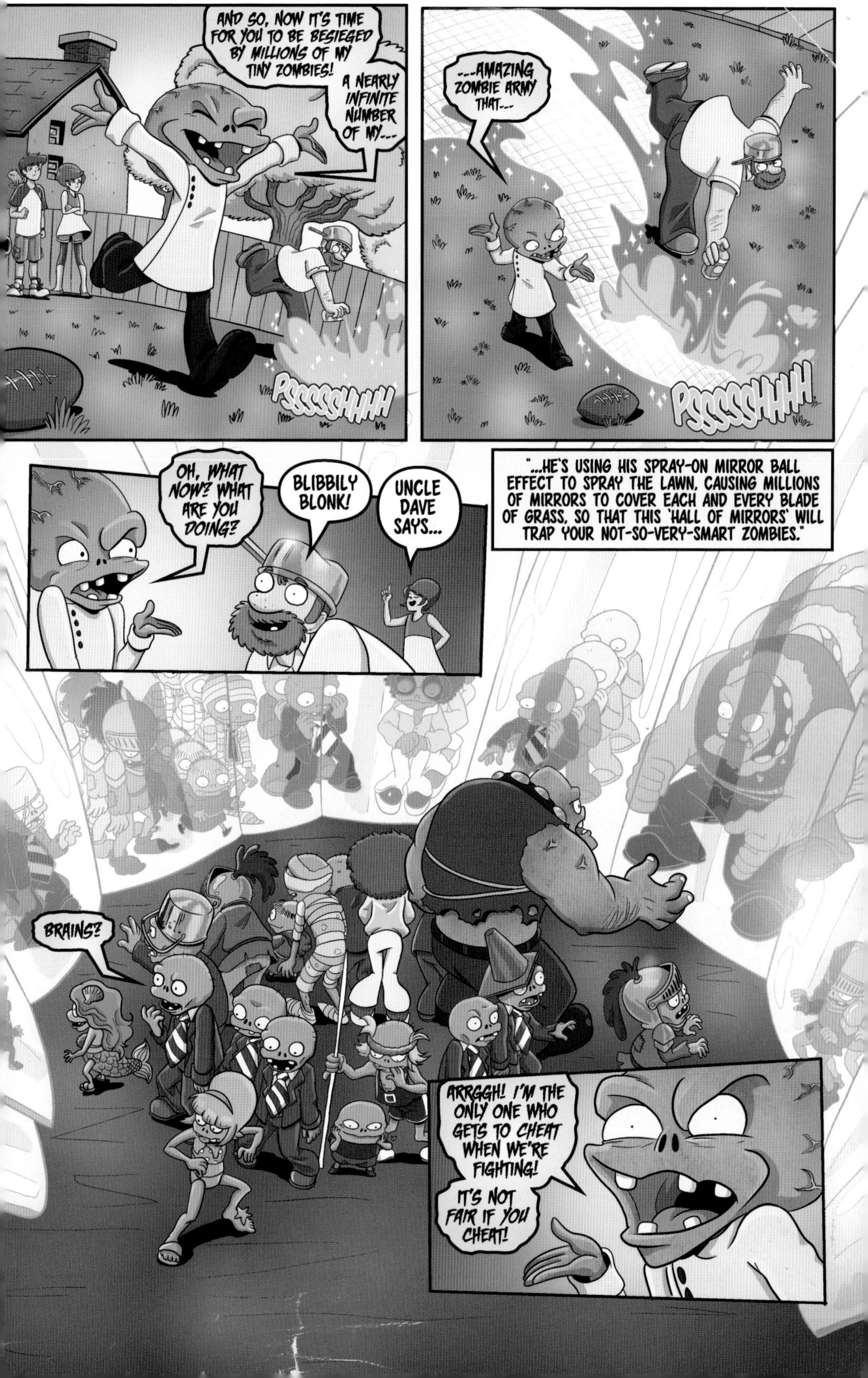
AND SO, NOW IT'S TIME FOR YOU TO BE BESIEGED BY MILLIONS OF MY TINY ZOMBIES!
A NEARLY INFINITE NUMBER OF MY...
PSSSSSHHHH
...AMAZING ZOMBIE ARMY THAT...
PSSSSSHHHH
OH, WHAT NOW? WHAT ARE YOU DOING?
BLIBBILY BLONK!
UNCLE DAVE SAYS...
"...HE'S USING HIS SPRAY-ON MIRROR BALL EFFECT TO SPRAY THE LAWN, CAUSING MILLIONS OF MIRRORS TO COVER EACH AND EVERY BLADE OF GRASS, SO THAT THIS 'HALL OF MIRRORS' WILL TRAP YOUR NOT-SO-VERY-SMART ZOMBIES."
BRAINS?
ARRGGH! I'M THE ONLY ONE WHO GETS TO CHEAT WHEN WE'RE FIGHTING!
IT'S NOT FAIR IF YOU CHEAT!

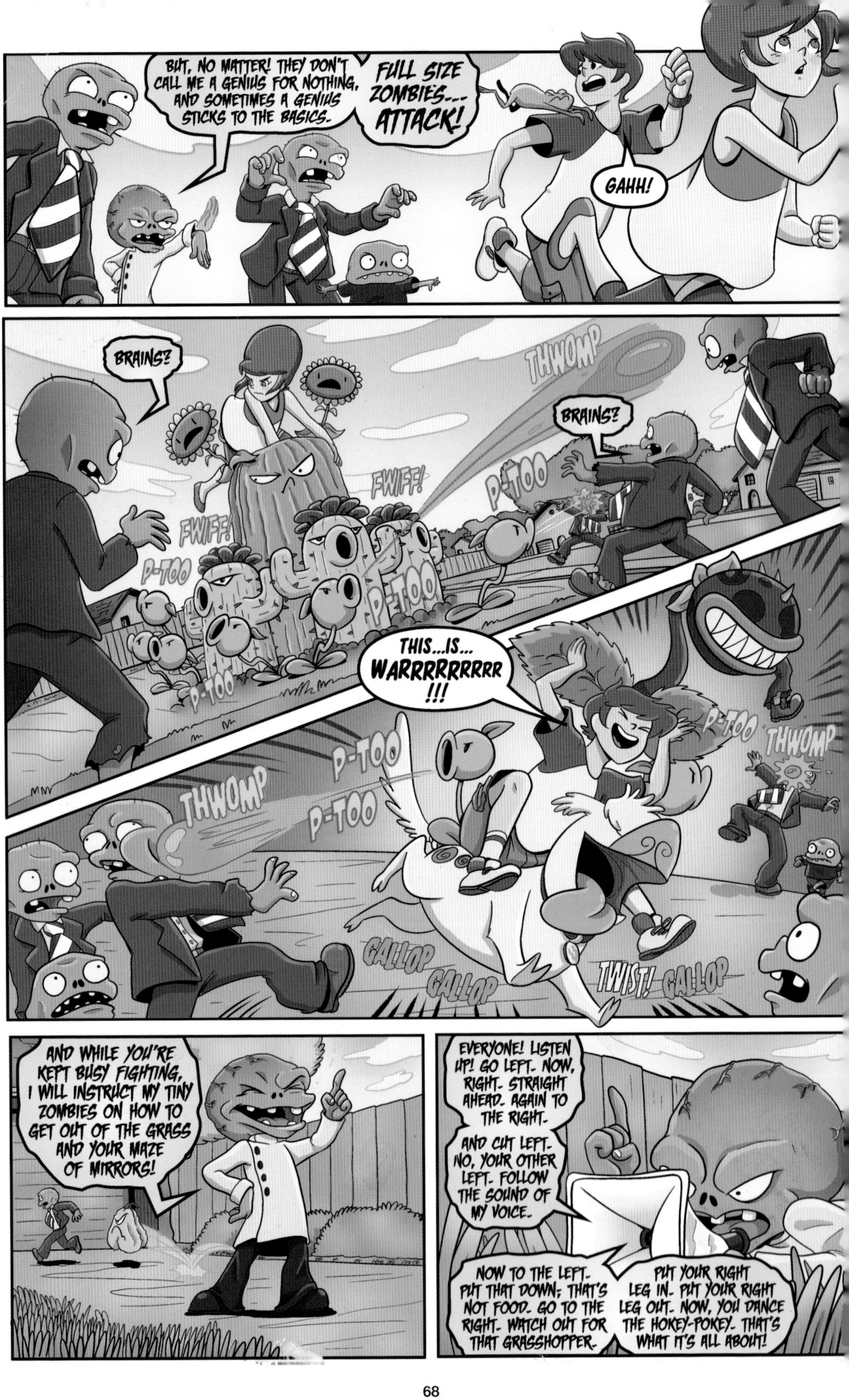

BUT, NO MATTER! THEY DON'T CALL ME A GENIUS FOR NOTHING, AND SOMETIMES A GENIUS STICKS TO THE BASICS.
FULL SIZE ZOMBIES... ATTACK!
GAHH!
BRAINS?
THWOMP
BRAINS?
FWIFF!
P-TOO
FWIFF!
P-TOO
P-TOO
P-TOO
THIS...IS... WARRRRRRRR !!!
P-TOO
THWOMP
P-TOO
THWOMP
P-TOO
GALLOP
GALLOP
TWIST! GALLOP
AND WHILE YOU'RE KEPT BUSY FIGHTING, I WILL INSTRUCT MY TINY ZOMBIES ON HOW TO GET OUT OF THE GRASS AND YOUR MAZE OF MIRRORS!
EVERYONE! LISTEN UP! GO LEFT. NOW, RIGHT. STRAIGHT AHEAD. AGAIN TO THE RIGHT.
AND CUT LEFT. NO, YOUR OTHER LEFT. FOLLOW THE SOUND OF MY VOICE.
NOW TO THE LEFT. PUT THAT DOWN; THAT'S NOT FOOD. GO TO THE RIGHT. WATCH OUT FOR THAT GRASSHOPPER.
PUT YOUR RIGHT LEG IN. PUT YOUR RIGHT LEG OUT. NOW, YOU DANCE THE HOKEY-POKEY. THAT'S WHAT IT'S ALL ABOUT!

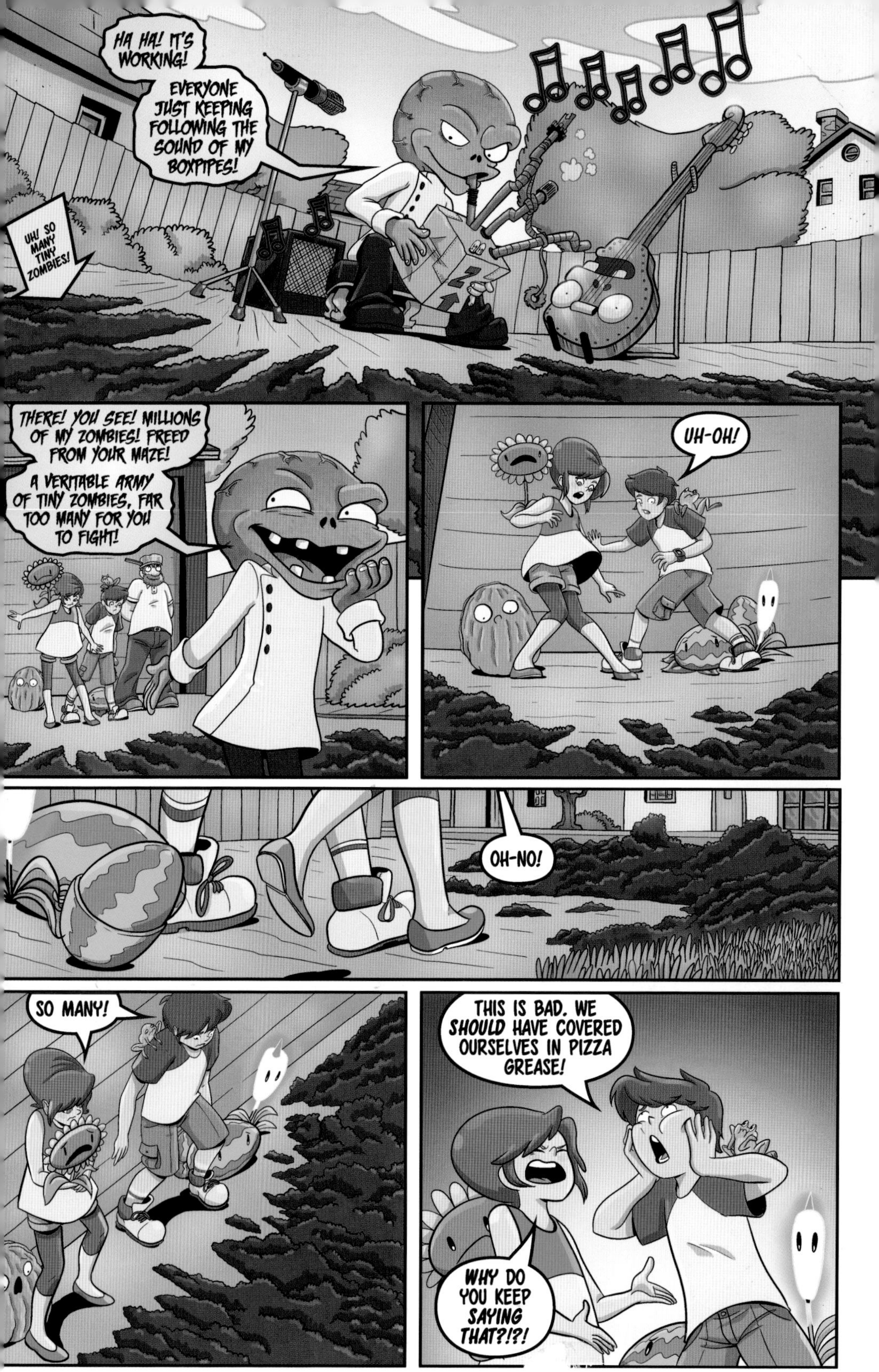
HA HA! IT'S WORKING!
EVERYONE JUST KEEPING FOLLOWING THE SOUND OF MY BOXPIPES!
UH! SO MANY TINY ZOMBIES!
THERE! YOU SEE! MILLIONS OF MY ZOMBIES! FREED FROM YOUR MAZE!
A VERITABLE ARMY OF TINY ZOMBIES, FAR TOO MANY FOR YOU TO FIGHT!
UH-OH!
OH-NO!
SO MANY!
THIS IS BAD. WE SHOULD HAVE COVERED OURSELVES IN PIZZA GREASE!
WHY DO YOU KEEP SAYING THAT?!?!

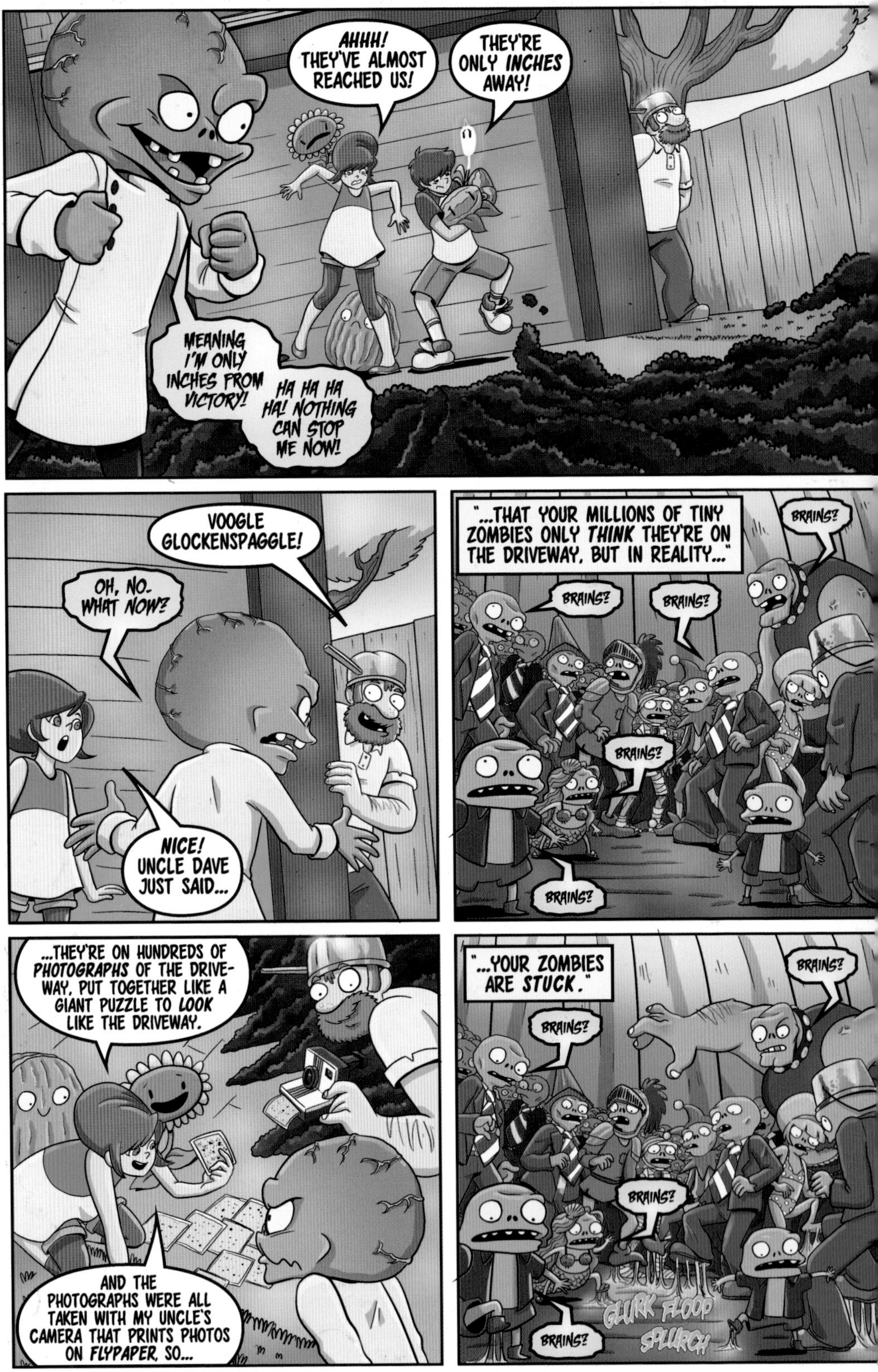
AHHH! THEY'VE ALMOST REACHED US!
THEY'RE ONLY INCHES AWAY!
MEANING I'M ONLY INCHES FROM VICTORY!
HA HA HA HA! NOTHING CAN STOP ME NOW!
VOOGLE GLOCKENSPAGGLE!
OH, NO. WHAT NOW?
NICE! UNCLE DAVE JUST SAID...
"...THAT YOUR MILLIONS OF TINY ZOMBIES ONLY THINK THEY'RE ON THE DRIVEWAY, BUT IN REALITY..."
BRAINS?
BRAINS?
BRAINS?
BRAINS?
BRAINS?
...THEY'RE ON HUNDREDS OF PHOTOGRAPHS OF THE DRIVE-WAY, PUT TOGETHER LIKE A GIANT PUZZLE TO LOOK LIKE THE DRIVEWAY.
AND THE PHOTOGRAPHS WERE ALL TAKEN WITH MY UNCLE'S CAMERA THAT PRINTS PHOTOS ON FLYPAPER, SO...
"...YOUR ZOMBIES ARE STUCK."
BRAINS?
BRAINS?
BRAINS?
BRAINS?
GLURK FLOOP
SPLURCH

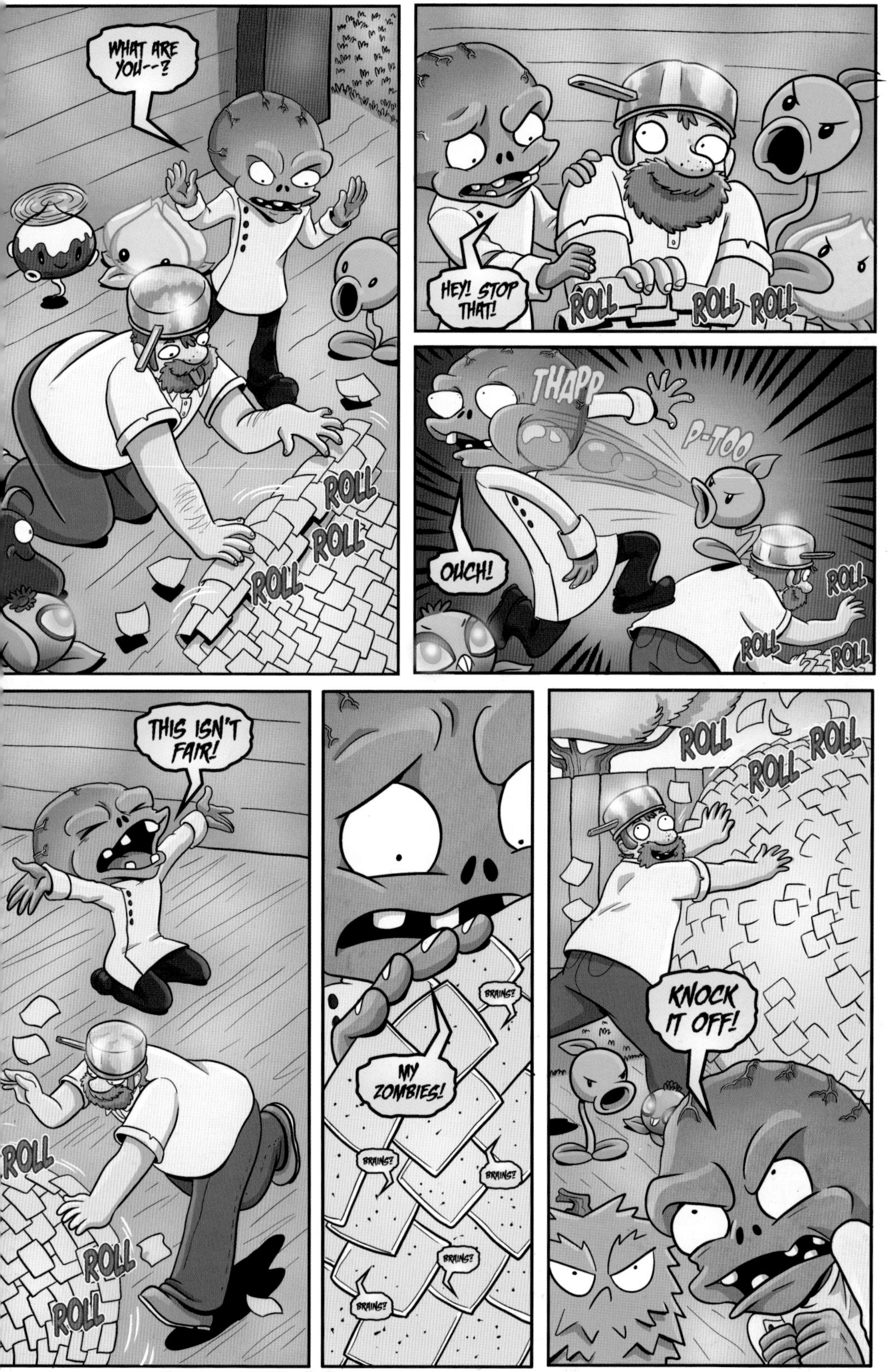
WHAT ARE YOU--?
ROLL
ROLL
ROLL
HEY! STOP THAT!
ROLL
ROLL ROLL
THAPP
P-TOO
OUCH!
ROLL
ROLL
ROLL
THIS ISN'T FAIR!
ROLL
ROLL
ROLL
BRAINS?
MY ZOMBIES!
BRAINS?
BRAINS?
BRAINS?
BRAINS?
ROLL
ROLL ROLL
KNOCK IT OFF!

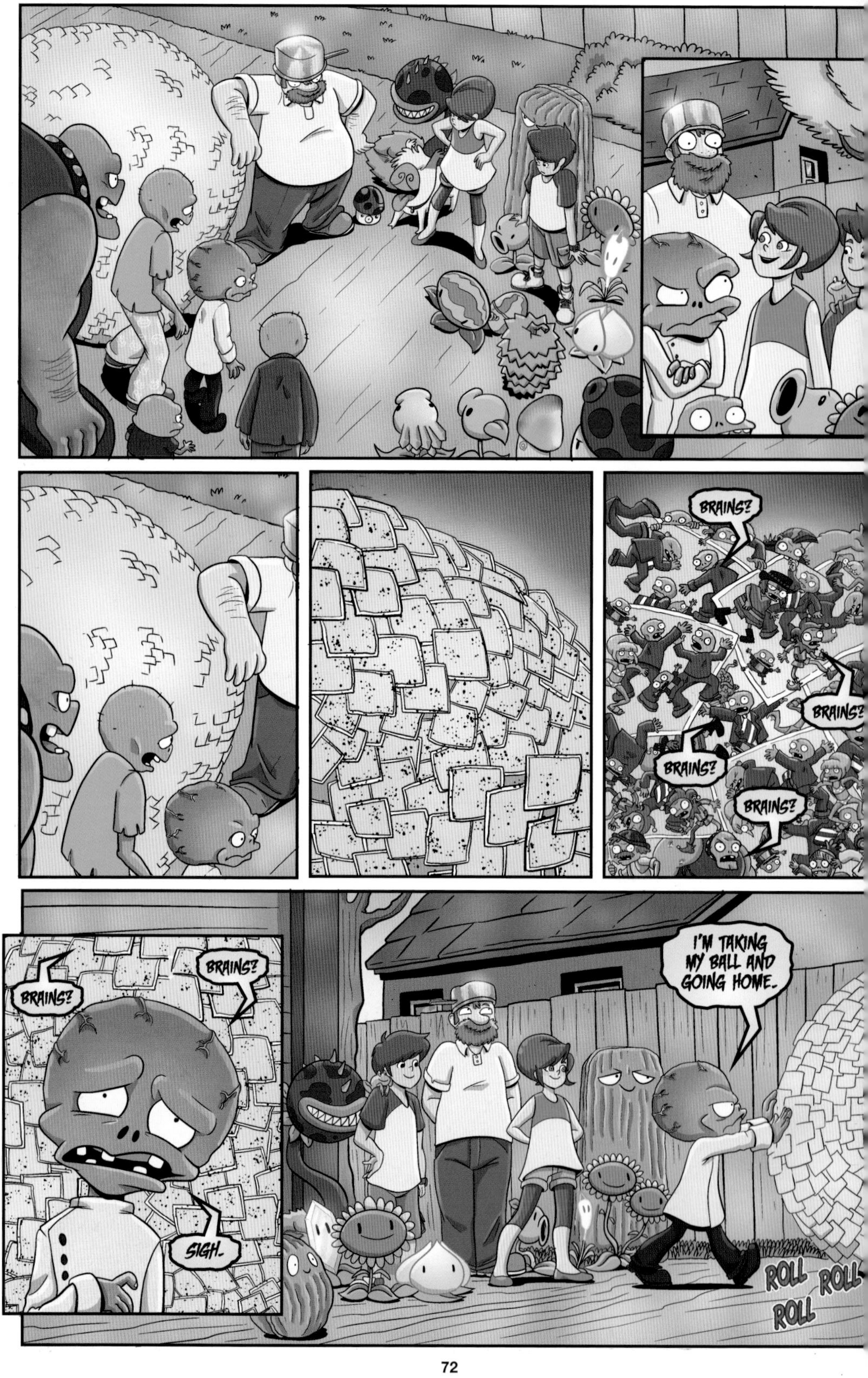
BRAINS?
BRAINS?
BRAINS?
BRAINS?
BRAINS?
BRAINS?
SIGH.
I'M TAKING MY BALL AND GOING HOME.
ROLL ROLL ROLL

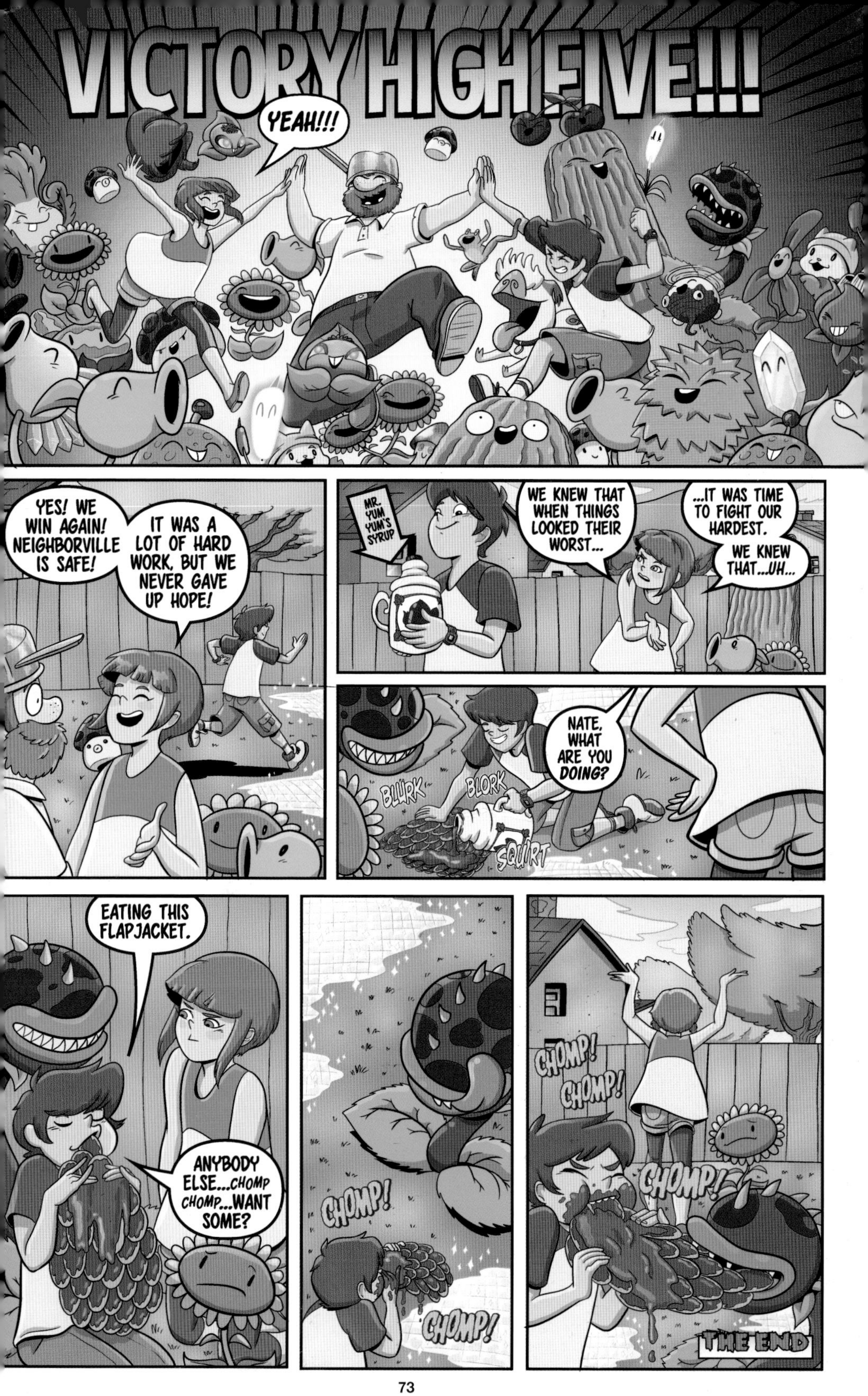
VICTORY HIGH FIVE!!!
YEAH!!!
YES! WE WIN AGAIN! NEIGHBORVILLE IS SAFE!
IT WAS A LOT OF HARD WORK, BUT WE NEVER GAVE UP HOPE!
MR. YUM YUM'S SYRUP
WE KNEW THAT WHEN THINGS LOOKED THEIR WORST...
...IT WAS TIME TO FIGHT OUR HARDEST.
WE KNEW THAT...UH...
BLURK
BLORK
SQUIRT
NATE, WHAT ARE YOU DOING?
EATING THIS FLAPJACKET.
ANYBODY ELSE...CHOMP CHOMP...WANT SOME?
CHOMP!
CHOMP!
CHOMP!
CHOMP!
CHOMP!
THE END

The Burping Advisory Board

Story by **Paul Tobin**
Art and colors by **Ron Chan**
Letters by **Steve Dutro**

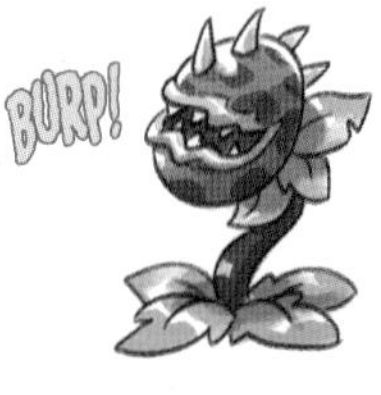
BURP!

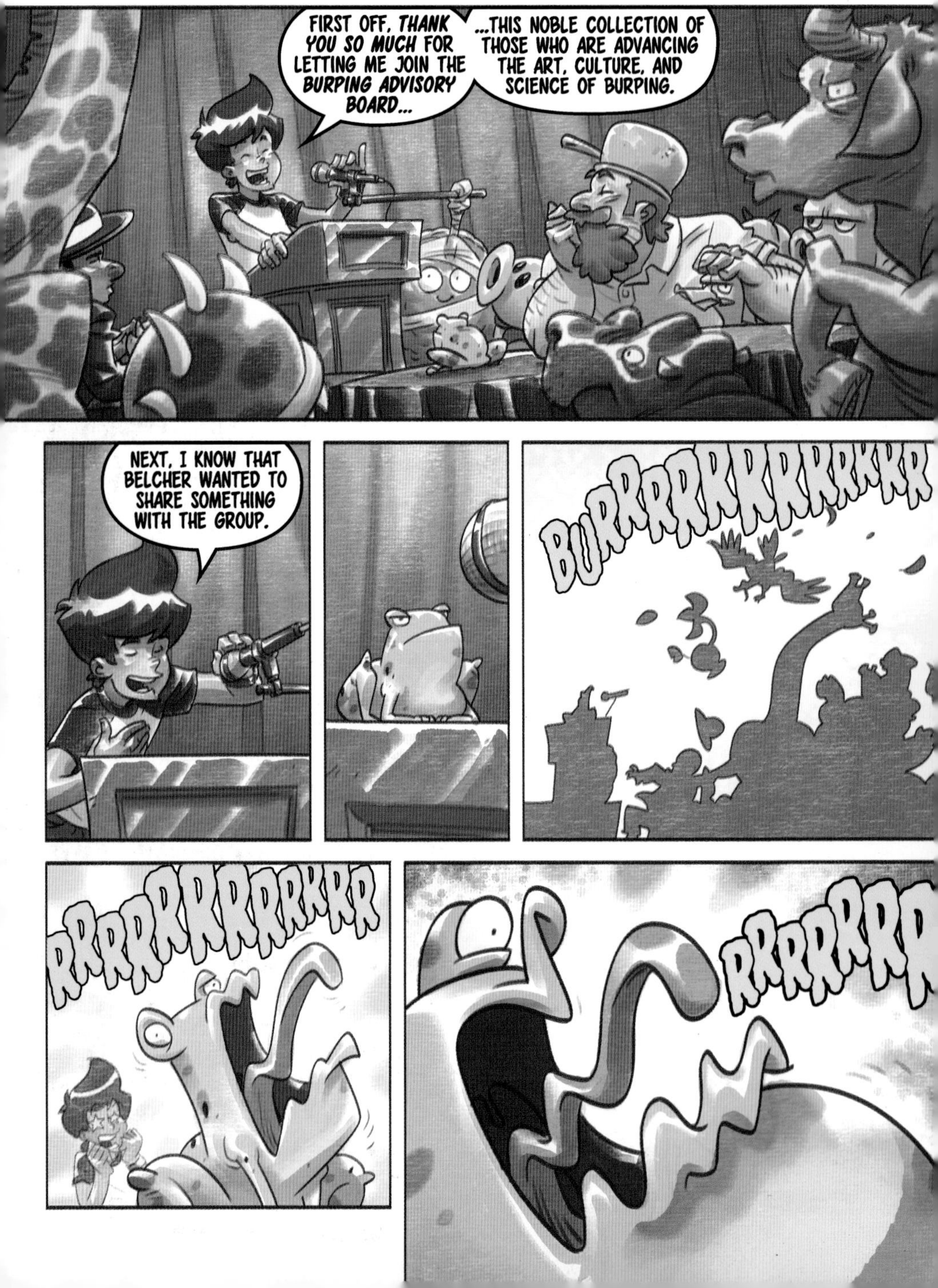
FIRST OFF, THANK YOU SO MUCH FOR LETTING ME JOIN THE BURPING ADVISORY BOARD...
...THIS NOBLE COLLECTION OF THOSE WHO ARE ADVANCING THE ART, CULTURE, AND SCIENCE OF BURPING.
NEXT, I KNOW THAT BELCHER WANTED TO SHARE SOMETHING WITH THE GROUP.
BURRRRRRRRRRRR
RRRRRRRRRRR
RRRRRRR

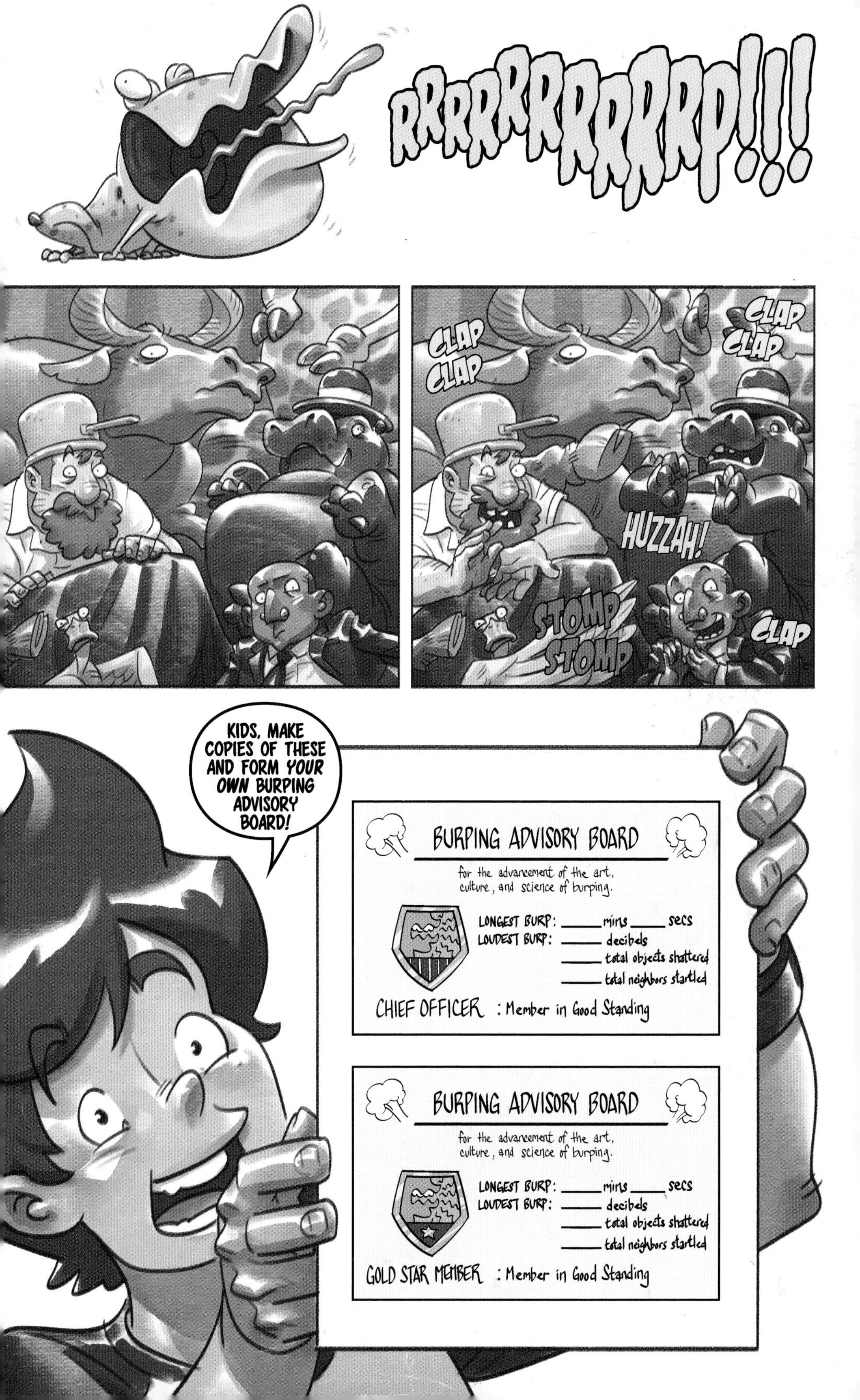
RRRRRRRRRRRP!!!
CLAP CLAP
CLAP CLAP
HUZZAH!
STOMP STOMP
CLAP
KIDS, MAKE COPIES OF THESE AND FORM YOUR OWN BURPING ADVISORY BOARD!
BURPING ADVISORY BOARD
for the advancement of the art, culture, and science of burping.
LONGEST BURP: ____ mins ____ secs
LOUDEST BURP: ____ decibels
____ total objects shattered
____ total neighbors startled
CHIEF OFFICER : Member in Good Standing
BURPING ADVISORY BOARD
for the advancement of the art, culture, and science of burping.
LONGEST BURP: ____ mins ____ secs
LOUDEST BURP: ____ decibels
____ total objects shattered
____ total neighbors startled
GOLD STAR MEMBER : Member in Good Standing

The Pizza

Story by
Paul Tobin
Art and colors by
Ron Chan
Letters by
Steve Dutro

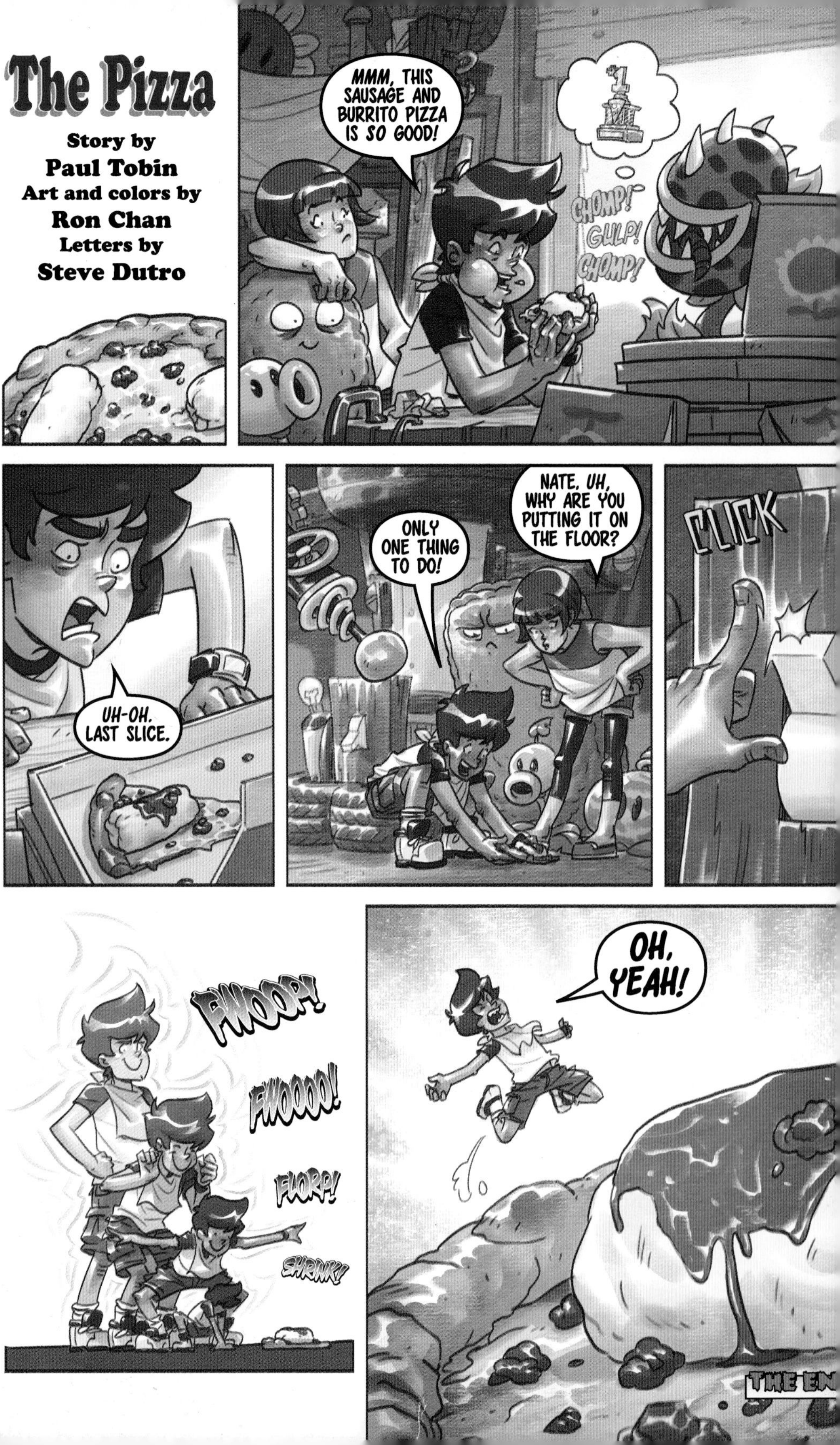
MMM, THIS SAUSAGE AND BURRITO PIZZA IS SO GOOD!
CHOMP!
GULP!
CHOMP!
UH-OH. LAST SLICE.
ONLY ONE THING TO DO!
NATE, UH, WHY ARE YOU PUTTING IT ON THE FLOOR?
CLICK
FWOOP!
FWOOOO!
FLORP!
SHRINK!
OH, YEAH!
THE EN

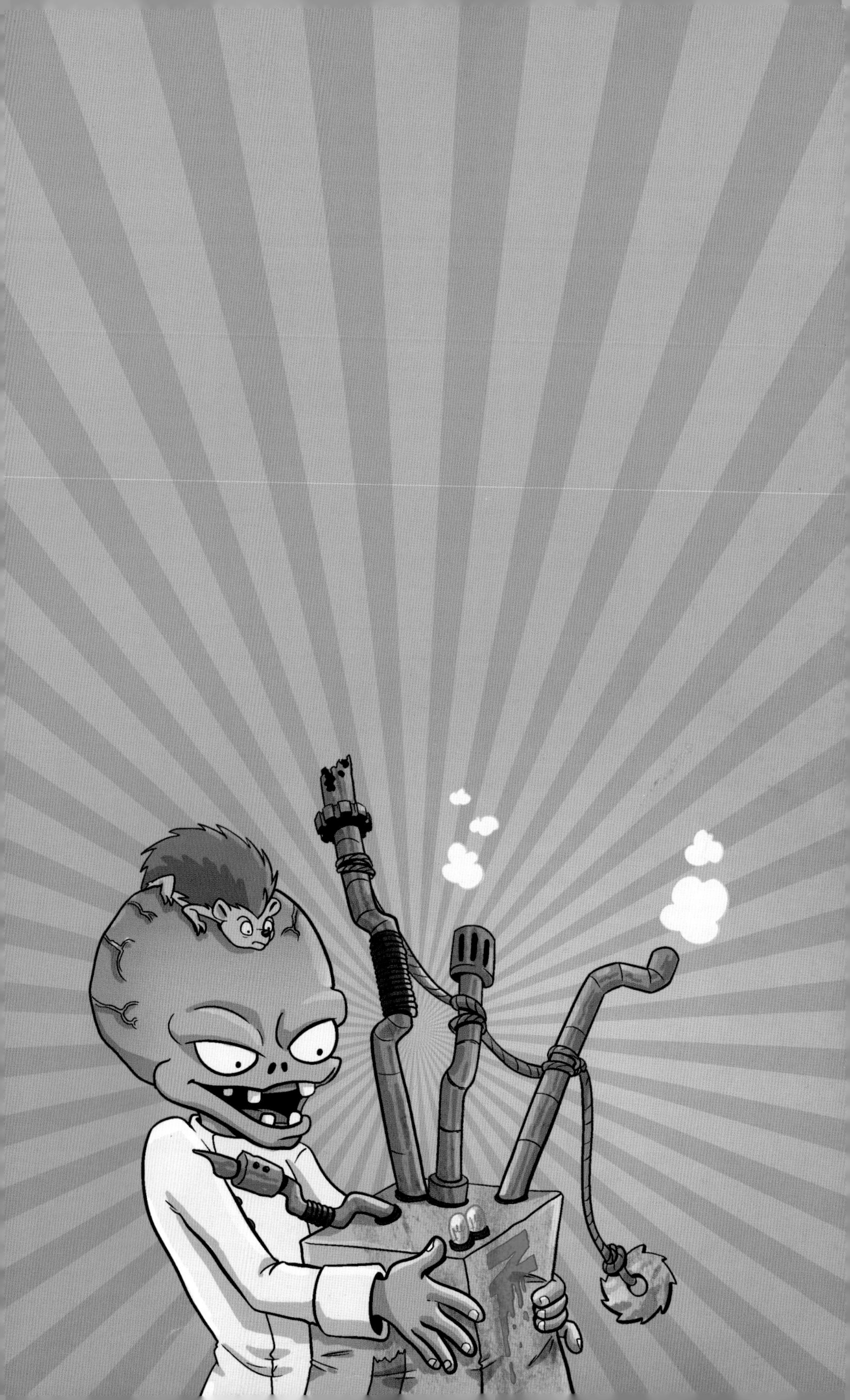

PLANTS VS. ZOMBIES: A LITTLE PROBLEM
COVER LAYOUTS BY SARA SOLER

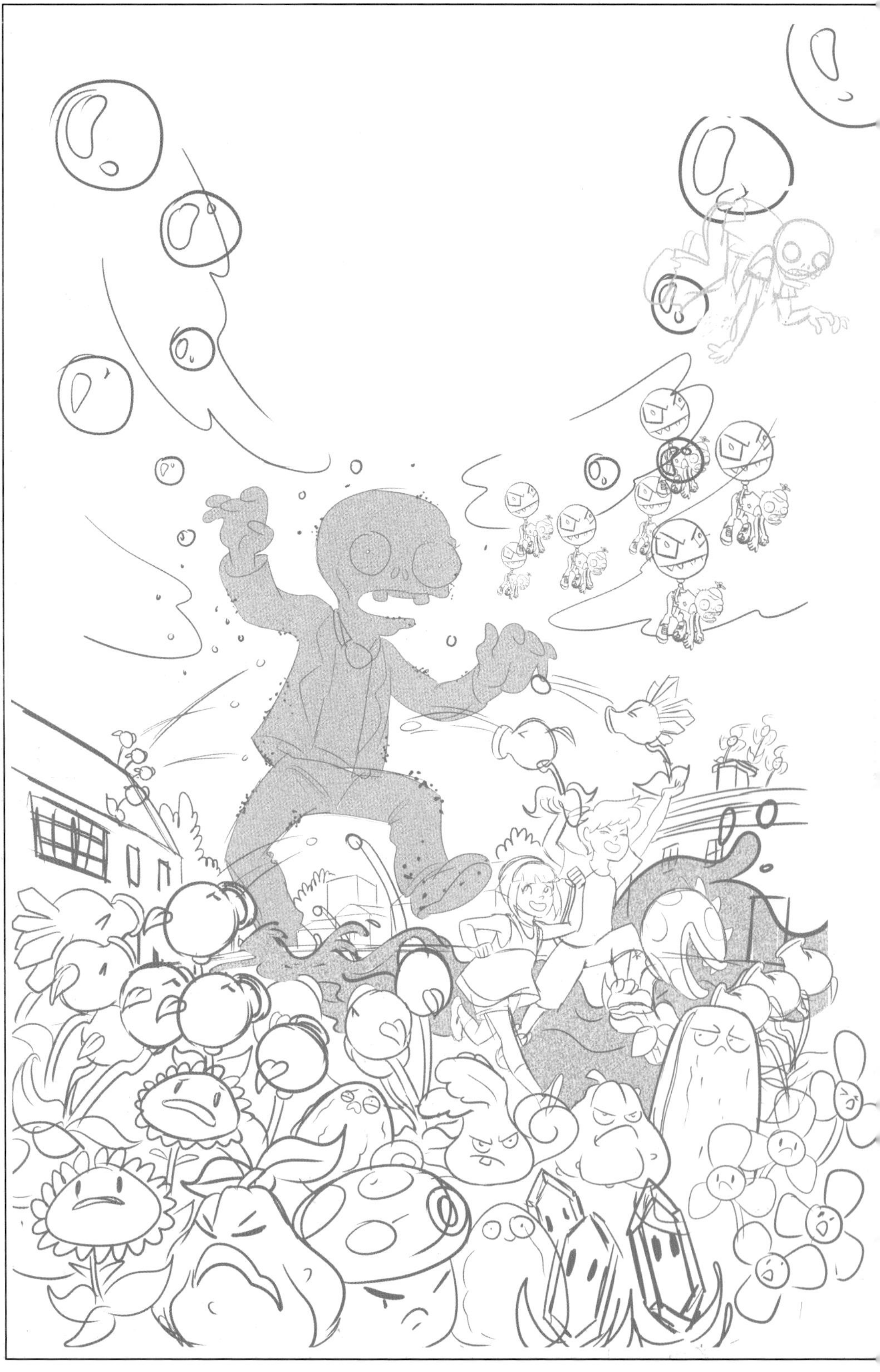

PLANTS VS. ZOMBIES: A LITTLE PROBLEM

COVER LINE ART BY SARA SOLER

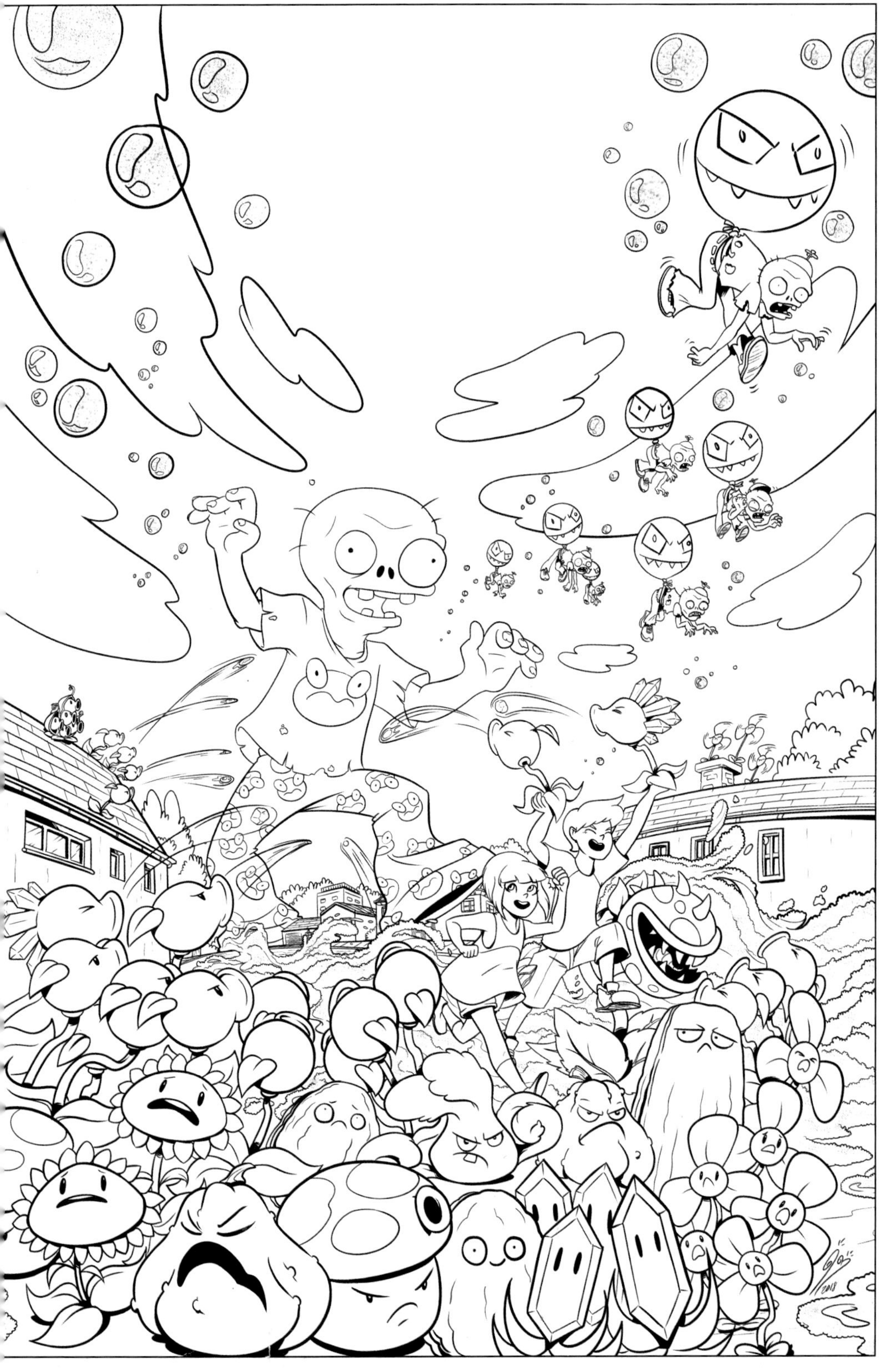

LINE ART FROM *A LITTLE PROBLEM* PAGES 41–44 BY ARTIST SARA SOLER!

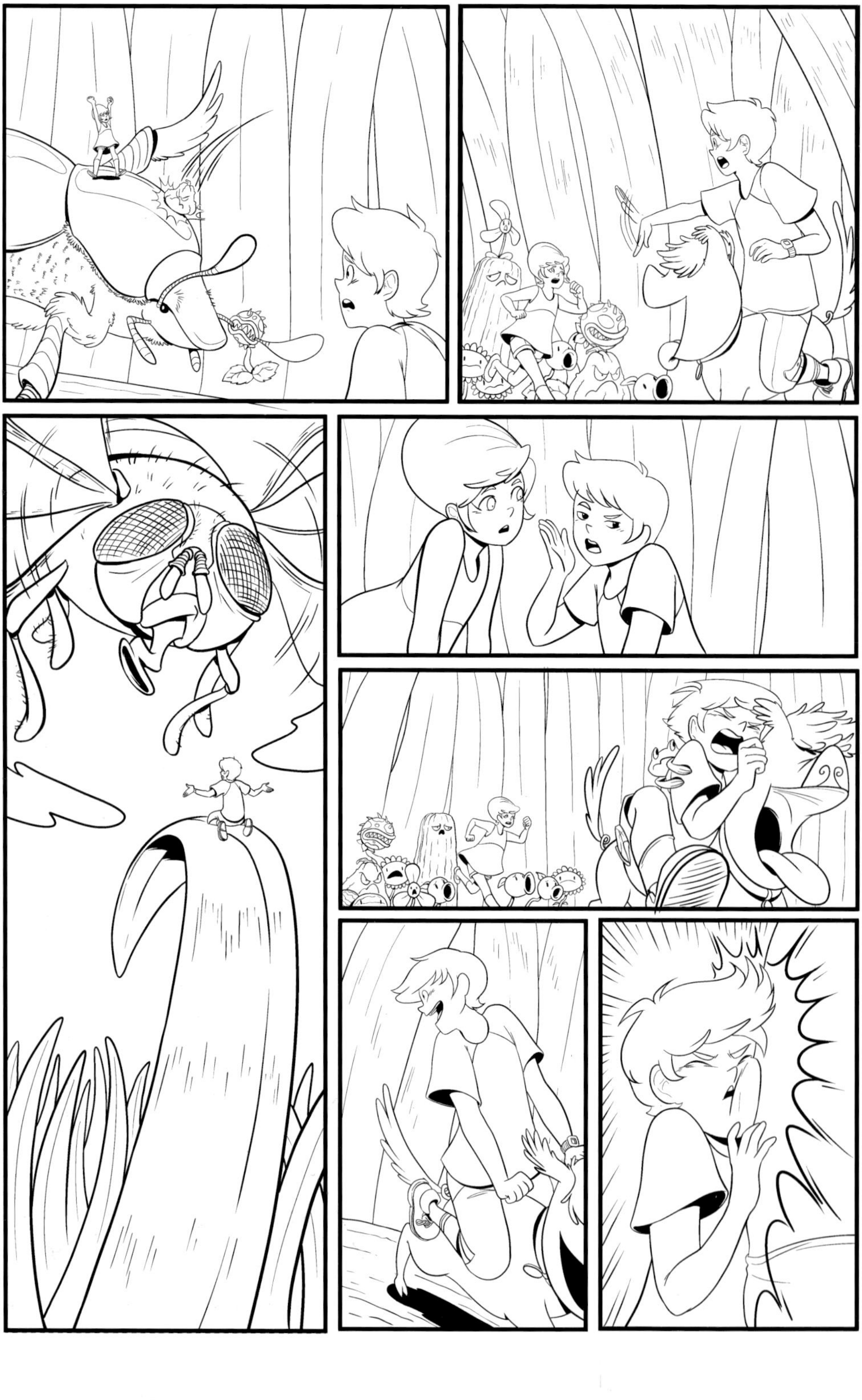

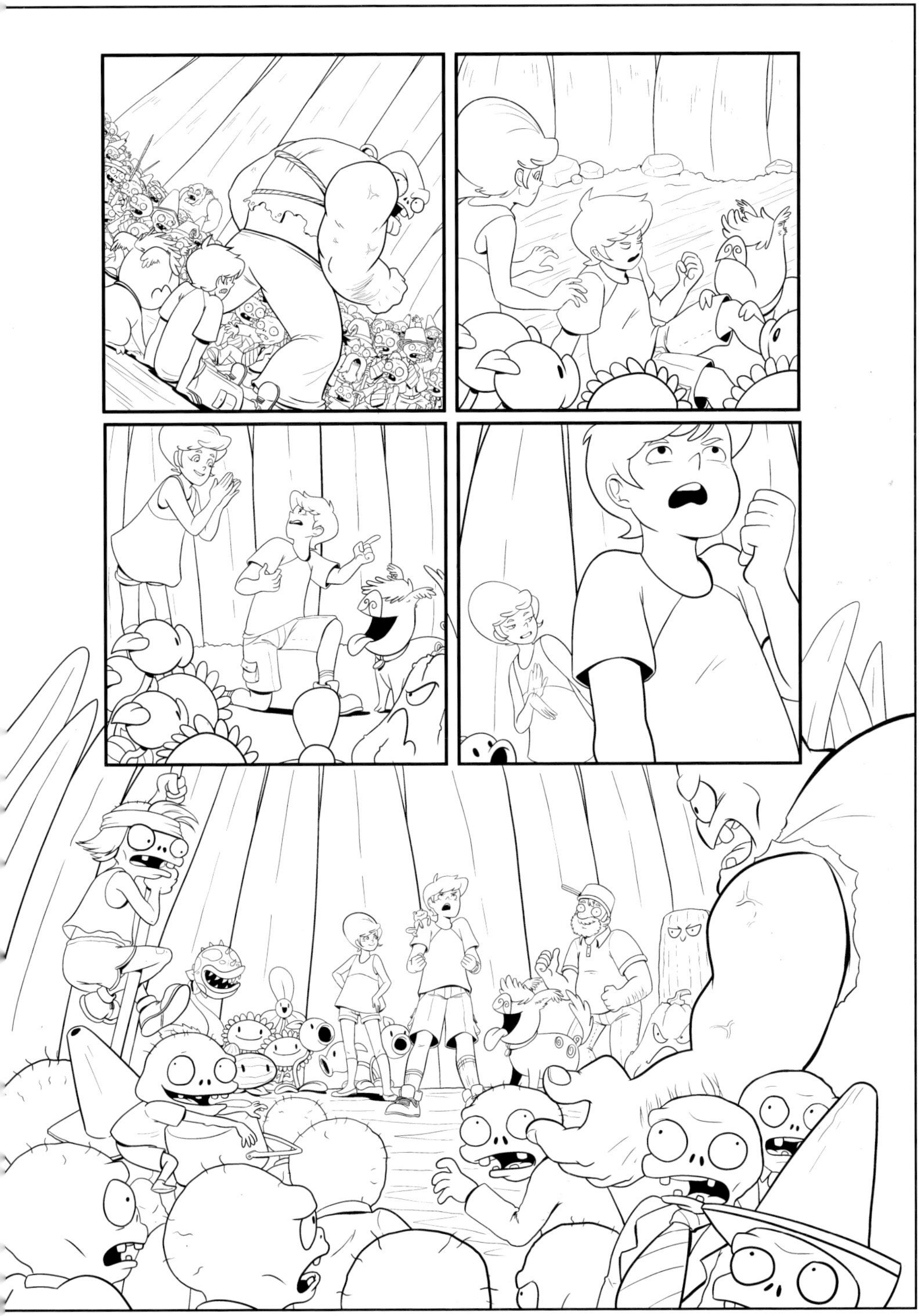

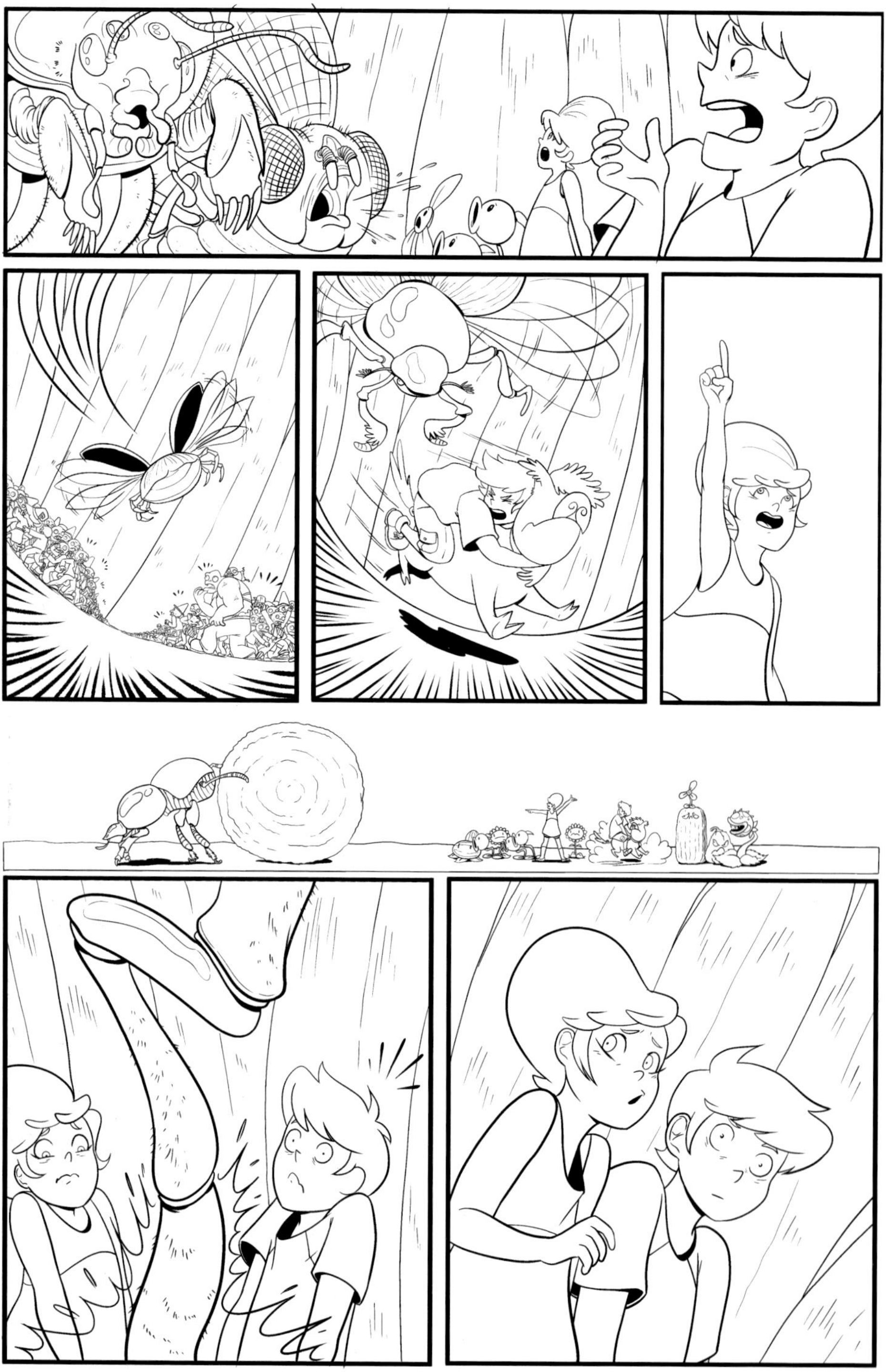

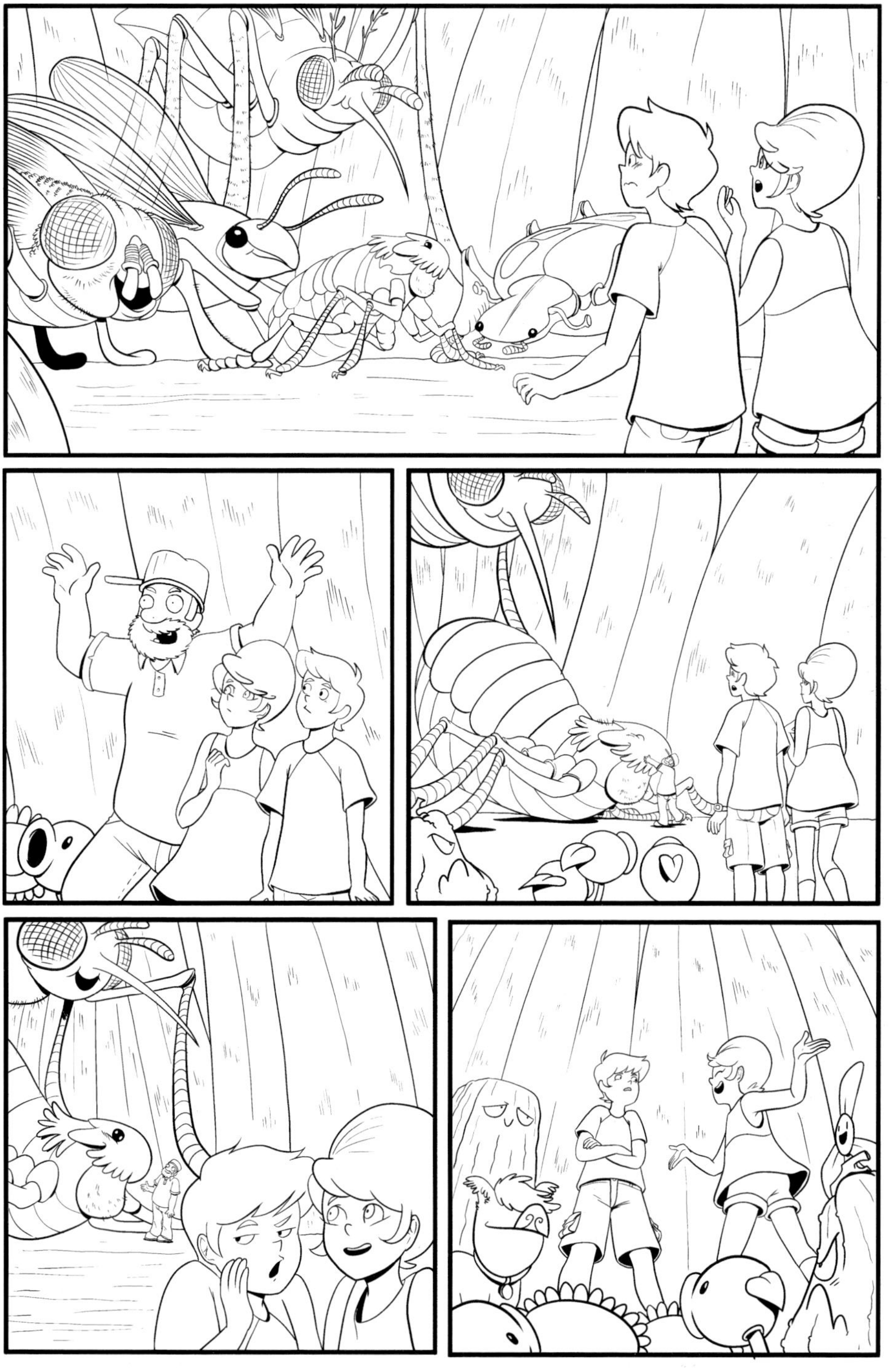

CREATOR BIOS

PAUL TOBIN enjoys that his author photo makes him look insane, and he once accidentally cut his ear with a potato chip. He doesn't know how it happened, either. Life is so full of mystery. If you ask him about the Potato Chip Incident, he'll just make up a story. That's what he does. He's written hundreds of stories for Marvel, DC, Dark Horse, and many others, including such creator-owned titles as *Colder* and *Bandette*, as well as *Prepare to Die!*—his debut novel. His *Genius Factor* series of novels about a fifth-grade genius and his war against the Red Death Tea Society debuted in March 2016 with *How to Capture an Invisible Cat*, from Bloomsbury Publishing, and continued in early 2017 with *How to Outsmart a Billion Robot Bees*. Paul has won some Very Important Awards for his writing but so far none for his karaoke skills.

Paul Tobin

SARA SOLER is a comic-book artist born in Spain and currently living in Barcelona, where she moved to study Fine Arts and complete the Graphic Arts course at Escola Joso. While studying, Sara started working on comic book art and writing short stories for several fanzines. She's also worked as a costume and stage designer and as a storyboard artist for animation studios. Sara worked as a background artist for the *Memorias de un hombre en pajama* movie adaptation of the graphic novel with the same name, created by Paco Roca. She started her professional career in comics as a writer/artist in 2017, when her *Red & Blue* graphic novel was published by Editorial Panini. Since then, Sara's worked for various national and international publishers—such as Norma Editorial, Planeta, and Dark Horse Comics. After drawing this volume of *Plants vs Zombies*, Sara has started to grow sunflowers in her backyard, just in case.

Sara Soler

Adi Crossa

After escaping the Escola Joso School of Art in 2014, **ADI CROSSA** has been coloring comic books and magazines and has worked for D.C. Thomson, Ideés Plus, and Insight Editions. Superhero action tales, revolutionary steampunk stories, and all-ages adventures are some of the subjects he's colored, and in his free time he likes to draw cute monsters and creepy girls!

Steve Dutro

STEVE DUTRO is an Eisner Award-nominated comic-book letterer from Redding, California, who can also drive a tractor. He graduated from the Kubert School and has been lettering comics since the days when foil-embossed covers were cool, working for Dark Horse (*The Fifth Beatle*, *I Am a Hero*, *Planet of the Apes*, *Star Wars*), Viz, Marvel, and DC. He has submitted a request to the Department of Homeland Security that in the event of a zombie apocalypse he be put in charge of all digital freeway signs so citizens can be alerted to avoid nearby brain-eatings and the like. He finds the *Plants vs. Zombies* game to be a real stress-fest, but highly recommends the *Plants vs. Zombies* table on *Pinball FX2* for game-room hipsters.

Ron Chan

RON CHAN is a comic book and storyboard artist, video game fan, and occasional jujitsu practitioner. He was born and raised in Portland, Oregon, where he still lives and works as a member of the local artist collective Helioscope Studio. His comics work has been published by Dark Horse, Marvel, and Image Comics, and his storyboarding work includes boards for 3-D animation, gaming, user-experience design, and advertising for clients such as Microsoft, Amazon Kindle, Nike, and Sega. He really likes drawing Bonk Choys. (He also enjoys eating actual bok choy in real life.)

ALSO AVAILABLE FROM DARK HORSE!

THE HIT VIDEO GAME CONTINUES ITS COMIC BOOK INVASION!

PLANTS VS. ZOMBIES: LAWNMAGEDDON
Crazy Dave—the babbling-yet-brilliant inventor and top-notch neighborhood defender—helps young adventurer Nate fend off a zombie invasion that threatens to overrun the peaceful town of Neighborville in *Plants vs. Zombies: Lawnmageddon*! Their only hope is a brave army of chomping, squashing, and pea-shooting plants! A wacky adventure for zombie zappers young and old!
ISBN 978-1-61655-192-6 | $9.99

THE ART OF PLANTS VS. ZOMBIES
Part zombie memoir, part celebration of zombie triumphs, and part anti-plant screed, *The Art of Plants vs. Zombies* is a treasure trove of never-before-seen concept art, character sketches, and surprises from PopCap's popular *Plants vs. Zombies* games!
ISBN 978-1-61655-331-9 | $9.99

PLANTS VS. ZOMBIES: TIMEPOCALYPSE
Crazy Dave helps Patrice and Nate Timely fend off Zomboss' latest attack in *Plants vs. Zombies: Timepocalypse*! This new standalone tale will tickle your funny bones and thrill your brains through any timeline!
ISBN 978-1-61655-621-1 | $9.99

PLANTS VS. ZOMBIES: BULLY FOR YOU
Patrice and Nate are ready to investigate a strange college campus to keep the streets safe from zombies!
ISBN 978-1-61655-889-5 | $9.99

PLANTS VS. ZOMBIES: GARDEN WARFARE VOLUME 1
Based on the hit video game, this comic tells the story leading up to the events in *Plants vs. Zombies: Garden Warfare 2*!
ISBN 978-1-61655-946-5 | $9.99

VOLUME 2
ISBN 978-1-50670-548-4 | $9.99

PLANTS VS. ZOMBIES: GROWN SWEET HOME
With newfound knowledge of humanity, Dr. Zomboss strikes at the heart of Neighborville . . . sparking a series of plant-versus-zombie brawls!
ISBN 978-1-61655-971-7 | $9.99

PLANTS VS. ZOMBIES: PETAL TO THE METAL
Crazy Dave takes on the tough *Don't Blink* video game—and challenges Dr. Zomboss to a race to determine the future of Neighborville!
ISBN 978-1-61655-999-1 | $9.99

PLANTS VS. ZOMBIES: BOOM BOOM MUSHROOM
The gang discover Zomboss' secret plan for swallowing the city of Neighborville whole! A rare mushroom must be found in order to save the humans aboveground!
ISBN 978-1-50670-037-3 | $9.99

PLANTS VS. ZOMBIES: BATTLE EXTRAVAGONZO
Zomboss is back, hoping to buy the same factory that Crazy Dave is eyeing! Will Crazy Dave and his intelligent plants beat Zomboss and his zombie army to the punch?
ISBN 978-1-50670-189-9 | $9.99

PLANTS VS. ZOMBIES: LAWN OF DOOM
With Zomboss filling everyone's yards with traps and special soldiers, will he and his zombie army turn Halloween into their zanier Lawn of Doom celebration?!
ISBN 978-1-50670-204-9 | $9.99

PLANTS VS. ZOMBIES: THE GREATEST SHOW UNEARTHED
Dr. Zomboss believes that all humans hold a secret desire to run away and join the circus, so he aims to use his "Big Z's Adequately Amazing Flytrap Circus" to lure Neighborville's citizens to their doom!
ISBN 978-1-50670-298-8 | $9.99

PLANTS VS. ZOMBIES: RUMBLE AT LAKE GUMBO
The battle for clean water begins! Nate, Patrice, and Crazy Dave spot trouble and grab all the Tangle Kelp and Party Crabs they can to quell another zombie attack!
ISBN 978-1-50670-497-5 | $9.99

PLANTS VS. ZOMBIES: WAR AND PEAS
When Dr. Zomboss and Crazy Dave find themselves members of the same book club, a literary war is inevitable! The position of leader of the book club opens up and Zomboss and Crazy Dave compete for the top spot in a scholarly scuffle for the ages!
ISBN 978-1-50670-677-1 | $9.99

PLANTS VS. ZOMBIES: DINO-MIGHT
Dr. Zomboss sets his sights on destroying the yards in town and rendering the plants homeless—and his plans include dogs, cats, rabbits, hammock sloths, and, somehow, dinosaurs . . . !
ISBN 978-1-50670-838-6 | $9.99

PLANTS VS. ZOMBIES: SNOW THANKS
Dr. Zomboss invents a Cold Crystal capable of freezing Neighborville, burying the town in snow and ice! It's up to the humans and the fieriest plants to save Neighborville—with the help of pirates!
ISBN 978-1-50670-839-3 | $9.99

PLANTS VS. ZOMBIES: A LITTLE PROBLEM
Will an invasion of teeny-tiny miniature zombies mean the party for Crazy Dave's two-hundred-year-old pants gets canceled?
ISBN 978-1-50670-840-9 | $9.99

AVAILABLE AT YOUR LOCAL COMICS SHOP OR BOOKSTORE To find a comics shop in your area, visit comicshoplocator.com. For more information or to order direct visit **DarkHorse.com** or call 1-800-862-0052

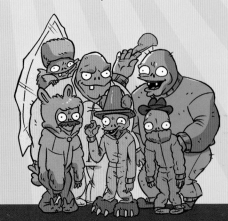

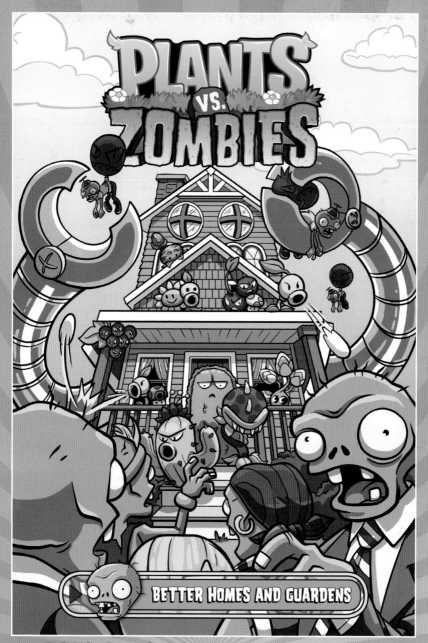

PLANTS VS. ZOMBIES: BETTER HOMES AND GUARDENS—
GUARDING YOUR HOUSE IN FEBRUARY 2020!

Get ready for an intense and persistent one-up battle of . . . *designing Neighborville dwellings?!* Plant pals Nate and Patrice suggest a brilliant idea: thwart any attack from the zombies by putting defending plants named "Guard-ens" inside homes, as well as in yards! But as soon as Mr. Stubbins informs zombie leader and Pop Smarts lover Dr. Zomboss, he quickly becomes obsessed with circumventing this idea with an epically evil one of his own—building cages disguised as homes to trap all the tasty brains (and the people they reside within) before the Guard-ens can get there. The plants, Nate, Patrice, and Crazy Dave must now counter Dr. Zomboss's havoc-filled scheme! Eisner award-winning writer Paul Tobin (*Bandette, Genius Factor*) collaborates with artist Christianne Gillendardo-Goudreau (*Plants vs. Zombies: War and Peas, Plants vs. Zombies: Rumble at Lake Gumbo*) for this standalone graphic novel!

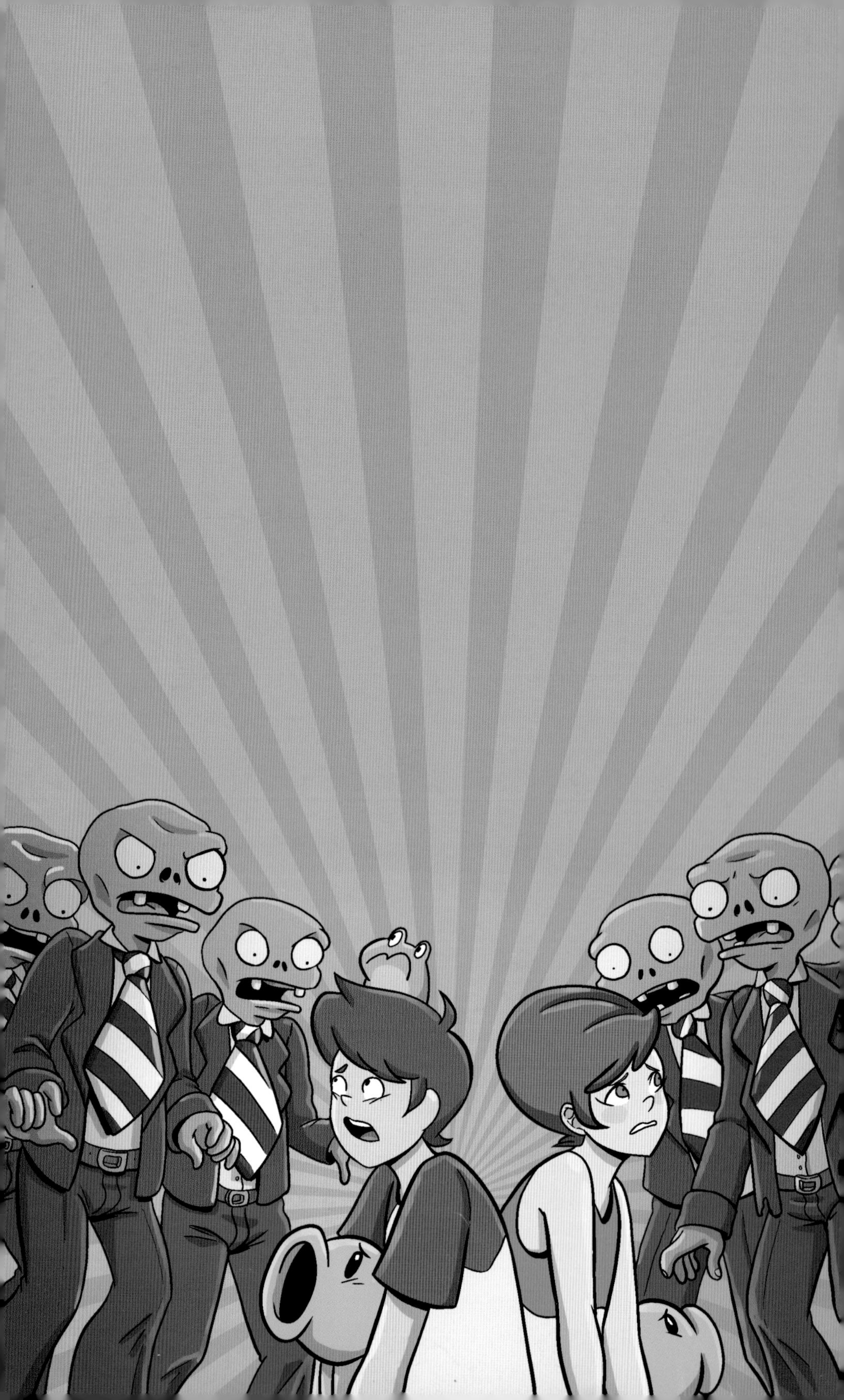

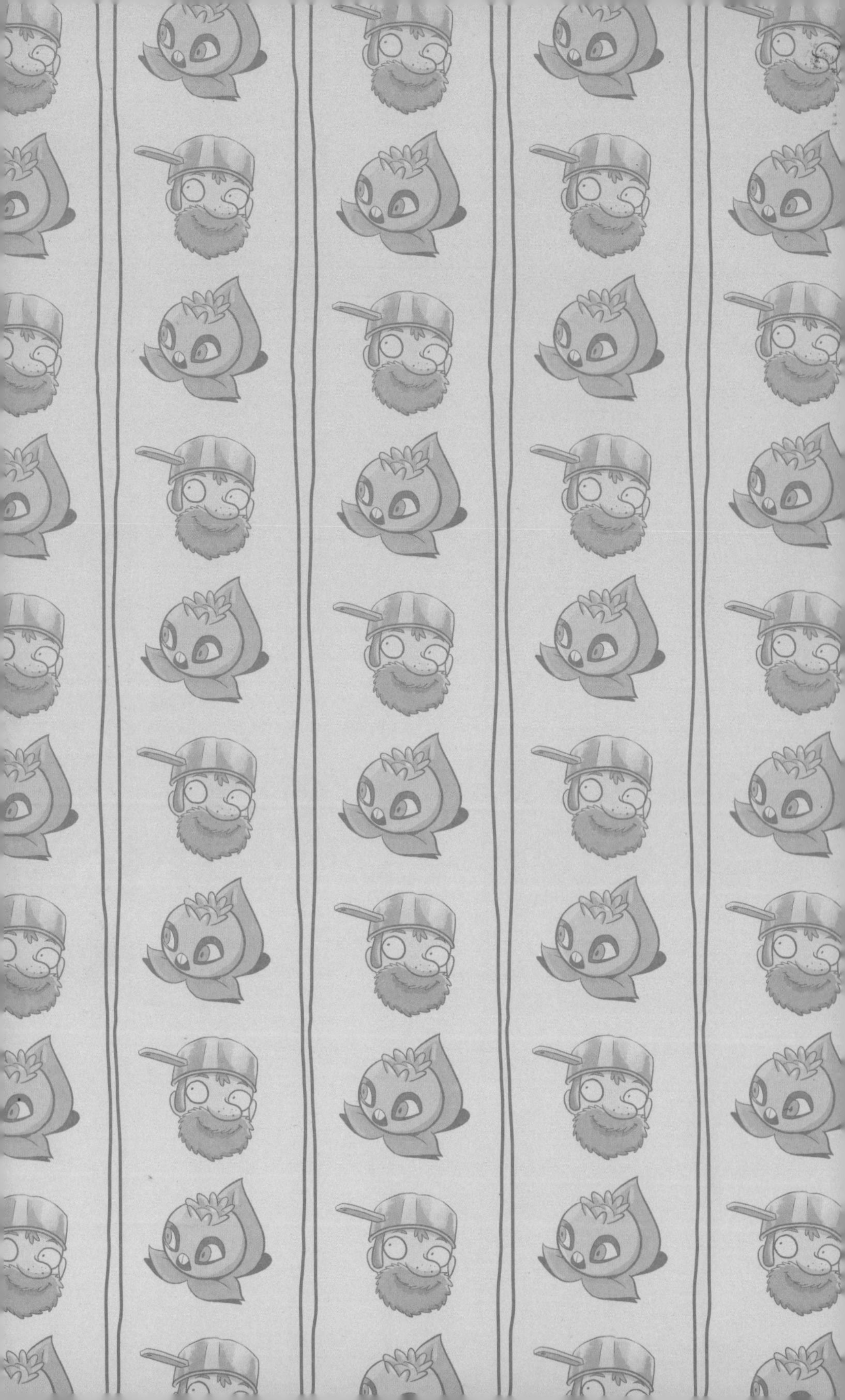